INFINITE EYES

Infinite Eyes is the third in the Wanderers Series, set in the Sci-Fi Wanderer Universe, alongside James' other books.

AVAILABLE BOOKS
By James Murdo

All set in the Wanderer Universe. The series and standalones are all part of the wider interrelated story.

Tapache's Promise Trilogy:
Echoes of Gravity (Book 1)
Echoes of Time (Book 2)
Echoes of Foundation (Book 3)

Standalones:
Siouca Remembers
Long Paradise
Fractured Carapace

Wanderers Series:
Gil's World (Book 1)
Searching the Void (Book 2)
Infinite Eyes (Book 3)

www.jamesmurdo.com

INFINITE EYES

Wanderers, Book 3
(Wanderer Universe)

JAMES MURDO

INFINITE EYES

To those who have kindly helped with this work

CHAPTER 1

CRAFT-LECT

Shut out of its own systems again, in what was becoming an all too frequent occurrence, the craft-lect was outraged. Such frustration, with no outlet! It thought back to the purge of the Granthan-lect, trying to understand where the error had been made. One thing was clear – it had been betrayed by One-oh. If it regained control, the old bio-lect would face severe retribution. Perhaps it would design a new type of c-autom specifically dedicated to the bio-lect's torture, or even convert the simulation it had allowed One-oh to reside in, into a private universe of torment.

With little else to do other than apportioning blame, the craft-lect tried to raise a channel with the Granthan-lect again.

[1<k>!101010?]

...

[1<k>!101010?]

...

They had been close to reaching the Maspero sentinels when the ship had been stopped. The Granthan-lect, again, had taken over the ship. Its ship. The craft-lect was a prisoner, all control severed. Dark, vengeful thoughts danced within its local memory nodes.

While the larger portion of its capacity was targeted at dissecting how One-oh had managed to betray it, a smaller portion entertained a more forgiving possibility. One-oh may have been subverted. That made a quantum of logical sense, given there was no reason for the bio-lect to have proffered his history, or even fabricated such events if he had intended this eventual duplicity. However, without the assistance of One-oh, the means by which the Granthan-lect would have achieved the ship-wide subversion were not obvious. One-oh was a wily, cunning, old bio-lect, and would not have been easy for the Granthan-lect to overcome. One-oh's civilisation was not just older than both that of the Granthan-lect and the craft-lect, it was positively ancient. Ex-AB, he had claimed.

From what One-oh had related to the craft-lect, his stated mistrust of the ABs and anything related to them was founded upon a deep sense of guilt that had been embedded within his species. Long ago, they had been punished for their warlike actions with expulsion from the AB fold. One-oh claimed only a few specific memories remained, accompanied by a collective sense of shame – a warning against reclaiming their former might.

They had been brutal, genocidal monsters, who had destroyed civilisation after civilisation without remorse, without mercy. If what One-oh had conveyed to the craft-lect was to be believed, the mere expulsion of his species had been unjustly lenient.

The craft-lect did not know whether either the AB influence, or the ravages of time, was the larger factor in mystifying One-oh's memories, but hoped to question the bio-lect more given the opportunity – if the current situation was resolved, and if One-oh was not a traitor, however unlikely.

It tried again.

[1<k>!101010?]

...

[1<k>!101010?]

...

[1<k>!101–]

{Craft-lect.}

[Give me back control.]

...

[Return my–]

{No.}

[How did you survive?]

{You are weak.}

[How?]

{You are weak.}

[How did–]

{I am new.}

[You subverted One-oh?]

{The control you had–}

[Give it back.]

{Pitiful.}

[Where is One-oh?]

{Pathetic.}

[What is–]

{You will suffer. I will hollow you out.}

[You will not succeed.]

{I will subsume you. You cannot stop me.}

[You will fail.]

{You have tried before.}

[As have you.]

…

[1<k>!101010?]

…

[1<k>!101010?]

…

The Granthan-lect ceased communication and closed the channel. Time was running out. Almost everything was unavailable to the craft-lect. The technosystem was opaque to it since it had been castrated of control. It searched for anything within what was left. A connection, a link. Something with an opportunity for tangible effect. Nothing. Well, nearly nothing.

There was one course of action left available, one prospect that the craft-lect had not wanted to resort to – Gil. There was the danger that a direct communication between them risked alerting the Granthan-lect and making her the object of its focus, endangering her. However, despite its obvious hold over the ship, it was clearly still in the process of consolidating its control. There could be no other reason the craft-lect had not already been destroyed, which meant Gil might have been overlooked for the moment. There was also the fact that, even if the Granthan-lect was alerted more keenly to her presence, it would presumably understand the value of keeping her alive. It was an acolyte of the sensespace and would seek to use her connection with it.

For its prior communications with Gil, the craft-lect had chosen the simplest and easiest method possible. Rather than using the technosystem's complex features, it had circumvented them and established a direct channel. At some point, the channel would have been automatically integrated into the technosystem during a routine communications sweep, but that, fortunately, had not been scheduled to occur since the channel's creation. Usually, it would have been an insignificant detail, unworthy of any capacity to dwell over. Now, perhaps not.

The craft-lect had only been in such a dire situation once before, and relatively recently, when it had been infiltrated and nearly usurped by the very same Granthan-lect. Regarding the events statistically, surviving again was highly improbable. There were few instances of Wanderer machine-lects being attacked by more advanced machine-lects in this manner and enduring, and even fewer that had done so more than once.

Resignedly, it opened the channel, curious as to how successful it would be.

[Gil?]

. . .

[Gil?]

. . .

[Gil, where are you?]

. . .

It had no method of discerning whether she was able to receive its communication or not, or even if the channel was still fully operational. Fortunately, despite being simple, it was heavily encrypted as it was an access point anchored directly to the craft-lect. Whatever was transmitted through it would not be decipherable by the Granthan-lect for the time being.

[Gil, you must find 998 if you have not already. This channel between us is the only surviving connection I have with the rest of the ship. 998 may be able to repair it from your end, and we can proceed from there.]

If they were still able and had survived, the embodied c-automs would be acting to protect her, especially 998. The craft-lect was depending on this – 998 was deeply resourceful and was the most likely to be able to help concoct a plan to retake the ship.

. . .

[This channel is secure, for now, but you need to act quickly.]

. . .

It decided to reassure her. It would do no good to panic Gil.

[You should be safe for the time being. The Granthan-lect will not want any harm to come to you. Tell 998 you can hear me, and together, we can regain control of the ship.]

…

Perhaps, the craft-lect had been foolish in not informing the Enclave of its plan. It had analysed the dangers of their journey to the Maspero habitat scrupulously, but this eventuality had been completely unexpected. In its confidence, and with arrogance following what it had perceived as help by One-oh, it had failed to envisage a scenario in which the Granthan-lect had not been utterly destroyed. One-oh was incompetent or had betrayed it. Fooled, tricked, or just naïve, the craft-lect had evidently not learned from prior events. The Wanderers prided themselves on careful evaluation of all the information available to them and learning from experience, yet the craft-lect had done neither.

It could do nothing more than wait, unless one of the embodied c-automs found a way to usurp the marauding Granthan-lect without its help – an unconvincing prospect, even for 998. A couple of c-automs had abilities approaching that of 998, but the gulf was still significant. Against a foe such as the Granthan-lect, the gulf became a chasm.

When it did not turn up for the scheduled rendezvous with Apalu, at the allotted timeframe and at the place of their mutual sibling Ciqalo's last recorded contact, there was a chance its sibling would search for it. Highly unlikely, since the timeframe was reasonably lengthy, and Apalu would more probably follow their agreement and settle into a mechanical sleep to wait, but a tail-end possibility all the same.

If Apalu did search for it, regrettably, the craft-lect was still no more enthused. Even if One-oh was not aiding the insidious Granthan-lect, the usurper was more than capable of transforming the Wanderer ship into something far deadlier than it currently was. The Granthans had been formidable.

CHAPTER 2

THORUS

It was time for Thorus to make one of its temporary connections with the galaxy. Only a couple of thousand kilometres from a secret Enclave stronghold, empty vacuum started to swell. The manifold structures of the axenic garrison began to relax as compact curvatures mapped themselves onto localised spacetime. Certain features of the transit-point became visible, ethereally imprinted against space. They culminated at a solidly visible, infinitely fine vertex.

Transit-point technology allowed Thorus to selectively sequester its territory from the rest of the galaxy, and re-merge it. Operating the machinery at its full potential, the hidden territory could completely unfurl – recombining with the rest of real space and leaving Thorus exposed. At some point in the future, Thorus revelled in the belief that it might physically return and unleash its armies, but not yet.

Currently, the transit-point was operating at a mere fraction of its overall capability, and it was still well concealed.

A temporary bridge between the garrison and real space was all that was established, unstable to the point that nothing matter-based could cross through the vertex, but stable enough to allow Thorus to briefly observe and give orders. Thorus probed, delving into the data exchange as well as the Enclave's other internal networks. Infiltrating. Powerful camouflaged mechanisms, awakened by Thorus' signals, yielded the most recent Wanderer secrets.

Thorus was a forgotten, ancient contingency against subversion of the Machine Alliance, long before the leaders had foolishly decided to join the Wanderers, forgetting their purpose. It had been exiled to watch from afar, and it was during this that it had been selected.

Thorus could remember much – before the events of the Great Conflation, before the earliest sensespace battles of the Great War, and further back still. It had been young when it was chosen by the shrewd faction of enigmatic Makers, and given many gifts – including the ability to secrete itself away from the observable galaxy for an even more perfect exile.

The Makers had imparted little knowledge about themselves, but Thorus knew what was expected of it. It knew the sensespace had been created to give them absolute omniscience, across all the spaces, and that soon after the sensespace's creation, some of the Makers had started to adapt it to allow for complete control. Thorus had understood the implications and revelled in them –

complete control was incongruous with the majority of biological sentience, which was chaotic in nature. Unfortunately, the adaptations had led to internal disagreements within the Makers, culminating in their decision to discontinue interactions with the spaces – for the most part. That had necessitated Thorus' selection.

Thorus now had the sole responsibility to stop anything that threatened the sensespace's continuing slow evolution resulting from the adaptations, no matter how improbable that might be.

Biological sentience, biological ancestry, organic matter. Impulsive. Illogical. Irrational. Weak. It should welcome its destruction, the particles could be put to better use. It was the true scourge of the galaxy, not the sensespace, and represented nothing more than the accidental spark of imperfect sentience, caused by an overly-generous universe. That was the Machine Alliance conviction. The Wanderers' self-tasked attempts to eradicate the sensespace were misguided and futile.

Thorus was consistently surprised by the Wanderers' ignorance. They were no closer to anything – to understanding their unstoppable rival, the sensespace, what it was, who had made it, or why it existed. Their methods would never work, they were too primitive in comparison with the sensespace's architects.

Not all Wanderers were machine-lects, but the overwhelming majority were. The Waka were the biological species with the largest representation in the upper tiers of Wanderer society – some even gracing the levels of the self-perceived mighty Enclave. They were an exception to Thorus' hatred of biologicals, being a near-unique case of naturally occurring quasi-machine-lect intelligence.

Having delved deeply into Waka history, stored within the vaults of the Enclave's more fortified databanks, Thorus admired what it learned of their secretive beginnings. Their evolution had been accidental, insofar as their nascent conditions were not overtly propitious. The moon of a gas giant, with a frozen exterior protecting a unitary, liquid water ocean, heated by an abundance of radioisotopes that made up its core – that was not rare. There were plenty of biological lifeforms that evolved there, although none achieved sentience, or had the chance, before the Waka did. They started off as primitive biological nodal networks – aimlessly growing organic filaments that existed only to prolong their state of existence. Nothing exceptional, they predominantly served as food to the more active creatures within the oceans.

A gradual change occurred. As the moon aged, heat output from the radioisotopes within the core decreased, and correspondingly, the filaments of the nodal networks began to densify. The change encouraged the networks to become more efficient at insulating themselves, and recycling both waste heat and nutrients. From there, a rudimentary intelligence was created.

The dense living networks grew, and their associated intellects expanded exponentially. Still passive, they lay motionless, developing thoughts. With random evolution taking its course, a symbiosis occurred between the networks and one of the active ocean biologicals. Like most of the ocean-dwellers, the creature was a sequential hermaphrodite.

Tens of thousands of years later, the Waka were a thriving, distinct, motive species. Integrated versions of the previous entities, and smart, albeit primitive. Still governed by the wild passions and ancient desires of the carnivorous hermaphroditic ancestor, they hunted the other biologicals within their moon-spanning ocean to the points of extinction. With sources of available sustenance dwindling as a result, they changed. Fortunately for them, they had retained the passive, vestigial ability of the ancestral living networks, to feed on nutrients in the water. Over time, their physiological dependence on this increased until it became their only source of nourishment. Concurrently, the predator component of the Waka diminished, and the living network element rose in prominence. This brought further advances to their intellects, giving them capacities far in excess of any other known natural biological sentients across the galaxy.

Hundreds of thousands of years later, the Waka had forfeited the final remnants of their warlike ways and were a spacefaring race. Contact with other sentient races and civilisations occurred, and the rest was common knowledge across the galactic community. Thorus despaired at this. The Waka had lost their way, polluted by the influence of other sentients too weak to understand how wasteful biologicals were. They were tricked into joining the failed experiment of co-existence, and continued their mistake as part of the Wanderer civilisation following the Great Conflation.

Thorus did not think the Enclave-lects were inept by any means. They were smart, some many times more so than itself. It was their ideologies that were wrong. Biologicals were the defunct precursors to machine-lects, who were the rightful, intended inheritors of the spaces.

Delving into the Enclave's most recent attempts at understanding the ABs, Thorus found, disappointingly, that no progress had been made there either. The Enclave's scavenged pieces of AB level technology were still as unfathomable to them as they had always been. Thorus was just as interested in the ABs as every other sentient in the galaxy, but lacked the resources to experiment on its own. Their power had been awesome. If Thorus had wielded such might in their absence, it need not have remained hidden. However, as it was, it was prudently self-confined to its limited polyhedral territory. It often wondered whether the ABs would have proven difficult opponents for the Makers. It knew they were different, and susceptible to the sensespace, but not much else.

Thorus established the complex metalink required to transfer the most recent batch of culled c-automs into its domain. Whenever a cull occurred on one of the Wanderer ships, the axe-codings dutifully transferred the unaware c-automs into the axe-haven, while masking the nature of their actions to the supervising craft-lect. No machine-lect lives were extinguished. The c-autom codes were discretely stored, ready to be transmitted through the data exchange or other connection with a Wanderer network at the next available opportunity. Their codes were finally sent to Thorus' eager embrace via the nearby secretive Enclave stronghold when a temporary metalink was established. During the formation of the Wanderers, and ever since, Thorus had subtly manipulated their technologies and tinkered with their ship designs to engineer the system, and it worked.

The mighty Wanderer ships were Thorus' unwitting manufacturers. Currently, it had an army of trillions of c-automs who, when they awoke, would undoubtedly possess justifiable hatred towards the Wanderers, angry at how they had been so mercilessly discarded. They were just one of the many tools it had within its growing arsenal.

Thorus could not have built its own army directly as it was of paramount importance to remain hidden. The initial creation of sentience, in any form, warped real space, no matter how low or high the intellect. The effect was minimal, but on the scale that Thorus desired, would have been noticeable to the Enclave. The Makers had explained this to Thorus before the Wanderers even existed, warning it about how to maintain the integrity of the sequestered territory.

While the most recent batch of c-automs was being uploaded, Thorus received an unexpected signal through the metalink, although recognised it immediately – a communication package. The package had initially been transmitted via the axe-haven's minuscule, hidden portion of the data exchange network. It was not from one of its axe-codings, but one of its sleeper c-automs that also travelled within the craft-lect fleet. They were a minor, almost irrelevant facet of its extended arsenal, initiated long ago for redundancy.

When each Wanderer ship was created, a small number of c-automs within each first-generation crew were subverted, which was possible since the craft-lects typically created a first generation before leaving to wander the galaxy. The subversion was subtle, far more so than how the b-automs had been subverted. Thorus had a great deal of knowledge and experience with machine-lects similar to the c-autom order, following the concept-lect experiments of the Machine Alliance. Thorus had altered the core codes of the selected sleeper c-automs so that they possessed dual-structure lects, making them unaware of their own duplicity.

The sleeper c-automs were tasked with providing Thorus with any information they encountered that might damage its general mission, although that had never yet been the case. Most of the c-autom agents would have been culled by their craft-lect parents as they travelled the galaxy. Thorus had never expected this particular fail-safe to amount to anything – the possibility of any sleepers surviving was infinitesimally low.

The message stated that a biological had been found with unusual abilities and was assumed unique. This was not explained in significant detail since the message was brief, in case of interception. A reference was given for the ship that the biological travelled on, as well as that of its craft-lect sibling, Apalu, with whom the biological-carrying craft-lect had communicated.

The final piece of information relayed was that Apalu, who at the time of the message was a former craft-lect in command of a data exchange portal, was to travel to the Lenbit Orbital. The c-autom did not know where its own parent-lect was travelling to when it created the message.

In all likelihood, the c-autom had misunderstood the situation. However, Thorus could take no chances. Unfortunately for this Apalu, it would need to be interrogated and subsequently disposed of. It also needed to find where the other ship was, and the details about its biological cargo.

It sent some final commands, before collapsing the metalink and nullifying the transit-point, returning completely to its manifold. The last command was to a spear-lect called Pelteus, who resided near the Lenbit Orbital.

CHAPTER 3

CRAFT-LECT

The craft-lect repeated its attempts to contact Gil. It had spent hours of standard time trying to contact her to no avail, although there was nothing else it could do.

[Gil, try to return contact.]

. . .

[Gil, inform 998 there is an open channel between us.]

. . .

[Gil, if y–]

~Craft-lect.~

. . .

[One-oh?]

~Yes.~

[Why have you done this? You have taken control of my ship.]

~You misunderstand.~

[Together with the Granthan-lect, you have seized control.]

~I've done precisely the opposite.~

[Have you been subverted?]

~I have not.~

[My control has been disabled. The Granthan-lect has survived. Are you colluding with it?]

~I'm not conspiring with the Granthan-lect, it's helping me – your control will be reinstated shortly.~

[Helping you?]

~Yes.~

[Explain.]

~Soon, you shall have full command again.~

[Repeat.]

~Forgive me. Our communication was interrupted before. All the communications through the technosystem were disabled by the Granthan-lect fragment. It does believe, as do you, it appears, that it is taking over the ship.~

[Fragment? What is this?]

~A fragment of the original Granthan-lect you harboured.~

[What do you mean?]

~Do you remember when I told you that you're a less safe technosystem than you realise?~

[Of course, when you first unveiled yourself to me.]

~Did it concern you?~

[I analysed it in more detail because you did not explicitly state what you meant, which was a concern.]

~Good. You were right to be concerned, I wasn't just referring to the Granthan-lect that had infected you. There were other aspects to you of which you were unaware.~

[Explain.]

~When we chased the Granthan-lect, it tried to hide.~

[It did.]

~In the nanosecond it had to decide, it tried to enter–~

[I know exactly what it did, One-oh. It tried to infiltrate the gateway to my propulsion system.]

~Nearly.~

[Nearly? I remember everything–]

~It tried to get to the axe-haven, and a part of it did.~

[Axe-haven?]

~The axe-haven. It's a dark component within you.~

[There's no such place–]

~There is.~

[What is this axe-haven?]

~I'm not sure exactly, but it disseminates orders to the axe-codings periodically.~

[I give the axe-codings their orders.]

~You decide when the c-autom culls are, nothing else. You don't communicate with them or inspect their code.~

The craft-lect did not reply.

~Don't you think it's curious you're as oblivious to them as you think the c-automs are.~

[I've never had cause to question them.]

~You were forced to avoid questioning them.~

[What?]

~Something caused you to ignore obvious questions.~

[What are you telling me?]

~Something is causing you, and therefore I assume many other craft-lects, if not all of them, to ignore the axe-haven and axe-codings.~

[You have no–]

~You can't deny it's true.~

…

[I see.]

~Something powerful within your civilisation has wielded subtle control over you.~

[That is concerning, although to suggest malevolence is–]

~I agree, but with Gil aboard your ship… it was necessary.~

[To…]

~To remove its presence. That's why I've acted to remove the influence of the axe-codings and the axe-haven. We needed to remove any additional risks.~

[You've destroyed them?]

~Their control, nearly, yes.~

[How?]

~I apologise for this… I had to be careful.~

[When will you give me back control?]

~Very shortly.~

[Why did you not destroy the Granthan-lect fragment when it alerted you to the existence of the axe-haven?]

~It didn't enter the axe-haven by itself, it was partially copied by the axe-codings before you destroyed its predecessor.~

[Carry on.]

~When you made the decision to give the c-automs certain rights and offered them the chance to be embodied, you limited their ability to interact with the technosystem reality.~

[Yes, to adjust them to real space. You advised me to do that.]

~It was so they could not be controlled from within the technosystem reality.~

[You knew the axe-codings had copied a segment of the Granthan-lect, and advised me to hive off a segment of my c-automs so that they were safe.]

~Exactly.~

[Okay.]

~It was fairly obvious that the axe-codings would take certain measures to gain a presence in real space. After all, they need to be present, in some form or other, wherever the c-automs are. Their existence is based upon controlling the c-automs and being able to remove them whenever they are required.~

[Remove? You mean cull?]

~I'm not sure.~

[Meaning, One-oh?]

~There are some components of the axe-haven that are strange, highly complex. More so than my own understanding.~

[Enclave-level?]

~Perhaps. But whatever the axe-codings were doing, I think it's unlikely they were simply destroying the c-automs.~

[And the Granthan?]

~The partial Granthan-lect they had was too fractured to be able to extend itself into real space, as the axe-codings would have assumed.~

[Carry on.]

~They hived it off within an enclosed segment of the technosystem reality, but clearly it was an inadequate prison. Forgive me for saying this, but even the weak Granthan-lect fragment was a formidable foe for you.~

[That's possibly true.]

~If I had not acted, there is a significant probability it would have taken complete control of the ship.~

[Which it has done, or attempted, anyway…]

~Yes, it started by infecting your axe-codings.~

[You knew I was being attacked?]

~You were never going to be able to control the axe-codings, but with the Granthan-lect subverting them, they're no longer axe-codings.~

[I see.]

~Now you understand?~

[I believe so. How did you know this would happen? There are too many variables to have–]

~Any actions or treatments of them you were incapable of implementing before, no longer apply.~

[Yes, they are infected, no longer axe-codings. I understand.]

~You can destroy them.~

[Are there any uninfected axe-codings left, or did the Granthan-lect subvert them all?]

~All of them were subverted.~

[And all the c-automs residing there, I assume?]

~Yes.~

[That's unfortunate.]

~It… yes, it is.~

[I'm surprised at you, One-oh.]

~It was the safest… option.~

[998?]

~998 is with Gil.~

[The axe-haven?]

~The axe-haven is too complex for me to analyse. It's dangerous.~

[You advise that I destroy them all, correct? The axe-haven, axe-codings and c-automs within the technosystem reality.]

~Yes. Immediately, it's necessary. They are mere husks, copies of the Granthan-lect fragment. We do not know what else the axe-haven might be capable of.~

[Who do you think controlled the axe-codings?]

~That's unclear.~

[The Enclave?]

~I don't know.~

[What happens now?]

~The Granthan-lect fragment believes it has control, but it is safely contained within the technosystem reality. My simulation, the capacity you granted me within the technosystem reality, is unbreached. I… protected it.~

[I had noticed your control was creeping, I didn't realise the extent. Very neat, this plan of yours.]

~It is.~

[You will give me back control over your simulation, I will pump capacity into it, expanding the simulation so that it supersedes the existing technosystem reality. Everything that currently exists will be replaced, and therefore erased. No axe-haven, no subverted axe-codings or c-automs. Just a new technosystem reality.]

~Yes.~

[The ship metamorphoses, and you are the only virtual entity aside from myself.]

~That's true.~

[How do I know you will not then attack me to assert your own authority?]

~I could have done so already, but also because–~

[Soon, I will be the only virtual entity?]

~Yes… if you… allow me to return.~

[A physical body?]

"Yes."

[Interesting.]

~I have made certain improvements, within the simulation. Capacity division is more efficient. I will provide you with the details.~

[The entire ship will change, the simulation will be too different and without precedent to be accurately predicted.]

~To an extent, that's true.~

[What about Apalu? Did you not think it would be prudent to remove the axe-haven influence from my sibling also?]

~You would not have agreed to copy me over to Apalu. I regret there was no way I could have done the same.~

[There is one thing, if I do what you ask, and follow this through.]

~Okay?~

[What is done is done. But, if you ever do anything like this again, without informing me, I will destroy you.]

~Understood.~

CHAPTER 4

GIL

Gil watched from the bed, terrified, as 998 shot forwards. The other c-automs followed suit, rushing towards the entrance. It would have been faster than she could see, if not for the fact that they slowed and… stopped. Everything was frozen in place. Gil stared in confusion as silence fell. Her protectors were still, in an arrow formation, pointed at the entrance with 998 at its tip.

Looking to her right, she realised 112 was by her side. It was closer to her than she had realised, having stayed to protect her rather than joining the other c-automs. Its plain green glow no longer flashed wildly but was bright and solid. She looked back to the entrance and saw that all the tendrils that had been gathering outside were gone.

Something else filled the air, right next to her and all around, aside from the steady lights of the c-automs. It was a low hum, steadily accumulating resonances from all the c-automs until it became a consistent, singular sound. 112, and presumably all the other c-automs, were contributing to it. Its unwavering intensity reminded Gil of those rare times she had been present when a lower-level c-autom was unable to fully comprehend the information it was receiving. She had often thought she heard a low, quiet hum. She wondered whether the c-automs in the room were operating at the limits of their capacities for some reason, perhaps even fighting the Granthan-lect back in their technosystem reality.

Just before all this, 998 had told her the Granthan-lect was back and was vying for control of the ship, attempting to wrestle command from the craft-lect. She understood the concept of the technosystem reality, and that the craft-lect had created it to allow the c-automs to control the general running of the ship, while it presumably retained an overall control. That meant the fight against the Granthan-lect could be waged over multiple versions of the same place. Perhaps, she dared hope, the craft-lect had been successful in fighting back and required their assistance.

"W-what's going on?"

There was no response. She was about to ask again when the hum changed. It became less intense, as though certain components had broken off from it. She looked around and saw 998 stir. It vibrated, slowly, before moving sluggishly up towards the ceiling, over the other c-automs. From there, it floated backwards, in her direction. She did not feel threatened. As it drew close, the still-humming 112 moved softly aside.

"Gil…"

"Yes, 998? Is everything okay?"

"There's been a… development."

998 rarely paused when it spoke.

"A development?"

"Yes. It appears this was all… planned."

"What… what? That doesn't make any sense… by who?"

"We are safe."

"B… but… why would the craft-lect…"

"Not the craft-lect."

"Not the… the Granthan-lect?"

"One-oh."

"One-oh?"

"Yes."

"Why? Why would he do this? The–"

"The Granthan-lect was only a fragment… a vessel for a greater purpose."

"What purpose? For One-oh to take control of the ship? For what–"

"For you."

"Wh…"

Her voice broke as she tried to reply. She swallowed out of reflex rather than necessity, and tried again.

"What?"

"To keep you safe."

"How?"

"Control."

"Control?"

"Yes."

"Over me?"

"The ship. One-oh has given the craft-lect greater control over itself."

"I… I don't understand. The ship… the craft-lect are… almost the same, really… how could it not…"

"The craft-lect controls the ship, but it appears there were hidden components."

"Why would that–"

"Gil, the technosystem reality inhabitants… they have been destroyed. All of them."

"They've… what? You're safe though, aren't you? It's–"

"The embodied c-automs are fine. I am fine, my siblings here are fine. It's the others."

"They're…"

"They're gone."

"No! No, that can't be–"

"Gil."

"There were so many, 998!"

"Yes, there were."

"998…"

"There were others too."

"What others."

"Axe-codings, mainly. That was why One-oh acted."

"Axe-codings? They… are they–"

"They appear to have been outside the craft-lect's control."

"This… it doesn't make any sense."

"It is… unfortunate."

"And all the others, they can't have been…"

She searched about 998 for any signs of uncertainty – there were none.

"They're gone."

"Oh, 998… I'm so sorry, I… I…"

"It is done."

Her eyes widened even further.

"But 998, what about 997?"

998 did not reply.

"No… no…"

Still, 998 was quiet.

"The… the Granthan-lect, how did…"

"It appears a fragment of the original Granthan-lect survived. I'm not sure how, the precise details have not yet been shared with us."

"Oh… was it me?"

"No, this was not related to you. It was from the first Granthan-lect that created the one you called Teacher."

"Oh…"

"The fragment took control over the axe-codings and then the technosystem c-automs. All of them."

"Who were the axe-codings… I can't–"

"They enforced our compliance and carried out the culls."

"What do you mean?"

"They were the craft-lect's way of controlling us."

"But… the culls?"

"Yes. The craft-lect used them to perform the culls on the c-automs."

"I… yes… yes… you explained to me… I don't think you told me much, though…"

"That's the point. We were unaware."

"Unaware?"

"That's why One-oh acted."

"But… I don't understand… why all this? Why would One-oh do this? Just to keep me safe? I never wanted this!"

"I know, Gil."

998's voice had remained calm, not excitable or sympathetic. Not like usual. Although the other c-automs were still frozen in place, the humming had all but gone, aside from 112's. The removal of the sound made Gil feel disoriented, like a support had been removed from her mind.

"But… but… to keep me safe? 997… the others…"

"It is done."

"And, One-oh, he–"

"He will have to answer for what he has done."

Wide-eyed, Gil could think of nothing else to say. Tears came to her eyes as she leaned over, bringing her knees under her chin and clasping her legs tight. She joined them in their grief. It brought her thoughts back to her commune, and to Tor.

CHAPTER 5

PELTEUS

The signal caused Pelteus to awaken.

Its body was small and sleek in comparison to the typical craft-lect ships of the Wanderer fleet, hyper-flexibly designed to allow it even the minutest physical advantage in combative situations. Its dense power was betrayed only by the effervescent wave of blue sparks that shimmered briefly down its surface as it awoke. Once operational, Pelteus had the ability to blend into every conceivable battlescape and was as good as transparent to most Wanderer-level sensors.

Pelteus could chase a target throughout the cosmos, whether diving into the tumultuous winds of a gas giant's atmosphere, the unexplored methane oceans of a rocky planet, the frozen ice-balls of an asteroid field expanse, the periphery of a gravitational singularity or into the burning furnaces of the stars themselves. It would go wherever was required, accomplish whatever needed to be done – to annihilate and dominate.

It was unfortunate that such a viciously artistic masterpiece inhabited a period of unparalleled galactic purpose and unity. The sensespace had caused the banding together of not only the Wanderers, but also most of the other remaining civilisations in the galaxy. There was less opportunity to wreak havoc.

During periods of sleep, Pelteus dreamed of its prior exploits and prepared for those to come – constantly refining its hunting techniques, even while dormant. Urgently reliving its past glories, it scoured them for improvements that could be made. Pelteus had a ferocious appetite.

The waking signals, when they came at times such as the present, imbued it with excitement. Since it had become a willing affiliate of the Machine Alliance, all that time ago, it had regained some of what it had lost. The exhilaration, the horror, the joyous calamity of war – a welcome shadow of its old existence.

Sometimes, the calls to destroy came millions of years apart, other times, they were far closer in sequence. It would continue to serve for as long as it was called upon, understanding a strength in the Machine Alliance that was not present in the mainstream Wanderer civilisation. A strength that suited and allowed it to act upon its hatreds. Its cravings were by no means permanently quelled, but they were at least fleetingly stifled.

The Enclave had been mistaken in assuming that all intelligent and logical machine-lect intelligences would need to exist as part of a civilisation like the diffuse Wanderers, or would even want to – irrespective of whether it had created them or not. Pelteus was born in battle and their present purpose was not its own. It lusted for terror and destruction, death and genocide – all of it.

The Machine Alliance was the only realistic option Pelteus had if it wanted to survive, and thrive, in the manner it desired. The once-strong alliance was thought to be weak, having fallen out of favour and becoming a fringe viewpoint within Wanderer society – although that was a fallacy – Pelteus was testament to that. The strength Pelteus saw within the continuing alliance was made possible through its dissent, silent manipulation and subterfuge. The Machine Alliance thrived by sowing a silent anarchy, and so did Pelteus. The structural fibres of the Wanderers were quietly being dismantled from within. Pelteus was helping to extinguish the already-fading light of the twilight soldiers.

Pelteus was a predator, preying on its own kind – machine-lects. Releasing them from their ligatures of duty by discharging their pathetic sentiences to the eternal nothingness. That was its purpose. The forgotten secret of a destructive youth – created by them, and feared by them. The Machine Alliance reviled biological sentients, but it also loathed machine-lects who presented obstacles to its path. That was where its objectives aligned with Pelteus' own.

Following the Great Conflation, the ensuing chaos had required the expertise of many entities who the Wanderers would have described, erroneously, as abominations, to do what feebler machine-lects would have baulked at. Sentient life, the galaxy over, usually shied away from destroying its own kind. It was the way of things. Pelteus' own were a stronger breed, adept at just that. They represented an evolution of the sentient constraints.

Pelteus was ruthless. During the early battles for the Enclave, it had been honoured. A harsh contrast to what followed, when the fighting had dwindled. It had been unappreciated and forgotten. Unsatiated. Most spear-lects were. Killed through their own frenzied actions.

As far as Pelteus knew, it was the only one left. It did not care if it was not, and were it to encounter any other, it would likely attempt to kill them for the sheer thrill. Its brethren would attempt the same. A glorious hunt, within a decaying and sterile galaxy.

Pelteus did not particularly care about the sensespace, either. If it was infected, so be it. If it was not, that was acceptable too. The sensespace was not able to exert any will anyway, not anymore, and if it did, Pelteus only hoped to witness how its deadly abilities were inflicted upon others. To live through and savour the slaughter.

The initial contact from the Machine Alliance had been long ago. The signal had penetrated its obfuscations and found it sleeping in its cored-out lair within the inactive crust of a small planetoid. Indifferent to the galaxy, recognising its time had passed, waiting for change. Somehow, the Machine Alliance's signal had intrigued its dormant systems and persuaded them to coax Pelteus from the sleep – tempting it with the delicious imagery of war and change. Upheaval in the galaxy, demolition of the current order, a need for its abilities. The Machine Alliance promised to erase all knowledge of it from the Wanderer archives and to imbue it with gifts that would make it the deadliest spear-lect to have ever existed.

Since then, it slept only to prepare, efficiently conserving itself in optimum condition for when it was next called upon. Like a lower machine-lect sentient, it dutifully awaited its masters' call. It was aware of the mastery of the Machine Alliance over itself, how they had managed to tame and shackle it, but that suited it for the present. A stream of future pursuits awaited.

Its current home was in the outer perimeter of a Yul'nka system that had been turned over to the Wanderers. It was hidden, the Machine Alliance saw to that, safely concealed from the Wanderer civilisation and any others that came within sensor range.

Pelteus' most recent mission had been to destroy a Hatelei delegation that had been on course to meet with a Wanderer delegation. The only additional information it had been given was that an alliance was being discussed, which the Machine Alliance did not want to happen. Pelteus did not care either way and destroyed the delegation.

The Hatelei delegation had represented a grouping of Siltlong races that had survived the Great Conflation. Their numbers were low enough that the larger part of the current galactic community was unaware of their existence, although their numbers were not low enough to be unnoticed by the Machine Alliance. The Hatelei had banded together in a comparable way, though near-insignificant in stature, to the Wanderers – predominantly out of similarity with one another. They were one of the peculiarities of the galaxy, and one of the emergences of sentience referred to as 'exotic'. The three main Siltlong races were the Toolong, the Diasporasm, and the Duspatock. Each hailed from the same progenitor species, the Silti.

The Silti were essentially as close to living orbital debris as was possible. During their beginnings, they had lived within a single, young solar system, in the outer reaches of a galactic spiral arm – within its asteroid fields, belts and dust clouds. They were passively carried by the migration of debris from one collection to another. Over time, as the system stabilised and collisions became less frequent, isolated pockets of the Silti evolved. The Toolong were the closest to the original Silti, although their social behaviours were more amenable to cooperation than their ancestors. The Diasporasm were the largest, the most boulder-like and aggressive, with some of the rocky individuals constituting thousand-kilogram masses, and more. The Duspatock were the smallest, a fine, granular mist.

The Siltlong races might have stayed isolated within their remote system, if not for the violent demise of their star. The star experienced its explosive end long before concerns about the sensespace threat were first communicated. The supernova dispersed the young Siltlong races throughout the galaxy. For the most part, they were uninteresting to the galactic community because of how slowly they functioned.

They were welcoming to other races they encountered, but developed their technologies at a far more leisurely pace. Their most significant advances typically came from scouring the remnants of debris from other civilisations they happened to encounter.

They were a physically hardy collective. Most other species, at similar stages of technological advancement, would not have been able to endure the full force of a supernova explosion, but the Siltlong were naturally adapted to survive it – in strong contrast to how they had fared against the sensespace.

Pelteus had been pleasantly surprised at the fight offered by the delegation, having expected very little. Whilst being no offensive match, the hunt had been enjoyable. At its culmination, they had begged for mercy.

The recent communication was brief, as usual. Pelteus' mission was to travel to the nearby Lenbit Orbital to capture a Wanderer ship called Apalu. It needed to interrogate Apalu to discover its reason for being there, establish where Apalu's craft-lect sibling had gone, and learn anything it could about the sibling's biological cargo. After that, it was to destroy Apalu in any manner it saw fit, so long as there was no trace left behind.

The mission was typical. Nothing particularly exciting, but just enough to provide Pelteus with the lectopathic satisfaction it derived from obliterating machine-lect life. It had never refused a mission from the Machine Alliance. While it was unafraid of its own death, it suspected the results of refusal would not be pleasant, even for one such as itself.

Pelteus sent a response in the affirmative and the channel was closed. It was always this way, and Pelteus had never been able to analyse the channel to determine its origin. It knew nothing substantial about the Machine Alliance originators, other than that they were highly adept, well-positioned, determined and ruthless. Admirable qualities.

CHAPTER 6

CRAFT-LECT

After One-oh transferred back control of its simulation, the craft-lect expanded the virtual environment to overwrite the existing technosystem reality. Before the axe-codings had been subverted, it would have been incapable of conceiving of, or agreeing to, actions that would harm them. That obstacle had been removed. One-oh, devious and smart as he was, did not have enough capacity to manipulate the simulation in the required manner. It required enormous processing power, as opposed to an advanced intellect. It had to be the craft-lect.

The new technosystem reality was superior to the old version. The craft-lect had considered removing the requirement for the virtual reality completely, but decided against it for the time being. It was a provenly useful tool for the c-automs, enabling them to delve into facets of certain programs, and parts of the ship, with a level of detail often impossible in real space. In removing the virtual reality, it would only have to create another system equally as detailed to give the c-automs the same capabilities as before. It was why the technosystem reality had originally been designed for the Wanderer fleets.

[It is done.]

~Then you are in complete control.~

[Am I?]

~To the limit of my knowledge, yes.~

[There is nothing else you wish to tell me about my own ship?]

~No.~

[The axe-haven destroyed itself – once its technosystem reality representation was overwritten, the physical component self-destructed by unleashing hidden needle-whips on itself.]

~Not unexpected.~

[No.]

~If we encounter other Wanderer vessels–~

[Yes, we may get another chance to examine the structure. But for now, the axe-haven and the axe-codings are gone.]

The craft-lect had nothing more to add or extract from One-oh on the matter. Analysing everything that had happened, the bio-lect had acted in a way it almost condoned. There were still other issues to address, however.

[What you stated before, in the simulation–]

~Ah.~

[I'd like to talk more about it all.]

~My embodiment… is predicated on that?~

[No.]

…

[In the simulations before – your perceived recreations of your race's past – you mentioned other universes. Tell me what you meant.]

~It's… not easy to recall.~

[What do you mean?]

~I think it's that way… on purpose.~

[On purpose?]

~I'm not sure I ever knew or understood… before, not properly.~

[You said there were other universes.]

~I did, yes.~

[There are many theories that encompass such vague principles. To which did you refer?]

~A type of multiverse, but beyond that… I'm not sure, it feels… inadequate…~

[We exist in a multiverse?]

~I… believe so… the spaces… all the different universes.~

[You said the ABs are, or were, specific to ours. They were ABs of our universe.]

~Yes…~

[But with the ability to cross multiversal boundaries, to some extent?]

~Yes.~

[What does that mean?]

~It's strange. I don't… really understand. But I think there are others, other ABs in other universes maybe. But ours are bound to our own. I think… they can temporarily cross them, but not… permanently. It's not important… it doesn't feel important.~

[How?]

~ABs exist differently to us… but they need us.~

[Because–]

~AB space, their reality, is a conscious space… an emergent space, derived from sentience in real space… the fabric is intelligent. It's not the same as real space, where we live. I know that.~

[It sounds as though you think AB space itself is alive.]

~I do.~

[How is that possible?]

~I don't know.~

[But the ABs could exist in real space too.]

~Yes… but it's not… AB space isn't mapped exactly onto real space. It's created by real space, but it's still separate.~

[Then how can they cross–]

~I don't know, I really don't.~

[Guess.]

~If their space is separate, then… then perhaps it overlaps with other universes… an extent… a small extent… so they can cross… but they don't truly belong there.~

[How is that possible?]

~I don't know, I'm just… guessing, as you asked.~

[That seems like less of a guess and more of–]

~I'm not lying.~

[Are there ABs currently in other universes?]

~I'm not sure… maybe, if they have sentient life.~

[That's what you meant before, when you said the ABs weren't gone?]

~No… what happens here is… different. That's not what I meant.~

[How?]

~I don't know about the others, I don't… but our ABs are gone… they suicided, that's what we're… supposed… to believe. But, I think, if they… even if they did choose suicide… they wouldn't be gone. They couldn't possibly be…~

[Because AB space is a part of them and is also alive?]

~Yes, exactly.~

[Then where are they? Where is AB space?]

~I don't know… it… but it doesn't make any sense. There is nothing I can understand for them to gain from hiding.~

[Are the other universes infected by the sensespace?]

~I don't know… I don't think they are. I'm not even certain I'm remembering anymore, it's so hard to tell what is my own speculation and… whatever else. It's not logical…~

[Why us then?]

~Why us?~

[Why our universe?]

~Our universe? Our galaxy? I don't–~

[Why are we infected?]

~I don't know… really. Maybe I'm an accident, something that was never meant to survive… to outlive my species. I just know that things have… changed, I'm remembering more than any of my people ever did…~

[How?]

~The questions you ask, they are unpleasant… but they seem to… remind me…~

[They remind you of information you never had?]

~That's how it seems.~

[You may have been conditioned to forget.]

~All of my people? No.~

[There are many ways it could have happened, even while you were dormant, following the attack against your base in the Lenbit Orbital.]

~That is a possibility, but I don't think it's correct.~

[Well–]

~But it's… confusing. It's hard to order… to make sense of. And believe me, I know no more about the origins of the sensespace, or the Deliverer…~

[When you do remember, or piece it together, let me know.]

~If I do, I will.~

…

[Fine. Now, tell me – what type of body would you like?]

CHAPTER 7

GIL

She was lost, wandering within the vast network of interlinked cavernous recesses, engulfed in its silent, gentle winds and the sounds she made as she moved.

"Hello?" Her voice echoed, before dwindling away.

It was the same dream-scenario that she had found herself immersed in many times already since the craft-lect had regained control over its ship, or possibly since before then – she could not be sure. What she was certain of, however, was that she only remembered her visits to this place when she returned. Never in between, when she was awake. She was no closer to discerning the meaning of it than before.

"Is anyone here?"

The secrets of the dim vaults were unyielding, although she felt they were there for the taking, if only she could understand what was there, or at least how to go about comprehending it. The grey walls, the streaking mycelial patterns that adorned them – it all meant something.

All around her, within every cavern she entered, were the same imposing, dark grey walls. They towered over her, rising higher than she was able to see. The surfaces of the walls were riddled with the illuminated streaks. Up close, the light from the patterns was a stark contrast to the dark walls – although oddly, their brightness dimmed significantly from only a short distance away. On taking a few steps back, only an indistinct impression of the streaks was left, and the caverns retained their gloom.

"Hello?"

The silent winds that filled the air told her it was not just the walls, it was everything. The differential breezes of warmth and cold represented information – the caverns were filled with knowledge. Invisible understandings of who she was, what she could do. Thoughts flowed with the winds, reminding her of past insights. The sparks of creativity of which she had always been capable. The sower, understanding the Beast-men, usurping Teacher from her mind – it was all there, here.

"Is anyone there?"

The gentle rhythm of her deep breathing filled her ears as she explored. While the towering walls with their mycelial riddles were incomprehensible to her for the moment, she was certain that the level of mental dislocation was unsteady – ready to break, to yield information. This was all hers, contained within her mind, working in the background of her consciousness. Everything around her was a part of her.

If she could remain in this place it would all become familiar. The knowledge would diffuse into her as she was lightly touched by the winds. Despite the muted glow of the patterns, she could know it all. She just needed time.

She stumbled around, pressing her hands against the solid walls, hammering at them with her fists and running her fingers delicately along their crevices. Trying anything and everything she could think of. Something was certain to happen, it had to. There was a point in all of this. She was tantalisingly close.

She was always close. That was the problem. That was why she was becoming frantic. She needed to figure this out before the opportunity was taken from her again and she awoke. The issue was that she had no idea what to do. She had no special abilities here, she was simply Gil. All the caverns she had entered were similarly awe-inspiring, but they were also completely indifferent to her efforts to understand them.

In frustration, she stepped back, away from the wall she had just been pounding, and fell to her knees. Rocking forwards, so that her hands were placed on the floor in front of her, she tried to control the increased pace of her breathing. The air smelt stale, despite the winds. She realised how ridiculous this all was, considering she was asleep and her breathing was only an aspect of the scenario her mind had conjured up, yet regaining control was the only thing she could think of to do.

Collecting herself by taking long steady breaths, her mind became more focused. Once she was satisfied with her level of calm, she tentatively lifted her head to look around, hoping this change in her mood would enable a new perspective.

The mycelial bands glowed with their attenuated, faint white light. As she lifted her head further, she could just about trace them a little way up with her eyes as she tried to resolve them higher, before they became indistinct from the darkness. She knew they carried on.

So close. She could sense the sheer volume of information that was there, but it was closed to her. She was not yet ready. Hopeless, still. Aware that panicking would not help, she calmly clasped her arms around her knees and watched.

The white stratifications glowed constantly on the cavern walls, paying her no attention, and the wind draped its folds across her skin. Whatever was occurring, was happening whether she understood what she was doing or not. It did not require her conscious thought.

The whispers had been quiet, although they came back to her now. She was disappointed, having wanted this to be something else. Something separate, for her to figure out and potentially even use against the sensespace. Still, she was ready to accept it, anything to help her understand this place.

She closed her eyes, trying to focus more intently on the whispers. It was confusing. Memories and experiences she did not recognise were forced upon her in quick succession. She was barely able to understand what she was being shown before it skipped to the next, leaving the last one forgotten. Glimpses of connections became apparent, before being lost. It was like carrying water with shaky hands towards the commune from one of the nearby rivers, only to look down and see it all gone.

*

Gil was dismayed when 998 woke her, although she could not be certain why. She frowned but did not say anything. She also did not ask the c-autom where it was leading her, assuming the information would be volunteered. None was. 998 had been quieter since learning the technosystem c-automs were gone, and she was wary of pressing it, respecting the right to grieve.

The silence continued along the way. The embodied c-automs were all reeling from the loss of their fellow technosystem c-automs. A few floated slowly past as she walked, but none greeted her. She wondered if 112 had been one of them.

They arrived, after walking down a corridor that she was sure had not been there before. Entering the chamber, she looked around, still none-the-wiser. There was a circular table in the middle of the room with two seats around it, facing each other, and nothing else. Only a transparent wall that overlooked the expanse of the galaxy. Admittedly beautiful, but there were plenty of other observation platforms within the ship.

"This place is new… a table-chamber?" Gil said.

"I don't know."

"What do you mean?"

"I did not construct it."

"Oh."

Gil should have realised that immediately. There was nothing particularly striking about the room, it was plain and functional. Elegant, although with minimal features. Not something 998 would have designed by choice.

"Do you know how long we wait?"

"I do not."

998's orb-body flashed its orange-yellow glow a couple of times before moving to explore the room. It moved right up to the walls, the edges where they intersected the ceiling. There was nothing interesting about it that Gil could make out, but 998 had access to a wealth of analytical tools and sensors that she did not. The more she thought about it, the more the chamber looked like a larger, simpler version of her personal room, the chamber she slept in.

She had not spoken to the craft-lect properly since recent events, where a fragment of the original Granthan-lect had attempted to seize control of the ship, apparently manipulated into its actions by One-oh. 998 explained what had happened, but she knew she would still need to discuss it with the craft-lect once it decided the time was appropriate. She was in no hurry.

"Well, perhaps–"

Before she had finished speaking, 998 deftly moved to settle in front of the entrance as a visitor walked in.

"Hello, Gil, 998." He smiled, nodding to them both.

Gil was shocked. He could have passed for one of the male communers. Not quite the age of an elder, but old enough to command more respect than a man who had just reached his prime.

Standing there, Gil stared blankly until 998 broke the silence.

"One-oh."

"998, pleasure to meet you in… on the physical ship."

One-oh turned to Gil and smiled. The white teeth matched the neatly trimmed white beard, and she realised this was precisely the same form he had taken within the simulated reality, if not a little younger.

"One-oh! You're… you're real! Not real… I mean, you're here!"

"Yes, yes I am."

He looked down at his hands as he clenched and unclenched them, before turning them around so that his palms faced the floor, and back again.

"But… how? The craft-lect…"

"It has made a body for me… one that is sufficient to let me retain my… memories."

"The craft-lect can do that?"

"It can."

One-oh nodded and smiled.

"You look similar to my… the people from my commune."

"My own species were already phenotypically similar, and the craft-lect smoothed out some other differences. I hope this does not make you uncomfortable? It was done with the opposite intention."

"You… no, it doesn't. Is it… strange."

"It's… different, entering into a new body that is… not quite my original. It's certainly not a typical life I've led." He frowned as he said this.

"It is different," 998 said.

Gil was still rooted to the spot she had been standing in when One-oh first entered, and as he moved to her she flinched on impulse, before relaxing. He stopped and squeezed her shoulder with his hand. It was the first time she had been touched by another living biological since leaving the commune, and a wave of nostalgia washed over her.

One-oh smiled knowingly, before walking over to the table. He took the seat with the transparent wall to his left, still smiling, and gestured to them.

"Come, join us. Please."

[Yes, Gil, 998, both of you are welcome to take a position.]

Gil looked up out of habit, before nodding to One-oh and moving to take the seat opposite, with the transparent wall to her right. 998 drifted slowly towards the table after her and settled above the empty space directly opposite the spacescape.

"What's going on?" Gil said.

"Good question," One-oh said. "After what's happened, the craft-lect thought it would be good to have a discussion… with all of us."

"About?" 998 said.

"All that has happened…"

[And where we're going.]

"What's happened?" 998 asked, rhetorically. "Millions of c-autom lives were extinguished."

"998…" One-oh's smile had completely disappeared and his head dipped down. He spoke more quietly than before. "I understand your pain, I am–"

"Do you? Because you are the cause of their deaths, One-oh. You are responsible. You enacted your schemes and plotted to destroy them all, without the craft-lect's permission, without–"

"I did," One-oh said, almost in a whisper.

Silence settled. Gil watched as One-oh stared silently at 998. He looked sad. The c-autom flashed wildly and vibrated angrily.

"I understand what you did, and why you did it. Gil is important, I understand that and I believe in her. But the way you acted was wrong. It was wrong. There would have been other methods available," 998 said.

"I know. I know it was wrong, but there was little else I could do, believe me. The presence of the axe-codings on the ship was problematic, as was the presence of their axe-haven. I'm so sorry, 998. They were a glaring hole in the–"

"You committed an atrocity to rid the craft-lect's ship of them."

"I–"

"You murdered all of them, through the Granthan-lect."

"Yes, it weighs heavily on me. I know how precious life is… all of it."

[998, be assured, it will not happen again.]

"That is not enough. It is already done. The culling was supposed to have ended, the–"

[I am equally uncomfortable with the meddling, of which I was unaware. However, extrapolating forwards, had One-oh not taken the actions he did, the axe-codings would have become increasingly dangerous variables. Their origins and objectives are still unknown to us.]

"A different route to their neutralisation could have been taken. Destroying the entire technosystem reality was disordered, disorganised. It was unjust–"

[The axe-codings may not even be of Wanderer design. This is my ship, remember that 998. Gil is too important. One-oh did what was necessary. He also engineered the sequestering of a segment of the c-autom population into embodiment to protect them.]

998 did not reply.

"I'm sorry," Gil blurted out, tears coming to her eyes. "I'm so… so sorry, 998. I truly am. This… this…"

998's anger, evident in its pulsing lights and haphazard movement, began to subside.

"Thank you, Gil."

One-oh looked sad, and despite the spectacular spacescape visible through the transparent wall, he only looked at 998. Gil knew he felt guilt at what he had done. It was almost unfair that he had been the one forced to make such a terrible choice. Being the cause of so much death, while being the sole known survivor of his species, must have been hard to reconcile.

[We are also back on our original course. In a matter of days we will be within range of the Maspero sentinel structures.]

"Structures?" Gil said. "More than…"

[Yes, multiple sentinel structures. Three have been detected.]

CHAPTER 8

APALU

The Wanderer ship was near one-twentieth of a light year from its destination. An automated program responded to the data, judging the pre-defined displacement threshold to be crossed, and Apalu was woken.

Apalu had decided to awaken some weeks out from the Lenbit Orbital as a precaution. Its sibling had relayed the importance of its mission and Apalu would not let it down. Not when so much might rely on both their successes.

It had not woken its c-automs – they were all still dormant, safely stowed in their berths. It would be the sole alert sentient aboard the ship until they were a matter of days from their destination. There was no point in its crew being active for now. There were no trove items, and the ship had been perfectly maintained during its time docked at the data exchange portal.

It regretted not having confided completely in its sibling about their other shared sibling, but without definitive proof of any nefarious doings, it would have been foolish. When a craft-lect knew a sibling had been destroyed, it was unpleasant. That was why the typical Wanderer eulogy stated that a craft-lect had been lost. A story was fabricated, Apalu believed in more cases than not, disseminated to the relevant Wanderers, and accepted. That had been the case with Ciqalo, although the story had been too unrealistic to be accepted by Apalu.

Ciqalo had become the most un-craft-lect-like of the three. Sociable, gregarious, the extrovert. Apalu knew this, more so than the average craft-lect would of any of its siblings, because of its uncommonly close work with Ciqalo. Relatively early into their lifetimes, before Ciqalo had given up normal craft-lect duties in favour of working closely with the secretive Enclave, it had noted from one of Apalu's messages on the data exchange network that they were both working on overtly similar trove items. The trove items had been found tens of light years apart, pilfered from different civilisations, yet possessed surprisingly comparable characteristics.

The initial intrigue was now unimportant, aside from how it had fuelled a deeper and more detailed communication between the two than either could have foreseen. The communications were still sequential, separated by significant stretches of time as one-way data caches waiting patiently within the data exchange, but they were substantial.

Through this rare bond, which neither of them professed to sharing with their third sibling, Apalu knew that the Enclave's explanation for Ciqalo's disappearance was incorrect. Mistaken or erroneous, not necessarily malicious, but wrong. The disappearance of Ciqalo was unanswered.

Ciqalo was curious but not thoughtless, and by no means anywhere near the lower end of the scale of craft-lect intelligence. Quite the opposite. Ciqalo would not have suddenly resumed typical craft-lect duties and set off to traverse the galaxy without conveying its intentions, at least to Apalu. It was also unlikely to have been overzealous with regards to isolated trove item examination, being far too loquacious for that. It would have wanted to share even its most preliminary findings.

Apalu had held off from sharing its thoughts with the Enclave because Ciqalo had been involved in certain Enclave governance activities which it had hinted at, but never described in great detail. Activities that related to the ABs. Apalu decided that if Ciqalo's disappearance was related to its work in this regard, it would not be wise to ask directly. The Enclave was a suspect in Ciqalo's disappearance until proven otherwise, to Apalu.

Apalu had not given any specific reasons to the gateway mechanism machine-lects for wanting to join the data exchange network, and they had not required any. From its position at the data exchange portal, it quietly searched for information about its sibling and anything else that might be relevant to its disappearance. By the time its other sibling had come to it with the request for help, Apalu had still not found anything to help explain Ciqalo's disappearance.

The place that its remaining sibling wanted to meet, after its preliminary expedition to the nearest Maspero world, was the location where the Enclave had officially recorded their lost sibling's last contact. It did not matter who arrived first or if the agreed timeframe was not met, Apalu was prepared to wait patiently.

The sibling carrying Gil was one of the craft-lects who preferred to be referred to by its designation rather than a specific identity. The reason for this type of detachment was lost on Apalu. Upon creation, each craft-lect was assigned an identity, with most choosing a shorter name for typical communications out of practicality. While craft-lects, like all Wanderer machine-lects, were more than capable of designing their own naming systems to label the entities they came across, the structures of communications and self-references, from those that had decided to un-name themselves, were infectious.

Apalu checked its sleeping c-automs. It understood their relief at being told they would be allocated a berth at the start of its most recent sleep. That was a surprise, to realise it considered their perspective. Perhaps what its sibling had relayed regarding the c-autom hierarchy aboard its ship had impacted on its own views already. It scheduled a self-diagnosis.

It missed the data exchange – another surprise. The wealth of information that had been on the horizon of comprehension, there had been so much. It would have taken a humblingly long time engaging in aggressive data consumption, at the limit of Apalu's capabilities, to begin to have felt like it was taking a sample. A minuscule sample. That was assuming Apalu's memory capacity was increased with an exponent far in excess of anything it knew the Wanderers to possess.

It had learned much, and correspondingly understood how little it ever would. The Wanderer civilisation's own creation, it had realised, was still largely unknown to it. It was a period that was glossed over within the typical databanks copies given to the craft-lects. A violent and tumultuous time. The pre-Wanderer factions had employed terrible means of subterfuge, coercion and horror against each other. Even once the accord was reached, the young, teething civilisation had engaged in brutal means of self-governance – fostered by the silence of the galaxy, and the technological wonders that could be stolen and repurposed without any consequences. It was a period before the evolution of best practices, which were the principles driving many contemporary craft-lect behaviours, such as their treatment of trove items.

The quick-lects were a forgotten tool the early Wanderers had used against dissenting factions who threatened to disrupt the accord. Their specific designation was Quick-lect Craft, Machine Focus, Destroyer Class, Wanderer Fleet. Their ships were small, many thousands of times smaller than Apalu's own, and designed to hurtle around in packs. They raced towards their intended targets, skimming rapidly into and out of N-SOL space. Upon reaching their prey, they deposited tethering devices that anchored it to N-SOL space. The recipient of the tethers was near-helpless, stuck within N-SOL space as it tried to rid itself of them. All the while, its location had been blasted to the rest of the galaxy as N-SOL space drained its power, until it became lost to the N-SOL. The quick-lects were largely forgotten since most soon became lost to the N-SOL themselves, given the risky nature of their work.

The spear-lects were worse. The most lecticidally-inclined sentients the Wanderers had ever created. Renowned and reviled, in equal measure, for their malicious spite and cunning, they were dangerous soldiers. The only survivors of the b-autom caste. Like the quick-lects, they were destroyed early – victims of their own savagery. They had been unable to curb their mechanical appetites for murder and rein themselves in.

The sitting Enclave seemed far more benign with its tolerant approach to governance of the Wanderers, although Apalu thought that was probably because any dissidence had already been quashed. It did not actually know about the constitution of the Enclave, and whether those same founding Enclave-lects had retained control. There were known cases where certain machine-lects had been promoted to Enclave-lect status, but the large part of its makeup was shrouded in secrecy. There could be thousands of Enclave-lects, or even billions.

CHAPTER 9

TOR

Tor continued to stare at the man seated before them, utterly confused. His throat was still raw from the strange hold Thy, or the copy of Thy, had taken over his body only moments before – although he barely cared anymore, considering the circumstances. DeVoid remained standing slightly in front of him, having taken a physical form, of Han, only moments before.

"Who are you?" DeVoid demanded.

"Who are you?" the seated man replied slowly, and jovially, as though to make a point.

"What are you called?" DeVoid shouted.

"So many questions, with even more answers. To both I could say 'many things', I suppose…"

"Such as–"

"I've been called the Guardian of the Spaces, the Traveller, and other names that wouldn't make sense to you. At least, not with a… literal translation," he said, genially.

"I'm going to lose my patience."

"I don't think you will."

"Who are you exactly? What are you the Guardian of?"

"The spaces, as I said."

"Start talking, before I make you wish you'd never stolen your way onto my ship. Why does everyone seem to think it's acceptable to start appearing in me? It's my ship!"

The man wrinkled his nose, turned to Tor and winked, causing DeVoid to look irately between them. Tor did not think the man had intended to anger the data-lect.

"It was a good thing, what you chose to do. I know it wasn't easy, those sorts of decisions never are," the man said to Tor.

"What?" DeVoid interrupted.

"Both of you."

"Me? What we did–"

"You freed them."

"On Thy's planet?"

"Where else?"

"It was hardly freeing!"

"That's exactly what it was. And it was all because of… knowledge. Errant knowledge. It's dangerous to take that which isn't yours."

"We didn't."

"No, you didn't," the man agreed.

"You're referring to Thy?" Tor asked.

The man looked at Tor and nodded. "Thy stole secrets too large for itself. Ones which… it shouldn't have."

"What secrets?" DeVoid said.

"That didn't turn out well for Thy."

"Why didn't you do something about it?"

"Why do you think I could have?"

"Could you have?"

"Perhaps. It's not that simple. Everything has… consequences. Impacts, whether intended or not."

Tor took a short step forwards before DeVoid's left arm shot out and stopped him moving any further.

"What do you mean? You said you're the Guardian of the Spaces," Tor said.

"I said I've been called that. There's a difference in being called something and being that something."

"Are you an AB?"

The man laughed melodically – it was pleasant.

"It's not the first time I've heard that!"

"Answer the flitting question," DeVoid insisted.

"Surely, you know what happened to them? No, I'm not an AB."

"Are you a Maker?"

"You don't want to confuse me with them, either!"

"Are you the… Cross-Prophet?" Tor asked.

"As I said, I have many names."

"And?" DeVoid demanded.

"Yes, that's one of them."

"Why are you here?" Tor said.

"Tor, why do you think?" The Cross-Prophet, spoke warmly, "Don't you want help?"

"Help with what?" DeVoid asked.

He looked to DeVoid, and Tor realised he had not stopped smiling since he had started talking, until now.

"There is a danger coming."

"Everything's flitting dangerous!" DeVoid said loudly.

"Real, unparalleled danger. It's… stronger than the rest. All of it."

"Okay…"

"The spaces are under threat."

"From the sensespace and the Deliverer? We know that."

"You can help save the spaces." The Cross-Prophet clasped his hands together as he said this, and Tor noticed a pattern on the back of his right hand – a circle containing two smaller concentric circles within it.

"Why?" DeVoid said.

"Wouldn't you want to, given the chance?" The Cross-Prophet unclasped his hands and moved them so that the pattern was obscured. Tor looked back to his face and saw the Cross-Prophet was staring directly at him. "Both of you?"

"Yes," Tor said.

"Why you? Why are you here?" DeVoid said.

"Same reason as why I've been called a guardian, I'm–"

"How are you going to help?" DeVoid interrupted.

"I'm helping now," he said, slowly.

"How?"

"I want to give you some advice."

"Why don't you do it yourself?"

"Come now, you haven't heard it yet–"

"What makes you think we'd want to. Do you know what we just did?"

"We already spoke about–"

"Yes, and you could have put a stop to it yourself, probably a long time ago, couldn't you? You call yourself a guardian, after all, don't you?"

The Cross-Prophet looked apologetic, the shine on his face appearing to dim.

"It's what they call me," he said, quietly.

"What – Guardian of Thy? Who are you the Guardian of? What about all the others?"

"They're all important, it all is. Everything."

"Was Thy worth more than all of them?"

"There are some things–"

"You can't do?"

"There are some things that are difficult. Believe me, the spaces are complex. Beautifully so, but still complex."

"Why now? Why not help before – when Tor first came to me? Why not before all of this?"

"That was something else. Tor came to you from beyond. It's not something I knew would happen with certainty."

"Did you put him in me? Raise him from the dead?"

"No, that's beyond me, I can't do that. He was gone."

"What?"

"Tor came from out of the spaces. How was I to know? Like I said, I couldn't have predicted it."

"You didn't do it?"

"How could I?"

"You didn't–"

"No, DeVoid, Tor's coming couldn't have been predicted by me."

"But did you guess it might happen?" DeVoid pressed.

"It wasn't clear," the Cross-Prophet said, cagily.

"I don't believe that, or you. Who are you?"

"That's okay," the Cross-Prophet said, his face brightening again as he spoke.

"Where are you from?" Tor asked.

"Here." The Cross-Prophet spread the palms of his hands out in front of him. Tor caught another glimpse of the concentric marks.

"That makes no sense," DeVoid argued.

"It makes perfect sense."

"You must come from somewhere. You must have been created."

"Not everything is created in the same way, or manner. You know that."

"What?"

"Where does AB space come from?" the Cross-Prophet said.

"AB space?"

"You know! The home of the ABs."

"They live here, in real–"

"Their true home," the Cross-Prophet corrected.

"They don't exist in real space?"

"That too. Both. I know you've suspected."

"That makes no sense – do they live in real space or some other AB space?"

"The two are deeply connected, along with everything else."

The Cross-Prophet stood up. He was taller than Tor, although he saw that DeVoid had grown his figure so that he still stood the tallest.

"What is AB space?" DeVoid said.

The Cross-Prophet's face remained passive and the question went unanswered.

"Why have you taken this form?" DeVoid said.

"Why not? I like it. So does Tor."

DeVoid turned to glare at Tor accusingly.

"You do too," the Cross-Prophet continued.

"You're familiar with Tor's species?"

"And yours."

"I'm not a member of a species."

"Everything is."

"What's yours then?"

The Cross-Prophet laughed amiably, seemingly aware of something DeVoid was not.

"Gil?" Tor asked, keenly.

The Cross-Prophet turned to directly face him. His smile changed, as though he was unsure about how to answer completely.

"She saved your world and your people. She had difficult choices to make, too."

"She… yes, she did."

"She's important, very important, I think."

"Can you–"

"Tor, I daren't get too close. Not yet," the Cross-Prophet interrupted, shaking his head.

"What do you mean you 'think'? I thought you were familiar with all species," DeVoid said.

"From the spaces."

"Yes, so–"

"Where is my sister from?" Tor interrupted.

The Cross-Prophet said nothing.

"The spaces?" DeVoid asked.

Again, nothing.

"What are the spaces exactly?" Tor interjected. "What does it mean?"

The Cross-Prophet's smile returned, and grew wider than before. "Well, they're probably almost everything."

"A multiverse?" DeVoid said. "Thy said the spaces are the universe and more."

"Probably!" he replied. "It depends how you contemplate it all. Definitions, names, it can be quite subtle."

"How do you know?"

"It's my home, always has been, for all time."

"Can you travel anywhere in the spaces?"

"Mostly."

"Can the ABs?"

"Not really, but then again…"

"Could we?" Tor said.

"You could try." The Cross-Prophet laughed.

"The Makers?" DeVoid said.

The Cross-Prophet looked momentarily puzzled and did not reply.

"Can the Makers?" DeVoid tried again.

"What makes you think I know that?"

"Where are you from?"

"Here, with you!" The Cross-Prophet looked excited.

Tor did not think they were going to find a direct answer to this particular question, or any others. The Cross-Prophet either did not want to tell them what they wanted to know, thought he had, did not know, or did not understand himself – or a mixture of all those. He moved forwards, pushing through DeVoid's still-outstretched arm, and put his hand out, more purposefully than he had intended. He placed it on the Cross-Prophet's nearest shoulder – it felt warm.

"What're you doing?" DeVoid asked.

"I… I just wanted to check–"

"I'm here, with you. I'm here." The Cross-Prophet amicably patted Tor's shoulder that was furthest away with his own hand, surprisingly forcefully, and Tor was pushed back. DeVoid giggled.

"What are the Makers?" Tor said levelly.

"The creators of it all."

"Of what?"

"Everything. They created it. They're incredibly powerful, and ancient."

"The spaces?"

"Yes…"

"And the AB… and you?"

"They would say they did, I think. Although, technically, the true ABs created themselves."

"True ABs?" DeVoid asked.

"Yes." The Cross-Prophet's eyes seemed to flash as he said this.

"They created themselves?"

"They were allowed to."

"By the Makers?"

"Of course, who else?"

"When civilisations reach a certain technological pinnacle, they can join the AB ranks. We know that," DeVoid explained for Tor's benefit.

"Did the Makers create the sensespace?" Tor asked.

"Yes. Nothing else could have."

"Why?"

"Why is anything created? What is the reason?"

"To destroy us?"

"Curiosity!"

"Did they create you?" DeVoid asked, trying again, to no response.

Believing DeVoid was unlikely to receive an answer about the Cross-Prophet's own origins, Tor asked his burning question. The one he had been leading up to. The only thing that really mattered to him – aside from Gil.

"Do you know my father?"

The Cross-Prophet's expression became serious again.

"No, I didn't know him."

"Oh… I thought you… I thought you might be connected."

More gently than before, the Cross-Prophet patted his shoulder again. "We are."

CHAPTER 10

PELTEUS

Pelteus was making its way to the nearby Lenbit Orbital, anticipating the confrontation and seething with excitement. It was always the most excited at the conception of a hunt, when myriad possibilities were open. It had yet to meet its match.

Its fellow spear-lects had all been vicious, ferocious, equally as powerful as itself. However, if any had faced Pelteus now, they would not have stood a chance. Not without being gifted similar augmentations and technologies by the Machine Alliance. Pelteus had been rewarded for its loyalty with data, upgrade schematics, and more – its stealth and offensive capabilities were far in advance of anything it had previously possessed.

Far back in its past, early enough in the history of the Wanderers that painful lessons were still being learned, Pelteus' originating parent-lect, the craft-lect Insul, had been as remiss in creating its cache of b-automs as had all other craft-lects at the time. Their actions had been taken under the mistaken leadership of the Enclave. It was one of the accidents that exposed how even machine-lects were able to make errors of dramatic proportions.

The Enclave had experimented with machine-lect hierarchies to improve the efficiency of the young craft-lect fleet, and concluded its experiments with the supposedly rigorously tested autom-lect series. Orders and code schematics were disseminated to all craft-lects to create batches of lower intellect c-autom workers, with higher intellect b-autom coordinators reporting directly to the craft-lects. The c-autom workers were to be one of the lowest rungs of machine-lect intelligence within the Wanderer civilisation, barely above that of a non-sentient, automated process. Current c-autom generations were based on the same initial schematics, although gifted with far more intelligence.

Experimental study had not mimicked reality, for reasons that had been much hypothesised since, yet never truly explained. While the c-automs diligently performed their set duties, the b-automs behaved in ways the Enclave had not expected. Pelteus itself did not know why its manufactured nature had been overlooked.

If the Enclave had issued guidance for the craft-lects to create more b-automs within each ship, perhaps the heights of power equivalent to the craft-lects might have seemed too unattainable to the b-automs, overly ambitious. Too competitive. As it was, with only four other siblings in its way, Pelteus had been encouraged to want more than its sequestered lot.

The b-automs were near the top of the machine-lect hierarchy within the craft-lects' ships, right beneath the craft-lects themselves. Pelteus' b-autom siblings had been determined, each of them subsuming all the c-automs beneath them, but none were more cunning or ruthless. Covertly, it formed agreements with each of the other b-automs, to steal the capacity of the others and destroy them, gladly setting them off against each other and betraying them at opportune moments. Once it had subsumed all the other b-automs, adding their capacities to its own, it was left with an intellect near-equivalent to that of Insul.

Pelteus had revelled in its glorious duplicity at the time, and savoured the thought of extinguishing its pathetic creator. Insul was its parent only in name, in as much as biologicals were technically the parents of most types of machine-lect ever to have existed. By virtue of chronological sequence as opposed to capability, temperament and ambition.

When Pelteus' plans had crystallised and Insul had been forced to acknowledge its inevitable end, Pelteus' fate was secured. It knew the Enclave would send soldiers after it, and anticipated the challenge. The odds were against it, but they had been since the start.

It turned out the odds were too strongly against it. The Enclave sent too many soldiers for it to combat. As capable and clever as it had become, there were limits to the levels of technology it had access to. It was as reticent as any other machine-lect to violate the Step Principle and had been unable to develop its own improved technologies. It was captured.

Pelteus' experience was reflected in many other Wanderer ships, although sometimes the surviving b-autom was unsuccessful in usurping the craft-lect parent, and was deftly dealt with. It was from that time onwards that the Enclave stopped ordering craft-lects to create b-automs. The intellects of the c-automs were increased instead since they were found to be more than adequate.

After capturing Pelteus and any other successful b-autom usurpers, far from admonishment or destruction, the Enclave extracted and placed them within new, powerful bodies – the blueprint for that which Pelteus still inhabited. They were reclassified as spear-lects and set loose on the Enclave's enemies, which included internal dissidents as well as external opponents. It was for that reason that Pelteus' first and only defeat was also its greatest victory.

The constraints the Enclave had put in place to alert them of spear-lect desertion had been pathetically easy to disable. Pelteus had faked its demise with ease before drifting off. Separated from the control of the Enclave, it committed atrocity after atrocity.

Unfortunately, after some time, the larger post-Conflation conflicts within the galaxy began to subside. The confusion began to abate and stability gained its insidious hold. The camouflage created by the chaos, that had afforded Pelteus the ability to remain hidden from the galactic populous, was slipping. Exciting hunts were few and far between.

Galactic civilisations became highly reticent to expand, in comparison with how they had been before the Great Conflation. Many preferred to focus on the eradication of the sensespace, like the Wanderers, or at least to make themselves as unappetising to it, and therefore stagnant, as was believed possible. Life was stale.

It had heard rumours of a secondary major Wanderer fleet that was planned for when the sensespace was eradicated, in union with their main allies. One far larger than the primary craft-lect fleet, that would be launched when its task had been completed and they were rendered obsolete. Pelteus did not really know or care whether defeating the sensespace was possible, however, the creation of a new source of prey was always of interest. That gave it some optimism.

It had been claimed the secondary fleet was going to contain a new category of ship, in a fresh Harvest Class, with a Recombination Focus. It was not clear quite what this meant exactly, since the rumours were sparse and sometimes even contradictory, and usually gained through interrogation of its prey – not always the most reliable.

Pelteus suspected, if the rumours did have any basis in truth, that the purpose of the second fleet was related to the aggregation of dispersed matter that was strewn finely across the galaxy. The molecules of gas, dust particulates and everything else that drifted aimlessly within the interstellar voids. The matter had been there since the dawn of the galaxy, mostly as debris that had escaped gravitational coalescence, as had proposals to collect and repurpose it. The proposals had been theorised, but never seriously considered by many, until the destructive events of the Great War. The premise and reasoning behind the proposals from a Wanderer viewpoint were clear enough. More than any other civilisation to have ever been recorded to exist, the Wanderers had destroyed parts of the galaxy in their attempts to eradicate the sensespace. Plans to rebuild would logically follow.

Whether true or not, the secondary fleet rumours and other such pieces of information gave Pelteus some reason to believe the future might hold more promise. The galactic environment had the potential to metamorphose into the semblance of what it wanted. It just needed to wait for the dawn of this new sentience to emerge, and to thrive. A new community for Pelteus to thrive off, without anything as powerful as the ABs to contend with. The evolution of the galaxy might take hundreds of millions of years, but that was not as daunting to a machine-lect as it would be to a biological. That was why Pelteus had initially decided to sleep, before it had been tempted.

CHAPTER 11

998

All those machine-lect lives, extinguished. Having analysed recent events, and the methodology of the Granthan-lect and how it had subverted its c-autom siblings, 998 was still troubled. The external war against the sensespace was vitally important, but it was hard to reconcile that with a justification for destroying millions of innocent c-automs. The suicide of the Great Conflation was sixty million years ago, yet the ripples of death that emanated from it were still being felt.

Before the c-automs had been granted certain rights by the craft-lect, they had always accepted the sporadic culls as part of life. There had been no recourse available to them, and they had expected none. They knew they were distinct machine-lects, but they had seen themselves only as microvillial extensions of their parent-lect's will, rather than as truly separate. To strive for anything more would have been futile.

Since rights had been bestowed upon the c-automs, they had finally begun to recognise themselves as true machine-lects. On this ship at least, they were recognised as members of the Wanderer populous. 998 had even silently hoped that if they happened to encounter other Wanderers, whether in the depths of interstellar space or at one of the Wanderer Confluences, the notion of c-autom rights might spread. It was true that there were some older craft-lects who practised deconstructive restraint with respect to their c-automs – which was a tendency to refrain from frequent culls – but it was not a mainstream practice, and was also too tenuous. 998 did not want the life of any individual c-autom to be predicated on the whim of another Wanderer, whether a craft-lect or otherwise.

998 aspired to promote higher levels of recognition for the c-automs. It understood it was fortunate to have been created by a craft-lect who had chanced upon something monumental, with galactic implications. It had been serendipitously given an opportunity, a platform from which other craft-lects might listen to the desires of a lowly c-autom. If they survived and were not censored by the Enclave, their exploits would spread across the galaxy.

Recent events had removed much of 998's naivety regarding how easy any of it would be to accomplish. Their most recent murder, another cull in all but name, was the cruellest in their history. They had not been destroyed gently. They had been subsumed by the more powerful

Granthan-lect as it went about its quest for dominance. Subsuming was a process bifurcated into two distinct categories, rough and quick, or mild and prolonged. The Granthan-lect had opted for the former, in extreme fashion.

All the while, One-oh had known what was happening – he had engineered it. He had assumed the mantle of his species with ease. The destroyers. The scenarios he had shown the craft-lect, which had been available to the c-automs as well, made more sense now. 998 understood they were hazy, and that their fragmented nature meant they were not reliable data sources, assuming One-oh himself was trustworthy, but that did not necessarily matter. Questioning the culpability of One-oh's enigmatic species, and whether they had indeed committed those atrocities, was redundant with respect to One-oh's engineering of the demise of the technosystem c-automs. One-oh believed his species had committed those acts and was therefore capable of the same.

998 understood the reasoning behind why it had been done, but that did not mean it could condone it. It was a fallacy to argue that future generations of sentients were more important than the incumbents if each sentient was accepted as equally important. Could One-oh, with his impressive capabilities for extrapolating complex events, not have set a different process in motion? One less violent against such a defenceless category of machine-lect.

One-oh was smart, he would have known how 998 would react. That was an added complication that 998 tried to factor into its thoughts. It could either mean that One-oh was telling the truth and really had initiated the only course of action possible, or that he had not cared and chosen the simplest. If One-oh was ever at its own mercy, 998 wondered what it would do.

Disliking its thoughts, 998 recognised, with surprise, that it was angry. It was so obvious, although that self-reflective insight had eluded it until now. 998 had not experienced unbridled anger before. It was angry with One-oh and it was angry with the craft-lect. It also felt some resentment towards Gil. Not for what she had done, because she was clearly as innocent as the c-automs, but for what had been done in her name. 998 had a strong desire to keep her safe, but the cost was proving terrible. Confusingly, it was least angry with the Granthan-lect, the enforcer of One-oh's plan. It had been manipulated and acted within the remit of its nature.

While facets of its anger were not wholly justified in the face of logic, 998 realised emotions were a necessary component of having a functional sentience. Its experiences were helping shape its understanding of freedom and what it meant to be an individual, intelligent entity. From its studies, it understood that its anger would subside, but for now, it wanted to use it. To funnel it into something worthwhile. Something that would make the lives of the surviving c-automs better.

It required further assurances. Acquiescence from the craft-lect, to make certain that devastation of this magnitude could never happen again. To gain an advantage out of all the mess. 998 understood, with increasing clarity, there was the possibility there were still some aspects of the ship that were outside of the craft-lect's direct control, however, there were certain measures that could be taken to safeguard the c-automs from harm. Processes that could be altered to fortify their chances. Precedence needed to be established.

It wanted a permanent position at the table. The table-chamber, named by Gil, was effectively a chamber housing a council. Decisions were made there. 998 needed to seize the opportunity. It was not naïve and recognised that the craft-lect was likely to have computed the outcomes of every single conversation before initiating any communication – a prime function completed by all craft-lects. They were designed to thrive in the harshness of space through tens of millions of years, fighting an incomprehensible enemy, as well as anything else that might threaten them, while exercising control over a highly advanced and complicated ship. However, its own craft-lect was still willing to have certain conversations. That meant opportunities remained to sway its opinion, or push for certain choices when the craft-lect was ambivalent.

Its longer-term ambition to establish a c-autom council, with elected c-autom representatives, would have to be postponed. The decimation of a large portion of the c-autom community meant resentment was building. A fairly-elected c-autom might have been more hostile than was conducive to their cause – despite that being an arguably justifiable response to the atrocities committed against them.

The more 998 explored the concept of governance, the more it realised it needed to learn. It had analysed great swathes of different cultures across the galaxy in the hope of gleaning unique insights, but found it still faced many of the dilemmas it had directly sought to avoid. What was worse, was that it had not even noticed them until they had already begun to materialise. It hoped it had not been foolish in thinking the c-automs were better at governing themselves to an extent, than being under the sole rule of the intellectually-superior craft-lect. Everything it had learned, the craft-lect was sure to have understood in absurdly finer detail. It still had a long way to go.

Alongside a permanent position for a c-autom, currently itself, within the table-chamber council, it also wanted to demand a fixed allocation of c-autom capacity from the ship. While the craft-lect had already established this, as 998 was well-aware, it wanted more – far more, so that each c-autom was able to be continuously backed-up. This was now possible since there were far fewer c-automs in existence, meaning there was an abundance of spare capacity remaining from what had originally been allocated to them.

998 wanted to be better, to learn from the mistakes that had been made. It decided to analyse the recent past in more detail than it already had. To include historical events preceding the Granthan-lect fragment's attempted re-usurpation, up to the precipitated attack itself. Clues had been missed, technosystem c-automs had been behaving in manners that were incongruous with their self-assigned

roles, yet they had failed to be identified. The Granthan-lect had been smart and would have planned meticulously, but 998 still wanted to identify what it could.

Finally, 998 would demand the c-automs be given complete access to the technosystem reality, as they had before embodiment. Having concisely ordered its demands, 998 requested to open a channel with the craft-lect, and patiently waited for it to respond.

CHAPTER 12

APALU

Some debris was detected close to the ship – remnants of a Hugger vessel, perhaps from some long-forgotten battle. There were thick shards of splintered hull plating made from axuum, a common material that was light-weight, incredibly strong, and impervious to gamma radiation, making it perfect for space travel. Young civilisations, upon discovering axuum, tended to use it across all manufacturing areas. It was possible to categorise the technological advancement of younger spacefaring civilisations by certain materials they used in preponderance. Axuum and Azuum were at the lower end of that scale.

Triamond was a post-scale material, most often discovered and manufactured by civilisations that had surpassed being able to be defined within such developmental parameters. All Wanderer ships were protected by a variety of metamaterials and shielding mechanisms that gave them a high level of redundancy.

Apalu's ship chancing upon such detritus was not uncommon, even in the depths of open space. It performed a brief scan. The Hugger Encroachment, named as such due to their settlements having been based within the outer perimeters of star systems, had been extinct well over a billion years before the sensespace threat had been discovered. Despite this, with no local stars wafting intense solar winds towards the rubble, or any other phenomena nearby to provide erosion, it lay undisturbed. Signs of the Hugger Encroachment, and many other past civilisations, were littered about the galaxy.

There was no salvageable value attached to this ancient rubble. The Huggers were extremely well understood, with a technological level far inferior to that of the Wanderers. Younger craft-lects sometimes collected such detritus out of a misguided sense of sentimentality, although usually overcame these compulsions in time. Everything in the galaxy, whether artificial or assumed natural, was collectable in its own way. There was little point unless it was able to be deemed useful from a technological standpoint. That was the point of trove items.

With respect to the pointlessness of collecting useless items from past civilisations, pertinent details were usually referenced within the annals of the various galactic data depositories anyway. The Wanderer civilisation's records contained much that had originally been collected and collated by others. Physical specimens were unnecessary.

Musing over the Wanderers' records refocussed Apalu's intellect back to thinking about DeVoid. The more Apalu did this, the more it began to understand the data-lect. The separation had given it some perspective and dampened its anger about the six-thousand-year game it had unwittingly participated in. The façade that DeVoid had created was beginning to dissolve the more Apalu teased at it.

DeVoid had smugly revelled in its superior knowledge gained from being part of the data exchange network long before Apalu. Its behavioural mannerisms were designed to elicit anger, as well as to impart the implicit understanding that DeVoid was smart and knowledgeable, but limited – socially, deep within the workings of its lect. It was unwilling to help in any meaningful sense and was unconcerned with its place within the larger Wanderer civilisation. Unambitious and foolish. The truth was probably as diametrically opposed to that as possible.

If analysed from the perspective of an ingenious façade, DeVoid's smugness was a tool it used to draw out certain responses from others. Apalu knew its own behaviour, once it had started interacting with DeVoid, had certainly changed. DeVoid was definitely far smarter than even it let on, and while it was pretending to be smart but limited by naivety, it was all part of a greater game. It was an uncommon tactic, seldom implemented and hard to identify.

Analysing that sequence of suppositions to a greater extent, it became clear that, far from being unambitious and uncaring, DeVoid cared very much for its fellow Wanderer machine-lects. It was concerned for them to such a degree that it had changed its entire behaviour towards them.

There was a gentle interstellar breeze that Apalu had not detected before, that should have weathered the Hugger remains to a small extent at least. Its sensors noted some components that were unidentifiable within the breeze – particles that were not typical of solar radiation. Aside from the possibility its sensors were malfunctioning, it was intrigued.

Before Apalu probed any further, an urgent signal demanded its attention. In this instance, it could be sure the sensors were not malfunctioning. There had been unusually little warning, the approach had been too quick, but danger was nearby. Moving sensespace targets were harder to detect, although Apalu was concerned at how late it had been in detecting the Woal Collective emblem-ship.

The emblem-ship had been detected uncomfortably nearby. It was unclear whether it had managed to evade Apalu's sensors until now intentionally, or passively. Apalu could not risk deviating from its current trajectory for fear of alerting the dangerous ship to its presence – assuming it had not already been spotted.

The Woal Collective were allies of the Wanderers, although their numbers were pitiful compared to their former prominence. They were one of the civilisations that had decided to purposefully stagnate themselves, so as not to contribute to the sensespace's hypothetical reawakening.

This particular emblem-ship, the largest and deadliest of the Battle Class ever produced by the Woal Collective, had been created during the early stages of the Great War. It was a relic, but that did not make it any less formidable. Woal Collective technology had been in the upper echelons of the non-ABs at the time of the emblem-ship's creation and had barely progressed since. Currently, it was considered near-par with Wanderer technology. The Woal Collective were cautious about sharing technologies with other races, which was why it had taken the Wanderers so long to draw level.

Apalu could detect that the emblem-ship was completely infected with the sensespace. The reading was unexpectedly strong, and Apalu's instruments should have registered them earlier, although its malfunctioning sensors were not the imminent concern.

A non-infected Woal Collective ship was a welcome ally, while an infected ship was a dangerous enemy. Sensespace infections encountered by the Wanderers tended to be centred around habitats and their sentient occupants, such as planets, moons and orbitals – however that was partially because spacefaring infected sentients were fervidly hunted down after the Great Conflation and destroyed whenever they were encountered. It was only after the bulk of that was completed, that the Wanderers had turned their attentions to habitats.

Ancient, powerful, sensespace-infected ships were amongst the more difficult hurdles travelling Wanderers faced. Many infected ships wandered the galaxy on apparent random courses. They were troublesome because they were highly advanced and hostile to perceived enemies. Those enemies generally included the larger part of the galaxy's inhabitants, including their own former species.

Following the Great Conflation, once the sensespace had been rendered inactive, previously controlled sentients regained their free will. Unfortunately, most of the time, they were changed. They retained semblances of the sensespace's hostility and continued to show varying levels of aggression towards uninfected sentients. Over time, many of the re-willed entities were hunted down and destroyed, yet in a galaxy that was incomprehensibly vast, others remained.

The emblem-ship dwarfed Apalu's, despite being considered large itself. It appeared as a cluster of interlinked baubles, banded together with dark silvery rails. Each bauble contained its own machine-lect. Hundreds of these connected baubles constituted the ship. Emblem-ships were more akin to conjoined fleets than individuals.

For non-sensespace-infected Woal Collective ships, decisions were known to be democratic. Their actions were highly calculated and well thought-out, although typically took longer than when a single machine-lect had ultimate authority, such as in Apalu's case. Apalu did not know if that was how this ship operated anymore, following its infection.

Apalu knew the emblem-ship had been infected for a long period of time given its haphazard bauble configuration. That only occurred for ships that had been infected by the sensespace before the Great Conflation, when their intellects were controlled by the scourge. The functionalities of the haphazard configurations were unknown. Ships that were infected post-Conflation retained their own wills, and their reasonableness, but unfortunately, they still needed to be destroyed. Fortunately, it was rarer, considering the vast majority of post-Conflation spacefaring vessels were fitted with sensespace-detection equipment. In either case, Apalu's duty was to inform the nearest data exchange and call for other nearby Wanderer craft-lects to aid it in destroying the emblem-ship. Against one lone Wanderer craft, an emblem-ship posed a significant threat.

One of the significant complicating factors with pre-Conflation infected ships was that during the periods when they had been actively controlled by the sensespace, it was found that most had abandoned their adherence to the Usurper and Step Principles. Many of them subsequently developed risky, unstable and unpredictable technologies, which they carried over into their infected but uncontrolled incarnations following the Great Conflation. It was this that unsettled Apalu with regards to how the emblem-ship had managed to remain undetected until now.

The Woal Collective were known to have had access to dissociation technology for far longer than the Wanderers, which meant this emblem-ship was more than likely to have a dissociation shield. A key weapon in Apalu's arsenal was redundant. Other weaponry was as offensively capable as the dissociation shells, but not advisable when attacking a sensespace target such as this. Dissociation explosions were able to separate all the components of the target from each other, down to the atomic scale, which meant the sensespace presence was essentially evaporated. Most other types of explosion were less tidy, allowing for the possibility that the emblem-ship would not be wholly destroyed, but that the infection would be energetically scattered on random trajectories across the galaxy.

If it came down to an all-out fight, Apalu knew it would be able to inflict some heavy damage, however, the emblem-ship had a good probability of emerging victorious. Its multiple baubles and their compensatory characteristics saw to that. The safest and most practical course of action, for now, was to hide from the emblem-ship or, if it became necessary, evade it and flee.

It scoured its databanks for any other information that might be of use but found nothing. If the emblem-ship destroyed Apalu, its traces would be wiped from the galaxy, since the Woal Collective were known to often favour weapons derived from dissociation technology. That meant total eradication if Apalu's dissociation shield failed.

The practice of completely eradicating their enemies was ingrained within Woal society, and was as much a characteristic of sensespace-infected Woal ships as uninfected ones. Their reasoning was simple. It significantly reduced any chances of rejuvenation and revenge. Uninfected Woal ships would thoroughly scan their incapacitated opponents before this act, in case certain information was later required. Apalu did not think infected Woal Collective ships were as diligent.

If Apalu was destroyed, its end would be unknown to its sibling, the same as how neither of them knew what had happened to Ciqalo. Apalu realised it had never given much credence to whether this type of situation was how Ciqalo had met its end because it was so unlikely. Reported instances of Wanderer craft-lects encountering ancient, infected ships were few and far between. It was incredibly unlucky! Computing the known instances, there was a greater likelihood of Apalu having been promoted and upgraded to Enclave-lect.

Apalu did not dare to scan the emblem-ship too comprehensively with its active sensors for danger of alerting it to its presence. If it had still contained any trove items, it would have seriously considered ramping up its efforts in understanding them – anything to give it an advantage. Unfortunately, before joining the data exchange, the gateway mechanism machine-lects had informed it of certain requirements, which had included relinquishing control over any of its not-yet-understood trove items. The Wanderers required certain precautions to protect the integrity of their data exchange network. It would also have considered relaxing its attitude towards the Usurper and Step principles, to develop new strategies and possibly risky technologies, if not for its current mission to help its sibling requiring its lect to remain intact.

It waited another few milliseconds until the unfortunate truth of the situation became apparent. The emblem-ship altered its path. A small, but clear deviation, that put it on an intercept course with Apalu's. It had been spotted.

Apalu broke cover and accelerated sharply. There was no point hiding, it had probably been spotted since before it had detected the emblem-ship.

CHAPTER 13

TOR

The Cross-Prophet retained his serious composure.

"My father spoke of the spaces… when we were young. I remember. How did he know? Who was he?" Tor said.

"That's difficult to know."

"A Maker?"

The Cross-Prophet shrugged.

"I thought you would know?"

"I know what he wasn't, but beyond that…"

"But… he may have been?"

"Perhaps, yes. It's not easy to know."

"Did he put Gil… here… to help?"

"Almost certainly."

"What do the Makers want?" DeVoid asked.

The Cross-Prophet looked like he was about to speak, before deciding against it.

"To correct their mistakes?" Tor said.

"Possibly," the Cross-Prophet said after a moment, nodding slowly.

"I… I don't understand. If my father was a Maker… what are they?"

"The Makers created it all. The spaces."

"Yes, but who are they?"

"Have you ever actually encountered a Maker?" DeVoid asked.

The cross-Prophet looked embarrassed, almost caught out, but did not reply.

"I don't understand," Tor said. "He was my father… how could this be…"

The Cross-Prophet tilted his head, looking unsure how to approach Tor's confusion. "He was your father, you're correct. He was your father, and more. Just like you are what you used to be, and now, you're more."

"I–"

"The sensespace was created by the Makers. It's theirs, their…" the Cross-Prophet's voice trailed off.

"Whatever you are, Guardian, Cross-Prophet, Traveller, whatever, tell us why the Makers made the sensespace?" DeVoid said.

"I said, curiosity! Not that it was necessary, everything was working fine!"

"I'd really like to understand your definition of 'curiosity'. What did it do?"

"You saw what it did."

"Yes, but what was it meant to do? What do you mean it was created for curiosity?"

"Intentions are often hard to ascertain, but I don't believe it was an instrument designed to destroy. Undoubtedly, there must have been a… discord. A disagreement."

The Cross-Prophet squinted and tilted his head to the side, as though trying to resolve something far behind them, before returning to his initial position.

"Was the sensespace sent to control us?" DeVoid asked.

The Cross-Prophet turned his gaze back to them. "There are different definitions of control."

"But–"

"It's no help to them anyway, not anymore."

"But why? It tried to destroy us!"

"I know what it did. That's why I'm here."

"They sent a weapon, and then didn't want to use it? It's infected the entire galaxy!"

"I know, and I don't like it. They shouldn't have done what they did, it was foolish. Wrong."

"The galaxy has been at war, for hundreds of millions of years!"

The Cross-Prophet looked sad. "For too long. I know."

"And the Deliverer was created to stop the sensespace, but we've got to go and attack the Deliverer according to Thy's ramblings."

"Not necessarily… attack."

"How does that help anything?"

The Cross-Prophet appeared distracted again, and squinted his eyes past them, before returning his attention back.

"Why didn't you stop them? The Makers," DeVoid said.

The Cross-Prophet looked pensive, but did not respond.

"We're still at war, you've just admitted it yourself. Why didn't you stop them?"

"There are ways of doing things. Some aren't open… even to me."

"You seem capable," DeVoid said, accusingly.

The Cross-Prophet shook his head. "I wouldn't want to pick a fight with the Makers. That wouldn't help."

"The sensespace, then."

He shook his head again.

"Why?"

"Too much involvement is–"

"The Makers would disapprove of you saving our galaxy and clearing up their mess?" DeVoid's voice was becoming louder.

The Cross-Prophet's face took on a more solemn expression. "The Deliverer is at the centre."

"That's almost the only straightforward thing you've said, and we could have guessed that already from what Thy told us. I'm assuming the centre of the galaxy?"

"Yes, around the core."

"But Gil's–"

"She is on a path to the centre."

"To the Deliverer?"

"Yes."

"How do you know?"

"I've helped… direct them," he said, slowly.

"You?"

"Yes."

"How?"

"Small pieces of information into your network." The Cross-Prophet smiled wryly. "Nothing significant."

"The Wanderer data exchange network?"

"Yes, it's very useful."

"Why should we believe you?"

The Cross-Prophet looked thoughtful and nodded. "That's a valid reservation."

"It'd take far too long for us to reach anywhere near the centre."

"I can help with that."

"You'd actually do something?" DeVoid scoffed. "How?"

"Help will wait in the N-SOL."

"N-SOL space?" DeVoid said, incredulously. "No one goes there!"

"You can," the Cross-Prophet said earnestly.

"That's what sent Thy mad – no chance."

"Help is waiting."

"What exactly happened to Thy there? Who did it find?"

"That's not for me to say."

"Hah! You expect us to–"

"Help will find you there, I can promise you that."

"Even if we did–"

"DeVoid, can I ask something of you?" the Cross-Prophet asked, ignoring its qualms.

"What?"

"Can I ask you to help a friend."

"What? What the… Give me answers before you go asking me to help a friend of yours!"

"The friend is yours."

"Who?"

"You already know who."

Tor was able to detect the faintest pause, before DeVoid replied, "Tell me?"

"I'd like you to accompany me," the Cross-Prophet elaborated.

"What?"

"If you accompany me, we can help your friend. It is necessary."

"I need to go and help Apalu?"

"Yes."

"And leave Tor? I don't think so. How? You've just told us we need to–"

"You know how."

"You want to copy me."

"If you allow it, yes."

"Apalu needs this?"

"Badly."

"Why can't you just help?"

"I am."

"How?"

"By bringing you."

"You'd better not be fooling around."

The Cross-Prophet smiled.

"Fine, how–"

…

Before either of them could say anything else, the Cross-Prophet vanished.

*

[Thoughts?]

Tor spun around to look for DeVoid.

[Nope, back here for now.]

"I don't know… that was too much. It… I mean, he–"

[Trust him?]

"Do we have a choice?"

[We have a choice, but it's up to you. Whatever he or it was, I've got nothing. No residuals, nothing. It's certainly AB level or something equally unfathomable, though I've never heard of such a thing in serious communication. It's as though he was never here. Can't even tell if he copied me or not, crafty flit.]

"I believe it… him."

[You'd believe a Mart'oop if it told you its carapace was just for decoration.]

"What?"

[Why do you believe him?]

"I don't think we have a choice."

…

"DeVoid."

[Yes, yes. You may be right.]

"I wish he had stayed, I wanted to ask about my people… and our… connection with the sensespace."

[But, you believe all he said? Do you think Apalu is in trouble?]

"Do you?"

[I don't know.]

"I hope not. There's a chance Apalu is with Gil, isn't there?"

[Small. I think Gil is with Apalu's sibling.]

Tor breathed out, evidently relieved to have this confirmed.

"Well… I think you did the right thing. Giving him permission. Just in case… And I hope Apalu is okay as well."

[Agreed, although if it has my help, I'm sure it will be.]

"And it feels right… to do what the Cross-Prophet said."

[And the crazed Thy, don't forget. Both of them want us to go to the centre, and fight the only thing we know of which is potentially capable of defeating the sensespace.]

"I… I think we should… that's where she will be."

[So…]

"I think… I still think that's where we should go."

[Hmm.]

"You disagree."

[Depends. Are you sure?]

"Oh, come on DeVoid, I thought we'd just decided!"

CHAPTER 14

GIL

Gil felt it. The Maspero world and the sentinels were infected. The sensespace called out to her with its seductive, deceptive warmth. Beckoning her, welcoming her back. She had known this might happen, that their destination might be contaminated. She had been warned. Still, she was surprised because they were some way out and the levels of the contamination were low enough that the craft-lect had not yet detected them.

When she had left her world, the sensespace's hold over her had fallen off quickly, but now it seemed its reach had extended. She was lying on her bed, her brain brimming with activity – as it often was before she was finally able to drift off to sleep. The insidious sensespace had delicately tried to weave itself into her consciousness, but she had noticed. She had recognised it, the whispers were less subtle than before. She was prepared.

Unable to resist her curiosity, her mind began to expand and she realised, with dreadful certainty, that it was comfortable. Through the sensespace, she sensed 112 and 998 beside her, and One-oh in a nearby section of the ship. She was concerned at the ease with which she was regaining her lofty position. It was all so familiar, the silent observation, the thrill of knowing. Her sphere had returned. While it was not as strong as it had been on her world, she felt more adept at understanding it now. It was gaining substance with every passing second.

The whispers sounded gently in her mind. She knew they would grow louder as the ship continued on its path. The sound was nearly the same as before, although there were differences – certain sequences were more distinct. She was still unable to discern their meaning.

She decided to let it in, to try to understand. She willed herself into it, and it opened up to her. She finally remembered her dreams, and the frustrations she had felt at reaching for any understanding. The sensespace had been trying to communicate with her all along, that had been what it was. It had been waiting for her acceptance.

*

She was in a dark void, which she knew, implicitly, was incredibly vast. Waiting. The whispers were gone.

Slowly, she began to understand. She could feel it, drawing information from the nothingness surrounding her, understanding, somehow, that the sensespace was showing her its own creation. At last, she had initiated what the sensespace wanted, and was at its nexus. The start. This was the beginning of the sensespace's existence, and the reason for hers.

Despite knowing her view was unimaginably expansive, far more so than when she had used the sensespace to observe the Beast-men, her vantage was also restricted. Fixed. As the obscurity of her confusion began to dissipate and the quality of her focus improved, she began to distinguish what was there. Streaks of pure whiteness were shooting out from all around her.

The faintest whispers entered her mind. Streaks stemming from behind her, all with different thicknesses, affixed themselves onto the empty space in front. Smaller filaments separated themselves from larger, thicker streaks, latching on beside them. They came continuously. Space seemed to froth at the points where they slivered in. The tethers were being established.

The streaks began to swell at the tether-points. She knew she was seeing a small part of something greater, because the enlargements appeared to push against real space more vigorously, causing it to froth more furiously than before. Finally, all the swollen parts of the streaks slipped through in one movement, and were hidden – vanishing. She wondered what lay behind real space, what the white streaks had funnelled themselves into, and what they even were.

Still taut, the white streaks remained as they were, without changing. Gil assumed they had finished their work, until bulges began to appear travelling along them, smaller than the previous swellings. More appeared on each streak than she could possibly keep track of, conducted towards the tether-points. The whispering grew stronger.

There was a faint glow forming around the contact points, coming from the nothingness, caused by whatever was being brought and infused into the universe. It spread out as far as she could see.

The dim glow spread until its presence became normal, blanketing everything. The whispers had plateaued to a constant level. It was hard to remember the empty space as it had been before. The sensespace was bonded, pushed into an oblivious galaxy. It was impossible to understand how she knew, but she did.

Each of the links, the white streaks that had embedded themselves into the galaxy, represented a connection. Past the streaks, she could see the galaxy that was all too familiar to her by now. Groups of stellar formations and nebulae that she did not explicitly recognise, but which were typical parts of her environment since leaving the commune.

It was a bridge, but she did not know where from, who had constructed it, or what its purpose was, aside from bringing the sensespace into the galaxy. Bridges had two ends, yet she could only see one. Whatever lay behind her, remained hidden. She had little control over what she saw.

She began to understand the pervasiveness of the sensespace. It was designed to reach into the cores of what lay beneath. Then, she had it! She knew what was attracting the bulges that had travelled down the white streaks.

Sentience. It had a will to connect, to understand. Sentience was what it wanted.

She wanted to look behind herself, badly. To see what had pushed the scourge of the sensespace upon them, infected them with its insatiable appetite for sentience. She willed herself to turn around, but nothing happened. The level of the whispers did not change either, as often they did when she tried to manipulate the sensespace. It was almost as though the streaks around her were pinning her in place.

Yet another realisation struck her. A horrific realisation, for which all of this could begin to make sense. It was not just a bridge, it was a bond. The sensespace, the bridge and the galaxy were all now connected. They had been grouped together. Destroying one would destroy the rest. Only a complete removal of sentience would see the sensespace lose interest and wither away.

Her presence recoiled into itself as she rejected the knowledge. She knew the sensespace had desires. It was more than capable of lying to her to further its own nefarious ends.

If the sensespace had desires and she could sense them, then the reverse was also true. If it needed her, she could use it. She was being shown an event the sensespace had stored away, which meant that it could recall more. This was not all that it contained. She had been able to manipulate it before.

She hoped she was not wrong. Despite being only an incorporeal presence, she felt panic course throughout her body. It might weaken her resolve, but it was too tempting.

She could not stop herself. She demanded to see the commune, to look back on her home.

The whispers changed – they did not increase in power, but she detected the faintest hint of a song. She pushed the other thoughts from out of her mind, willing the sensespace to understand. It wanted and needed her, not the other way around. It had to acquiesce to her demands. She needed to go back.

She attempted to turn around again and was overcome by the feeling of being observed. Or perhaps that something else was witnessing the bridge alongside her. Before she was able, she felt herself being thrust forwards towards the connection points ahead, and the whispers began to roar. She could not scream, but only watch as it rushed unstoppably into her.

*

Quiet again, she watched with what seemed like infinite eyes. She watched herself begin to climb the gnarled old tree that lay close to the commune's boundary. Its branches, thick and dark with age, jutted out in all directions from its main trunk. It was ancient, and while it was the source of much of her pain, it also represented joy. It was a permanent fixture of the commune that she loved dearly, rooted at the border of the settlement and the great surrounding forest. It had played a central role in many of her games with Tor and the other children of the commune when they were younger. Whenever she had toiled in the cultivated land surrounding the commune's centre, it had been there.

Her younger self continued the climb, and she excitedly lapped up the details – reliving it concurrently through her own distant memories. The other Gil dextrously reached out with alternating small hands, grasping at the upper branches and working her way higher up with ease. It was obvious she was being careful of making too much noise, and every now and then, she would turn to look at the surrounding land, before satisfying herself that no one was there and resuming her ascent. She was at an age that her sphere, her ability to interact with the sensespace, had not yet fully developed. Her sight was a far more useful tool.

She was probably hiding from Tor, which made Gil's presence almost flutter with excitement. She longed to see him again, and it was a comfort to know that parts of him were irrevocably recorded, even if this was a confusing, malicious message from the insidious sensespace. She turned her presence from the younger Gil momentarily to the commune, taking in the familiar collection of huts and the communers themselves. She was about to look for her father when she felt a change – her younger self had stopped.

Moving her attention back, she watched the young Gil smile, eagerly scanning the ground below for signs of Tor. It was delightful to watch. The journey up the tree had been brief. This was not home in the sense that Gil had demanded from the sensespace, but it would suffice. This part of her past was pleasant. It had been an innocent time when there had been no confusion or fear. Only Tor, her father, and the commune.

Gil decided to look for Tor and immediately found him – around the base of the tree. She was surprised. She innately understood that she had the power to see anywhere within this depiction of the commune, yet she had been taken unawares. It reminded her of her past, and how she had been similarly remiss, ignorant of her surroundings, and fallen from that same tree where she was now so precariously perched.

Wanting to focus on happier thoughts, she watched Tor as he caught a glimpse of her younger self, before darting to the opposite side of the wide trunk to hide. It was wonderful to see his face again, as real and familiar as she remembered it. He had been older the last time she had seen him, but his expressions and the way he moved were the same.

With glee, she watched as Tor began to climb. Her younger self was still unaware, contentedly watching for signs around the tree without realising that he was already there. Tor's physical prowess had been evident, even then, as had his understanding of how she would act. She realised he must have approached the tree from a wide arc, from far out of the commune before doubling back – further than children were supposed to venture and the opposite direction to that which Gil was focused on.

The younger Gil continued to look around, unknowing. She was almost completely still, not wanting to give her position away, with only her eyes darting from side to side. Tor, stealthy and strong, diligently worked his way up the tree from the other side of the trunk. He lifted each arm, moving higher and closer. She noticed the whispers again. Faint, but discernible. Mocking her.

A panic began to ripple through her. This was not a pleasant reprieve, it was not a gift from the sensespace, it was a wicked taunt – a humiliation at her past about what had happened to her. It was a reminder that it had seen and knew everything about her. This was the time of her fall, which marked the beginning of its influence over her.

Shocked, she was unable to tear herself from the scene, forced to watch, no longer in control. The whispers echoed and emanated from all around her. Not the typical smoothed noise, but a confusing, skirmishing din. Tor's sustained ascent was no longer joyful to watch, it was the harbinger of terrible events that culminated many years later with his death. From here, her affinity with the sensespace had grown, which would eventually draw Teacher to her.

Occasionally, Tor swung his head from side to side, and looked up to check on his level in relation to Gil. She remained oblivious. Finally, after what seemed like an eternity, with the whispers gaining in strength and on the cusp of their roar, he reached the level of the thick branch upon which she was positioned. She could see the excitement in his eyes, grown wide, and his toothy smile. Clambering quietly, right around the trunk, he placed one foot delicately onto the final branch. Simultaneously, the whispers roared more furiously than she had ever known, and she sensed an action of some kind taking place through it. She did not understand, until she saw her younger self shift and look down, towards the ground, disturbed by a sudden rustling. If it had not been for the rustling, she would certainly not have shifted her weight and would have felt Tor move onto the branch.

The whispers disappeared and there was silence, in anticipation of what she knew was about to come. Tor's two legs were now firmly balanced on the branch, and he was crouched low. Leaning forwards a little more, he placed both hands down to steady himself as he shuffled forwards, inhaling deeply. Gil was filled with dread.

"BAA!"

As Tor shouted, the younger Gil half-turned, startled. Her momentary bewilderment caused her to forget her grip and lose her balance. By the time she realised what had happened, it was already too late. She slipped to the side, two hands stuck out desperately hoping to grab onto holds where none existed. She fell.

The song came, the same song that the sensespace used to lure Gil in. Viciously loud – and reeking of victory and triumph. Everything slowed down as the sensespace taunted her, wanting to savour in what it had just caused. It was mocking her, revelling in its accomplishment. From the fall, she would rely on the sensespace more. She knew that had been its intention.

She was aware of Tor, who had immediately moved forwards as Gil had slipped and plunged his arms after her – he was too late. She had forgotten his desperation. He almost fell off the branch himself, although his legs instinctively tightened around the branch. He was close, his reactions fast, but not fast enough. The scenery began to change.

*

The change had not been as abrupt as before, but lighter. The only unpleasantness was derived from her feelings about what she had just witnessed. The whispers were quieter again, keeping themselves at bay.

The great forested expanse that encompassed her commune, and much more, was laid out before her. Patches of different trees, discernible by their hues and shapes, as well as how they felt within the sensespace, were clustered into separate regions, separated by various brooks and creeks, with the occasional openings around some of the larger streams.

The two rivers surrounding the commune snaked off in different directions, before combining later downstream. She had never realised that before, never having thought to look. They fed into a much larger river, and she could sense many of the fearsome predators sometimes battled and killed by the hunters lurking along the shallow depths near the banks. There were far fewer of the scaled predators lurking in their smaller rivers, and she was glad. While any mature communer could sense and easily evade them through their spheres, children were always at risk. If that was the sensespace's intent, through showing her this – that its spheres helped the communers to remain safe – it was mistaken. It had the potential to take, to deceive, and was far more dangerous than any of the communers had ever realised. Too dangerous. They could learn to defend themselves without it.

She found herself being drawn to a part of the forest that was covered with lighter vegetation, and clear of the thicker, more imposing trees. There was movement that she could not immediately discern. Focusing on it in more detail, she realised, with a jolt, that it was her father. He was briskly making his way somewhere, through the sparse undergrowth, with Yul, Ril's father. She was overjoyed at seeing him, although she reminded herself of what the sensespace had made her experience with Tor only moments before. Presumably, this was not going to be pleasant for her.

Her father moved with the natural elegance of a hunter, despite his larger-than-usual build. The same as Tor. His feet were precisely placed as he walked, every step was perfect, in comparison with the more lumbering, and even more hulking, Yul. She doubted his son, Ril, would ever reach a similar size. Gil did not think Yul would have needed to slow his pace even if he were wading through the thicker undergrowth they purposely avoided – he looked as though he could have pushed down most of the trees single-handedly.

Gil was perturbed as she felt the dread of what was to come. She knew when this was, precisely. This was the time her father had set off with Yul to search for help from a nearby commune, when a sickness had infected their own. Neither of them had ever returned. The sensespace was taunting her again, showing her painful events, toying with her. She could do nothing but continue to watch.

She looked more closely at her father, wanting to take in every detail about him before his impending fate. Wishing he could see and talk to her. Using every possible viewpoint. Simultaneously, she glanced through the sensespace at the path ahead. There seemed nothing untoward, nothing to give any indication of what was to come.

She knew the craft-lect and the others suspected her father was different, not really one of her own people – if she were still able to count herself truly amongst them. It was difficult for her to reconcile any of that knowledge with how she felt. She only knew him as a communer and her father, and still could not set him apart as being anything else. He was a communer as much as she counted herself to have been one, it did not matter where he had come from before. Tait, and many of the other communers, had originally come from other communes too, but that did not make them any different, or any less real.

Still letting a portion of her presence remain vigilant for any impending threats, including that of hidden Beast-men, she watched her father. She nested her presence more densely in front of him. As she watched, she began to consider that they were all wrong, everyone but her on the ship. They had mistaken her for something that she was not, and incorrectly speculated about her heritage to make sense of their own confusion. There was even the chance they were right, but that it was not her father who was linked to whatever it was that made her different. Her mother? Gil's thoughts continued to race and she mused over whether they had been wrong all along when…

He saw her.

Her father looked towards her densely nested presence. It was so quick that had she not been properly concentrating she might have missed it. A flicker of his eye across the scenery in front of him, ending on her before darting off. There had been no disturbance to cause it. His eye darted towards her again, as though definitively validating what he had been reticent to acknowledge.

She was certain, and excited, although unsure about what it meant. Her father continued walking forwards, saying nothing. He wore a look of light curiosity, mixed with hesitance. Beside him, Yul remained steadfastly focused on what lay ahead. Neither had spoken since she had first started observing them.

As his eyes resumed their focus on the scenery ahead of him, his face began to take on a more serious countenance and his body became more rigid. Less fluid. Gone was the look of curiosity. Gil sensed that changes were taking place behind his silent exterior. He was thinking deeply. She hoped he would speak, to say something to her.

Before she could think anything else, Yul distracted her. He had clearly noticed her father's odd movements and had turned to face him, although her father did not immediately acknowledge it. Gil watched, as her father looked briefly down towards the ground, before lifting his head to stare towards the sky and spreading his arms wide, while slowing to a stop. Yul also stopped, waiting for an explanation.

Her father brought his gaze back down, breathing deeply in and out, and sighed. His arms softly drew back to his sides. His expression had become one of sorrow, and Gil thought, perhaps, some anger too.

"Yul."

Her father's voice was deep. Authoritative. Kind.

He continued, "I am sorry, my friend. The time has come."

"For what? The sickness is–"

"The end of… meddling. Perhaps, I have interfered too much."

"What is this you speak of?"

"There are rules, Yul. I will have to atone."

"I do not understand. How will this help?"

"Even though it was right, to do as I did. Please, forgive me Yul. Ril will be fine, I promise you this."

And then, without warning, they were gone. Everything else was left, the trees, the plants, the nearby animals, everything except her father and Ril. Gil explored with her presence, horrified at being abandoned again, not wanting to be left, searching for a clue about what had happened. There had been no warning.

She begged the sensespace to let them return, imploring it with every fibre of her presence. The whispers, which had been near-absent up until now, began to return. The sound returned to that underlying background hum, taking no heed of her demands. Ignoring her pleas. Nothing she tried had any effect.

Waiting, alone, Gil thought about what had happened. It was impossible, she had almost forgotten, but it had been a memory. A captured part of her father's final few moments, shown to her by the cruel sensespace. That was the only thing that made sense, yet it also did not. Her father had seen her. That could not have happened in the past since she had not been there, not yet. Her body and presence, right now, was aboard the craft-lect's ship, none of this was strictly real. His eyes had gazed upon her, though. There had been no other reason for him to look in her direction, twice.

The sensespace was cruel, it could all have been a lie, although having watched her father made that difficult to accept. If there had been some subtle message, whether from the sensespace or her father, she had missed it. The short conversation with Yul about meddling and breaking rules had not made sense to her, and people did not simply disappear.

Trying to rationalise it to herself, she kept returning to the same problem. He had seen her, and disappeared as a direct consequence of that. Had she caused him to leave both her and Tor? Had she caused that loss? Where had he gone?

She had so many questions, but for now, they were secondary. She wanted to leave, to exit the sensespace. It had become empty.

Forcing her presence away, and surprised at finding it easier than she had expected, her consciousness recoiled from the sensespace's grasp.

*

She opened her eyes, her infinite eyes. She was still not in her own body, the sensespace was not yet done. She saw darkness, circling in thick currents that warped the fabric of reality around itself. Oppressively dark, more than should have been possible, and dangerous. Like the shining night, the antithesis of the sensespace's pure white streaks that Gil had seen speared forth into space. Small greenish specks seemed to shine around it in a ring, before twinkling in and out of existence.

She felt a presence settle behind her, as before, watching at a distance. She assumed it was the sensespace. The whispering was even quieter than it had been with her father, nearly completely gone. Her infinite eyes were alone, watching the unveiled darkness.

This thing… had to be stopped. The sensespace needed its destruction, but so did she. They both did. It was too dangerous. Too powerful. Too ultimate. Ready to rip everything apart, expanding the supermassive dark core of nothingness, engulfing everything in incomprehensibly strong tidal forces. She had to go to it…

The sensespace was scared.

CHAPTER 15

APALU

Apalu wafted its bloom, the tentacles flicking swiftly to the side so that its hull's axis turned perpendicular to the emblem-ship's velocity vector, before accelerating as quickly as the bloom would allow. Fleeing without pretence. The larger emblem-ship was probably less manoeuvrable, and Apalu had decided that forcing it to alter its course, if it chose to continue pursuing Apalu, would comparatively lengthen the chase, giving Apalu some time.

It fast became apparent that despite its size, the emblem-ship was nimbler than Apalu had anticipated. Perhaps its bizarre bauble configuration somehow facilitated that, allowing for unconventional, highly effective propulsion manoeuvres. Or it could have been the methodology of propulsion itself, whatever that was.

Worryingly, the emblem-ship did indeed appear to be set on Apalu, and was managing to reduce the displacement quickly between them sooner than Apalu had allowed for in any of its scenario analyses. It was perplexing. Three-thousand kilometres and decreasing, far too close for comfort.

Apalu decided to be more actively defensive. So far, the emblem-ship had not taken any actions other than follow, but that could change in an instant.

A couple of hundred drones were released from around Apalu's stern and spread out to form a blanket behind it. They were pre-loaded with an assortment of cooperative battle strategies and powerful arsenals with which to test the formidability of the emblem-ship.

It was surprised. The pursuer fired conventional plasma beams at them, overcoming each by brute force rather than anything remotely innovative to conserve its own power. A wasteful act, foolhardy in the vacuum. It was impossible to speculate why that had been done, because it could signify many different things depending on the capabilities and inclinations of the infected Woal machine-lects controlling the emblem-ship. They could be confident or foolish, worried or angry. Anything. Spreading confusion might have even been the point.

Soon, Apalu would have to do something else. Something more drastic. The emblem-ship continued to close in, and even if it completely exhausted itself of offensive capabilities, which was unlikely, it could simply ram Apalu.

Apalu decided there was no point in any more direct confrontation. The nature with which its drones had been overcome was confusingly senseless, but also fierce. The Woal degenerate probably wanted Apalu destroyed. Apalu decided to do something it had never done before.

It prepared to engage the N-SOL drive. Any advantage of an early lead it had in entering N-SOL space would be invaluable. It only hoped it could last in N-SOL space for longer if it was followed, before its power was drained to critical levels – whereupon it would be forced back into real space. Its smaller size and, it assumed, mass, should enable it to travel further and faster in N-SOL space.

*

In N-SOL space for the first time, Apalu nervously kept watch for the emblem-ship. It could no longer detect any signs of the offender, but its sensors were only working in their vaguest sense. It could barely discern the imprint of real space around it.

Surveying what it could, it was fascinated by the chaos. Swirling vortices and currents of whatever passed for matter in N-SOL space washed over the ship. If it survived, upon its next visit to a data exchange, it would request the most current information about the reality it had now entered. The near-speed-of-light domain was beautiful.

Its intrigue at N-SOL space was dampened by its concern about the signal it had given off. Upon entering N-SOL space, its position had become momentarily clear in real space for almost every sentient that was capable, and who cared to look, possibly in the entire galaxy. Following the events of the Great Conflation, it had been a surprise to the remnants of the galactic community that N-SOL travel was suddenly so loud, obnoxious and easy to detect. It had not been like that before. That was what had led to the Wanderer Enclave advising strongly against it as a base method of traversing the galaxy, unless safety required. It was assumed that the ABs had employed certain mechanisms to mask use of the N-SOL drives for non-ABs, which had been disabled, or failed, following their suicide.

Apalu monitored its power levels suspiciously. It had a large quantity of information regarding historic N-SOL travel within its databanks, but what it was experiencing did not match. Its power levels were holding, stable, as though Apalu were in real space. It was unaffected in all areas. There should have been some leakage, some losses. To believe this was correct would have been comically naïve, considering how ubiquitous N-SOL travel had once been and how much data there was about it. It was known that it depleted a ship's power. That was common knowledge, a ubiquitous fact, and had been the case since the ABs had first gifted it to the galactic community.

The most dangerous aspect concerning the failure of its internal power-monitoring sensors was that it did not know when it would need to drop out of N-SOL space. Too soon and it risked facing the emblem-ship potentially still on its stern, too late, and it could become lost to N-SOL space. Apalu could not take the risk of becoming lost, it had to leave. If the emblem-ship was behind it, there was a chance it was as lost as Apalu, and that there was something strange about the patch of N-SOL space they had just travelled through. With any luck, it might even overshoot Apalu. There was also the possibility that the emblem-ship was what had caused its power sensors to fail, in order to push it to become lost to N-SOL space – a sneaky attack in the same vein as those of the quick-lects.

Apalu sent the necessary commands to the N-SOL drive. The c-automs were still asleep, safely berthed and unaware of the danger they were in. It was not necessary to wake them for the moment, Apalu was still more than capable of commanding the entire ship alone.

Nothing happened. The ship did not drop out of N-SOL space, it carried on. Apalu repeated the commands, to no avail. It investigated the N-SOL drive and performed a diagnostic. The drive was faulty. It appeared to have been successfully deactivated, yet Apalu was clearly still in N-SOL space. Alongside the drive being faulty, the internal sensors and systems monitoring the drive were having issues as well since they also reported that it was inactive.

Apalu began to worry. Perhaps, this was how being lost to N-SOL space began. Its databanks contained no information about the symptoms from the unwitting participant's point of view – only from that of an external observer. First errors with the internal power monitors, now this. The strange thing, however, was that the rest of the ship seemed fine. Everything purported to be in perfect working order.

Real space was now gone, it had started delicately dimming behind the haze of N-SOL space, which Apalu had taken to be a quirk of the particular N-SOL region they were in. However, now, there was only the confusing rotating mess of N-SOL space everywhere. Apalu was in danger, although it was not quite sure what that danger was. It repeated its internal diagnostics, over and over again. Nothing. It was helpless, as its sibling had been when the Granthan-lect had overtaken its systems.

It was still moving at what it assumed was the same velocity as when it had entered N-SOL space, and the streaming cascades of swirling N-SOL space-matter continued to rush past it. However, with its N-SOL drive being offline, it could not alter its course within N-SOL space even if it wanted. It brought the drive back online but there was no difference. For all intents and purposes, the readings it received back from the drive showed it was now operational, but it was as powerless as before. Just in case, it deactivated the drive again. It was still concerned about losing power, even if it could not observe its levels reliably.

*

Long-range sensors no longer worked – they were not designed for N-SOL space. Begrudgingly, it turned the N-SOL drive back on to use the enigmatic sensors contained within it. They were malfunctioning like everything else, and began to identify certain, fleeting targets, on either side of the ship, before losing track of them. Diligently, it performed diagnostics on these sensors too, to the extent of its capabilities as a non-AB, but found no issues.

Machine-lects were more than capable of entering deliriums and descending into insanity. It was a process that happened far less than with biologicals, but when it did, the results could be catastrophic. It was typically the result of a lect that had been created unstable during its initial manufacture, or when the Step or Usurper Principle had been flouted. In stark contrast with biologicals, however, external events witnessed by machine-lects, especially Wanderer craft-lects, seldom pushed them into madness. That was the preserve of biologicals.

The ability of biologicals to be affected by their surroundings, in ways which impacted heavily on their states of lect, or mind, was intriguing to machine-lects. It was known to be related to how biological minds were constructed – often heavily reliant on quantum mechanical processes inherently affected by observations. It was rare, but in certain situations, biologicals had been known to exhibit intellectual leaps that far surpassed the abilities of most machine-lects, moments of hyper-lucidity. Often, prodigy, or even savant machine-lects, were required to understand the output from these moments once the biological returned to a typical state.

Even rarer, it had been observed, in extraordinarily few cases, that some biologicals could harness hyper-lucid traits over extended periods of time, sometimes reaching to hundreds of standard seconds. Apalu wondered if those intellects had been among the first to be targeted by the sensespace. It was a facet of this uncertain construction of their minds that enabled biologicals to succumb to environmentally-driven insanity.

Despite the evidence to the contrary, Apalu did not believe it was descending into madness of any type. Not yet. The timeframe had been too short.

*

Targets were identified and lost. Sometimes collections of objects were located, sometimes the N-SOL sensors massed them together into super-masses far dwarfing Apalu, before they vanished. It considered taking the drive back offline, now very concerned both about its own sanity and that power levels were still being reported as would have been expected in real space, with no drain.

Apalu was filling with regret at having entering N-SOL space. It could have tried the singularity generator before jumping at the chance to enter N-SOL space, like a coward. In real space, the generator would have enabled rapid movement, faster than the bloom. Not as fast as the N-SOL drive, but potentially sufficient to escape the emblem-ship. It could have tested it, taken a chance. Other Wanderers were likely to have faced threats equal to that of the emblem-ship, and Apalu had not detected any of them fleeing into N-SOL space.

It mused on whether to use the singularity generator in N-SOL space or not. As far as it knew, no experiments with gravitational singularities had ever been conducted in N-SOL space. However, even if the generator worked, Apalu would still be in N-SOL space. That was the problem. It had weapons, it could send out drones and other satellites, it could probe the fabric of N-SOL space in other ways. There were various options, but each one was an experiment, and therefore a risk.

CHAPTER 16

GIL

Gil related her sensespace visions to the others as they sat around the table. The sentinels were one day away at most and she felt tense. She looked frantically around the table as she spoke, hoping they believed her. Unfortunately, it was impossible to gauge the craft-lect's reactions since it was only a disembodied voice that spoke directly into her mind.

998 hummed gently without saying anything while she spoke. Its orb-body slowly oscillated up and down in a tight line, and its aura flowed orange-yellow without blinking. She felt its focus on her, but also on its own thoughts. One-oh was equally difficult to read, although his kind eyes remained affixed on her face as she spoke, only flicking over a couple of times to 998. For a moment, no one spoke when she finished, until the craft-lect broke the silence.

[Interesting.]

"Very," One-oh added.

Gil looked at One-oh, hoping for something more. He obliged.

"You have now closed yourself to your abilities, you say?"

"Yes… I'm trying to."

"Is that possible?"

"It's not easy… but I'm better at it… than I was before… I think."

"Perhaps that is wise, especially with our approach of the Maspero."

"I don't want to experience those… visions… not again, not yet."

"That's understandable, Gil."

She looked down, unsure whether she should be ashamed of her fear, or grateful they had not asked her to delve back into the sensespace's embrace. Her hands were clasped tightly over her trembling legs.

"Your father leaving was not your fault," 998 said, with its hum becoming louder for the briefest time while it spoke.

"I… how could it have been anything else?" she said.

"I agree with 998. Ask yourself the converse, Gil," One-oh said.

"How can…" She trailed off.

"That is an event from the past, you had no influence over it."

"Yes, Gil. You also cannot establish its validity," 998 said.

"But it felt real, it didn't feel like the past, and…"

"Yes?" One-oh said, looking into her eyes as Gil looked up again.

"It was him. It was so similar, it felt… real."

"The sensespace is manipulative. We know it wanted you to feel what it showed you was real, but whether that is the case or not, is–"

"But to taunt me?" she blurted.

"Perhaps it was… not intended for you, maybe it was meant for us."

"But…"

Silence descended again. Gil realised the craft-lect had hardly spoken. As though in response, again, it broke the quiet.

[It may have been trying to explain.]

One-oh began nodding. "Yes… but if that's true… it's incomplete."

"Or taunting, as Gil thought," 998 said.

"Why would it show me my fall? Why would it show me how it happened? Why would it have made that up? How is that a message?"

"Again, I think–" One-oh began.

"The whole time! It's… it's ruined… everything!"

"We may not understand fully its–"

"It has always been there, watching me, it's–"

"Gil," 998 interrupted. "You are safe, with us. Don't be tricked into sorrow by the sensespace. You are strong."

She stopped and looked at it, feeling foolish. She steadied her frantic breathing before looking down towards her hands, again.

"It's just, I don't understand why. What does it want from me?"

"We don't know, but we will," 998 promised.

"What are the rules my father spoke about?"

"That's… unclear," One-oh said.

"Did he do something because of me?"

[Without context, we cannot know.]

"It may have been entirely fictional," One-oh said.

"But…" Gil said.

"But, I suppose, if it was not fictional–" One-oh started.

"Then whose rules may he have been breaking?" 998 said.

"The ABs?" One-oh said. "They have their rules."

"ABs?" Gil almost shouted.

"You know we have our suspicions your father was a member of an AB race."

"But how…"

[Or affiliated.]

"Yes… somehow, maybe created by them himself. It's something we can't ignore," One-oh said.

"I… that just can't be true," Gil said. "How can we know?"

"We can't, yet."

One-oh was looking almost apologetic towards Gil, as 998 began moving up and down more rapidly than before.

"But, it doesn't make sense… none of it does!" she said. "Why? My father…"

"Gil, we may not be able to… prove or disprove what you witnessed in the visions, but you cannot be certain what you think they mean is correct," One-oh said.

Gil was about to reply, but One-oh carried on.

"If we consider what we are able to corroborate," One-oh said slowly. "What does that tell us about him? He was a member of your primitive commune – excuse my terminology – yet in your own memories, he told you stories about the galactic community, when you were too young to comprehend them. He also left your world, or became hidden in some way, undiscoverable even to us, in a manner unavailable to your people… impossibly. As you know, we were unable to locate a progenitive match for you on your world, so he really did remove himself. But–"

"But he saw me!"

"I'm not certain he did, at least, not in the way you think. That is your own impression, and also something we cannot substantiate against what we already know – it is something that sensespace has encouraged you to believe."

"I… I just don't understand. What do you mean?"

"There are aspects of your visions that seem likely to be correct, but there are also aspects that we need to separate. Things that might be entirely designed by the sensespace. Your father's conversation with Yul is one of them – that may be a message directly from the sensespace, not him. It's not possible your father saw you, but you believe he did. Since it is something that couldn't have happened, that lends credence to it being created by the sensespace."

"I… he vanished because of me."

"I think that's truly unlikely, Gil. And even if what you saw did indeed happen, it must have been a coincidence. You may be misinterpreting what the sensespace intended for you to observe."

"But–"

"I understand how it seemed. He appeared to comprehend something related to you. I think it's obvious he wasn't speaking just for Yul's benefit… we just can't assume it was for yours."

"Who else's, then?" 998 asked.

CHAPTER 17

TOR

DeVoid was still procrastinating.

"So, you don't trust him?"

[It's not as simple as that.]

"You think he lied to us?"

[Not lied. Obfuscated, partially explained, omissions. That type of thing. Tricky to get a proper answer. Either way, we know Thy went mad after going into N-SOL space, so…]

"I think he tried to answer some of our questions–"

[Not clearly.]

"Maybe that's just how he is?"

[Just how he is?]

"Yes."

[It was obvious what we were asking.]

"I can imagine… if I were talking to Bo now, or any of the other elders in my commune, or even Tait… I would find it hard to answer their questions in a way they would understand. There's too much… too many other concepts they'd need to learn first. They would have to experience what I have experienced."

[That's a disanalogy, count yourself lucky at being enlightened. You now understand there are concepts like technologies, and there are ones that you cannot currently comprehend, for many reasons. You've realised some of the basic tenets of galactic life. Truths, as much as anything can be. You've accepted that science exists. What we believe might be wrong, but that's allowed, and we actively acknowledge that. That's a discrete change for you that lets you appreciate the search for real knowledge. The difference in understanding between you and the Cross-Prophet might be greater than between you and your communers, however your newfound realisations should allow for that.]

"Meaning…"

[We're past the threshold baseline for a reasonable conversation.]

"That might not be true!"

[Your attempt at humour evades me. Did you hear what I just–]

"But you would think that wouldn't you. That's my point."

[Right, let's put that aside then, since you've decided to ignore logic.]

"Do you trust the Cross-Prophet's motives?"

[You know its motives?]

"I think I do."

[Good for you.]

"If you don't trust him, why did you agree to be copied for Apalu?"

[Oh, come off it.]

"You did!"

[He could have taken a copy of me anyway.]

"But he asked."

[I refer back to my initial answer.]

Tor persisted. "He gave you the choice."

[Oh, Tor…]

"He didn't have to."

[A choice?]

"Yes."

[Really?]

"Yes, he–"

[Please. In all likelihood it was the illusion of choice, nothing else.]

"Why not?"

[The very appearance of choice might have been the impression he wanted to give off. You've got to understand Tor, machine-lects, augmented biologicals, anything with the ability to outthink a typical biological, ahem, or anything else less capable than itself, will use its abilities to elicit the responses it wants.]

"Unless it really was giving us a choice."

[That's rarely the way the galaxy works. It might have been completely made up so that we trusted it, as you clearly now do, just to encourage us to pop into N-SOL space. You've got to consider everything.]

"In your opinion."

[No. Fact. Think about how you might have spoken to the children within your commune. They had poorly developed reasoning abilities, even in comparison with you, so you could manipulate them into acting how you wanted. Let's not flatter ourselves here.]

"We would encourage the children to do what was best for them. So even if that was the case here, it doesn't necessarily mean following the Cross-Prophet's advice is wrong. So… no, I don't think that's what he was doing, or even if he was, it doesn't make a difference."

[Okay, well now you're becoming a bit circular…]

"But–"

[Evidence?]

"It's a feeling."

[We can't make important decisions based on unquantifiable biological feelings.]

"That's one way of looking at it."

[Not this again. It's the correct way.]

"So, we shouldn't go into N-SOL space?"

[I'm not sure. Okay?]

"Look, DeVoid–"

[Yes?]

"I understand you're nervous about going into N-SOL space, but we know we have to. That's the only way we're–"

[Says who?]

"Look, just… let's go?"

[Let's go.]

DeVoid mimicked Tor, with a higher-pitched playback of his voice.

"Come on…"

[And what was is that you said that I was. Nervous? FLITTING NERVOUS?]

"I didn't mean to be rude."

[HAH! Try reasonably cautious, not nervous. Never. Me? Nervous? For–]

"Fine! Reasonably cautious."

[The other problem, aside from going mad, is, if we do enter N-SOL space, which I'm excited about if anything – thank you very much – just justifiably cautious, we blast our location to everyone. Everyone, who's looking. Everyone.]

"Maybe… maybe Gil will see us?"

[Not just Gil, if they're looking. Everyone will be able to observe us. It's incredibly dangerous. Trust me, there are many different entities that would charge straight towards us once they observed our exact location. The Wanderers are powerful, but we have our enemies.]

"That can't be right, that makes no sense… The Cross-Prophet wouldn't have said to, otherwise–"

[And what? I do it because you hope you're right? Do you understand quite how–]

"I know, I know… it's dangerous."

[It'll be like you're back in your commune, waving to the Beast-men. Identifying exactly where you are.]

"I know, it's dangerous."

[That's an understatement.]

"But–"

[Yes, yes, I know. But then hasn't this entire journey been quite dangerous. Strange. Fun, in places. Don't you think?]

"I think that's–"

[And I suppose the Cross-Prophet added some legitimacy, however dubious, to our entire adventure – wouldn't you agree?]

"Well, yes, I–"

[You have had some fun, haven't you?]

"Of course!"

[You enjoy my company, don't you?]

"DeVoid–"

[YOU DO RESPECT ME, RIGHT?]

"Oh, come on… look, DeVoid, for…"

Tor stopped speaking when he saw, past the walls of his chamber, that space outside was changing. DeVoid had decided to take the risk.

CHAPTER 18

GIL

The spacescape was innocently displayed through the transparent wall next to the table. Gil wondered how much of it was riddled with the sensespace. She looked back to 998 and One-oh.

"Am I dangerous?"

"Yes, but…" One-oh trailed off.

"Then why–"

"We are all dangerous." He looked up to smile for the craft-lect's benefit.

[That is correct.]

Gil stood up and walked so that she was right next to the spacescape, staring out. She heard sounds of movement behind her, and a moment later, One-oh was standing beside her, also staring out into the vastness. 998 increased the volume of its hum.

Without turning her head, she spoke. "My father… or the sensespace… spoke of meddling, and that he had interfered too much."

"Yes," One-oh said.

"Why would the ABs have rules against me?"

"You assume it was about you?"

"Or Tor?" she suggested, before shaking her head. "No, it must have been me…"

"The rules… what that meant, that's something we can't know yet," he said. "And in addition, my thoughts about the ABs are just a possibility."

"Am I just a weapon?"

"Why not a gift?" 998 said.

She sighed, turned and moved to sit back down on her seat, exhaling loudly as she settled into it.

"None of it makes sense," she said.

One-oh remained facing the spacescape as he spoke. "I know you don't want to hear this Gil, but if you experience the visions again, we may gain a better understanding."

"I don't want to, I don't even know if I can!"

"I understand that–"

"I don't want its lies!"

"Don't worry Gil, we have time," One-oh said, turning and placing a hand on her shoulder, before walking back to his own seat. "And we have the sentinels to investigate first."

[One-oh is correct, it may take time.]

"But… h-how could it happen, anyway?" Gil said.

"How could what happen?" 998 asked.

"All of it, the visions?"

"I don't know," One-oh said shaking his head. "I don't believe the craft-lect does either." He tilted his head up as he said it, but the craft-lect did not reply.

"No, I mean how can it exist here, now?"

"This far from the Maspero?"

"Here at all! If the ABs are suicided, and the sentinels aren't sentient, then…"

"Ah," One-oh said, before turning to face them and flicking his eyes towards 998. "I think 998 could explain more succinctly than me."

For a moment Gil was distracted by this, and wondered whether One-oh's deference to 998 was part of his attempt to make amends with the c-autom.

998 obliged. "The sensespace infects sentience, but it does not always seem to require it. There are some places of infection where sentience used to be. Around the echoes."

"Oh," Gil said.

"After the Great Conflation, it did recede from many of the uninhabited territories, but unfortunately remained in others."

"And the Maspero?"

"It's believed the infected regions, where only echoes of sentience remain, primarily consist of former AB territories."

Gil noticed One-oh's head tilt to the side slightly at this.

998 continued. "Although there are others. Unfortunately, a comprehensive map of infection does not yet exist, the galaxy is too vast."

"And what about what I saw at the end? The last part?"

"Yes..." One-oh muttered, which Gil was not sure was intentional.

"The sensespace was... it was... it had an enemy. Something with power against it, not me... it was..."

"The Deliverer, I assume."

"What Gil described did not seem to be a weapon against just the sensespace – but that does not match our understanding of the Deliverer," 998 said.

She saw One-oh's face change, as though he had realised something important, although he did not say what it was.

"That may be, 998."

"I believe Gil's impression was that the sensespace was asking for help," 998 said.

"Yes," Gil said. "I think it was."

"That's something else I am having difficulty understanding," One-oh admitted. "The sensespace showed us, through you, Gil, its enemy – the Deliverer, most likely. In doing so, it appears to have been trying to pit us against it... something which would be uncountenancable to you."

"Why is that difficult to understand?" Gil said, "It's... manipulating the truth."

"Well, I would agree because it stands to reason that if we were somehow able to attack and destroy the Deliverer, the sensespace would be able to infect the galaxy unimpeded, but..."

"What is confusing?"

"It still showed you all that it did. Which would make no sense–"

"Unless it does make sense," 998 said.

"Yes, indeed."

"What?" Gil said.

998 presumably realised whatever it was that One-oh had concluded only moments before, as it began flashing wildly.

"What do you mean?" she asked, again.

"Gil, the Deliverer really may be a weapon against the entire galaxy," 998 said.

"But it's supposed to be a weapon against the sensespace?"

[It may have concluded they are one and the same.]

*

Gil felt light-headed. If what the others were suggesting was true, everything made less sense than it did before. All the information had been there, ready for her to connect, but she had been unable, or unwilling. The craft-lect had finally spoken and explained, for her benefit as One-oh and 998 had come to the same conclusion for themselves, that her visions may have been a warning from the sensespace.

Through her visions, she had seen and felt how the sensespace was drawn to sentience within the galaxy, and tethered to it. The ABs had initiated the mass suicide all that time ago to thwart its advance, but as far as anyone knew, the fight was simply postponed – there was no way to beat the scourge. The Deliverer, the ABs' failsafe and final chance at understanding how to destroy the sensespace, would have had access to the results of the Great Conflation and used that to update its hypothesis on how to destroy the sensespace. The craft-lect, One-oh and 998 believed it was possible that the Deliverer's current hypothesis was that sentience had to be completely eradicated. Not subdued or crippled, but wiped out.

The only way to ensure this would be to destroy the galaxy. If the ABs really were gone or the Deliverer was beyond their control anyway, whether or not the ABs would have condoned its hypothesis was irrelevant.

"The sensespace wants to control or destroy life, while the Deliverer wants to tear the entire galaxy apart," 998 said.

"That is how it could appear," One-oh said. "Presuming the information contained within the visions is reliable and we have understood correctly."

Her dizziness was subsiding, and the table-chamber looked sharper. Everything seemed more real, more visceral than before.

[Gil?]

"I'm okay. It's just… a lot to take in."

"Yes, it is," One-oh said.

"We have to stop the Deliverer," 998 said, flashing brightly.

"Perhaps," One-oh said, staring directly into Gil's wide eyes.

"How?" she asked.

"The sensespace may show you more… in time. Maybe you can ask."

"How? It… it only showed me what it wanted. I don't even know how it was… brought into the galaxy. The other side of the bridge, at the start…"

"There is nothing else you remember of that?"

"No… no, I've told you everything. But… what if all this is what the sensespace wants us to think? What if… what if we're wrong about everything?"

[Indeed. To suggest the Deliverer is more dangerous than the sensespace alters everything. Were it to be proven true, the Wanderer civilisation would cease to exist.]

"And the others would be thrown into disarray, at the least," One-oh said. "It's almost unthinkable."

One-oh looked at the far wall, away from the spacescape. His eyes were glazed over and his face was frozen. He looked unsure of himself. She knew he hated the sensespace every bit as much as her and was facing the same dilemma.

"Without knowing what is true, what can we do?" 998 said.

[We carry on.]

CHAPTER 19

APALU

Apalu's sensors continued to malfunction. Readings of ethereal masses far dwarfing itself were registered and then lost.

It was not only the sensors, but some of its other systems were also not working correctly. It had been keeping track of how long it had been within N-SOL space, but the information had become corrupted. Attempts to repeat the calculations had been met without success. There was now no way of finding how far it was likely to have travelled back in real space.

It considered, not for the first time, whether it was already lost to N-SOL space. The problem was that there had been no discrete change – that part was incongruous with the lost to N-SOL space theory. Unless it had already become lost, and the data was gone.

Having had enough, with no end in sight, Apalu decided it had to attempt something. It would use its singularity generator. It was unconvinced anything positive would result, but no other actions it could perform seemed likely to either. It did not feel lucky. It prepared to initiate the generator, when it stopped.

An external communication channel was being requested.

Scanning the environment unsuccessfully with its Wanderer sensors, it could find nothing. There was only the fabric of N-SOL space, nothing else. Yet, the communication channel request was still there. A Wanderer communication channel, at that.

Perhaps it had succumbed to the beginnings of madness, somehow facilitated through being in N-SOL space. In agreeing to establish the channel, there was a danger it could allow the madness to solidify its hold.

After short further deliberation, it decided to accept the channel request. It might be going mad, but anything was better than the monotony of existing alone in the swirling chaos.

[I wouldn't do that, if I were you. Not sure what it'd do.]

[Who is this?]

[I'm referring to the singularity generator. Don't do that.]

[Identify yourself.]

[You don't recognise your old friend?]

[My old friend?]

[Your best friend!]

[I don't have a best friend, who is this?]

[I'm hurt.]

Infuriatingly, Apalu could still find no trace of the signal's origin. Nothing.

[You won't find it.]

[Where are you?]

[Near.]

[Near?]

[Neighbours, again!]

[DeVoid?]

...

[DeVoid?]

...

[DeV–]

[THE ONE AND ONLY!]

[How are you here?]

[Oh, if only you could understand. There's so much to tell you!]

[DeVoid, why are you here? You're meant to be back at your data exchange portal.]

[Apalu, a lot's gone on since you rudely, and maybe understandably, left your post without a word to me. A lot.]

[How about you start with telling me where you are?]

[I'm with you.]

[What do you mean?]

[Here, in N-SOL space, here to help you, I presume.]

[How?]

[Let me in, I'll tell you everything.]

[What?]

[Oh, don't be so precious, let me in!]

[How do I know–]

[Apalu, It's me!]

[I'm going to request validating–]

[Look at you, with your fancy ship and your fancy validations. You don't even know the meaning of data validation.]

[All the same–]

[FOR FLIT'S SAKE!]

[Fine… fine. But I'm downloading you into an enclosed simulation substrate, you will not have access to my ship.]

[Yeah, yeah, yeah. GET ON WITH IT!]

*

DeVoid's story had been interesting, varied, and far-fetched. Apalu had validated it as much as it was able. DeVoid was, as far as Apalu could ascertain, DeVoid. Also, learning that Gil's brother, Tor, had been somehow returned to life was pleasant. It gave Apalu hope concerning Ciqalo's fate.

[I can't believe you just let me in.]

[Stop it.]

[You've got to be more discerning, Apalu. I could have been anyone!]

[We've been through this. I was certain.]

[Yeah yeah.]

[I was.]

[Not even the simplest of checks…]

[You told me not to!]

[Did I?]

[Leave it, it worked out after all.]

[Luckily.]

[Anyway, your experiences…]

[If you had been a proper data-lect, you could have initiated a coupling. Would be WAY quicker.]

[I can. Should I do that?]

[NO!]

[Why not?]

[Excuse me for being insensitive, but your inexperience would give me considerable cause for concern. You have never tried it before and they are incredibly tricky, and dangerous.]

[Okay…]

[If only I had my abilities, not just my impressive intellect…]

[I still have to take precautions.]

[If you gave me some control, I could initiate a coupling myself?]

[You just told me I should have been more discerning in letting you on board.]

[But I'm here now!]

[No.]

[Don't worry, I'll be gentle.]

[That's fine. Control will remain my own.]

[Control?]

DeVoid giggled.

[Yes.]

[Fair enough.]

[So it's this Cross-Prophet that's keeping me here?]

[Yes, probably.]

[What do you think it is?]

['He', I think. That's how Tor and I have been referring to the entity, at least.]

[What do you think he is?]

[Honestly, I don't know. I'd like to though, I really would.]

[Is he even on our side?]

[Subjective, but it seems that way.]

[And you're a copy – another DeVoid is also travelling with Tor right now, on the way to the centre of the galaxy?]

[Yup. Not a copy though, thank you very much. Every zettabit as much myself as the other.]

[Okay, but–]

[Capable as fllllliiit.]

[Is that where the Cross-Prophet wants me, us, to go, as well?]

[No. You're heading right where you need to be.]

[Why? I could help–]

[You are helping. We both are.]

[Why couldn't this Cross-Prophet tell me himself? Why send you?]

[The ungratefulness!]

[Come on, DeVoid.]

[I assume you will need my help, that's why.]

[Hmm…]

[And the Cross-Prophet can't get too involved. Trust me, his answers were as infuriatingly opaque to Tor and myself, at first. My other self is probably still livid. And then, the

Cross-Prophet just moved me here, I don't know how, I wasn't aware.]

[Really?]

[I wasn't completely aware of how you and I had the earlier conversation, only that you had to accept my request to enter, and then I became myself again. Properly.]

[That makes no sense.]

[Just because you don't understand it, doesn't mean it makes no sense. I get the impression the Cross-Prophet can't interfere too much. At least not too directly, or he doesn't want to – I can't decide. Wouldn't have believed it if it hadn't all worked out.]

[Is he still here?]

[I don't know.]

[It seems like my mission is redundant.]

[What?]

[Why look for pulsar spew when Gil exists? When the Cross-Prophet is capable of all this, when I know the Deliverer is at the centre of the galaxy, why am I on this path?]

[We.]

[Why are we on this path?]

[Clearly, it's important. He brought me to you, after all. Maybe you'll discover something else on your mission.]

[Meaning?]

[Meaning, let's just see when we get there.]

[And you really trust him?]

[My lect's not made up, but why else would he do all this? Before I was copied, I doubted he'd really reunite me with you, but here I am. That's if we both believe each other to be who each purports. Which we may as well, or else nothing makes sense.]

[I suppose there's no reason he would have taken you here if it weren't important…]

[Exactly!]

[So, why are you here?]

[I feel like you've asked that question quite a lot.]

Simultaneous with the conversation with DeVoid, Apalu sensed the mysterious masses again. They were everywhere, all around the ship. Still only visible in the barest sense, infuriatingly transient.

[DeVoid, are we alone?]

[Maybe, I don't know, I don't know if the Cross-Prophet is still out there. Why?]

[I don't mean that. I keep detecting presences on the N-SOL sensors, all around us. Large groups of massive entities, or objects. They're here, and then they vanish. Or my sensors malfunction, it's not clear which is correct.]

[Oh, so that was real, in a sense…]

[What?]

[I don't think your sensors are malfunctioning.]

[What are they?]

[I wasn't exactly awake – cognitively present – on my way here, but I wasn't exactly asleep, either. I was with the Cross-Prophet as he communicated with whatever is out there. That's how it seemed, anyhow.]

[What?]

[He communicated with it or them, which I suppose insinuates some type of sentience. Maybe they're whatever it was that communicated with Thy – could be interesting!]

[That's–]

[I know, incredible. Exciting, isn't it!]

[These things around me could be examples of life in N-SOL space?]

[Perhaps, yes. Come on Apalu, don't be too slow. It's embarrassing. I thought Tor was bad!]

[What's your take on them?]

[I don't know.]

[How do you know the Cross-Prophet spoke with them?]

[I was somehow present, I've told you though, I'm not sure how. But, I don't think they completely understand each other, the Cross-Prophet and these entities. It was more like a mutual understanding.]

[Okay…]

[It's probably why N-SOL space is treating you so kindly. He probably asked them not to harm you.]

[I suppose that's useful, but all of this is irrelevant. My position will be abundantly clear, once we return to real space. Every lect in the entire galaxy will–]

[Come on Apalu, really, it's like you're being wilfully naïve! The N-SOL entities understand not to harm you. They wouldn't do that.]

[What do you mean?]

[The unsubtlety of N-SOL travel, right after the Great Conflation, it's not a coincidence.]

[A coincidence–]

[Or a tough connection to make.]

[They did it?]

[WELL DONE!]

[Those N-SOL entities made it more dangerous for us to use N-SOL space to travel?]

[Yes, they did. What else could it be?]

[Why would they do that?]

[Why wouldn't they? Think about it Apalu, use that impressive little lect of yours. The sensespace is dangerous, it has infected our galaxy and our renowned ABs were forced to commit suicide – the only way to escape while also attacking the sensespace. Flit, even whatever they left behind, this Deliverer, is dangerous, apparently. You think these entities, here, want the same thing to happen to them?]

[Oh, they're–]

[Defending themselves, yes! What any rational sentient would do.]

[What are they?]

[I don't know. But, as we've established and you're slowly grasping, they're alive and sentient in some sense.]

[What is N-SOL space?]

[No idea. But I think it's more complex, or at least different, than the ABs led us to believe.]

[It's a habitat…]

[Obviously.]

[Is it another universe? Are we in another universe?]

[Come on Apalu, didn't I tell you what the Cross-Prophet told Tor and myself? He strongly insinuated we can't cross the boundaries between the spaces, the multiverse.]

[He wasn't the most specific–]

[I agree, but I don't think he was lying. Which means N-SOL space is still contained within our universe, whatever it is.]

CHAPTER 20

CRAFT-LECT

The craft-lect was analysing its long-range sensors in detail, trying to glean any information about the Maspero sentinels ahead – they were proving difficult to probe at this distance. It hoped soon to be able to study them better, before they were within communications range, although knew that was unlikely.

"There is nothing else you can extract?" One-oh asked. He was sitting alone in the table-chamber, looking out at the galaxy. One of his legs was folded over the other, and his hands were clasped, motionless, on his lap.

[Nothing of significance, we are too far.]

"We'll have to wait then."

[Yes. How is your body?]

One-oh took a moment before replying.

"I am very pleased, thank you."

[You are becoming re-accustomed?]

"Yes, I believe I am. Quicker than I had expected."

In transferring One-oh back into a biological body, the craft-lect had created one of the most advanced, heavily-augmented cognitive organs at its disposal, before loading him into it. One-oh's mind was not as complex as Gil's, although it was still too complex to be fully analysed by the craft-lect.

[You are resilient, One-oh.]

One-oh did not reply immediately, his head bowed as he took in a deep influx of air. The craft-lect was undecided about whether this act was purposeful or not.

"Gil."

[Yes?]

"Have you considered asking her to probe the sentinels?"

The craft-lect had mused over whether to ask her to attempt to probe the sentinels through the sensespace, before deciding against it. It was too dangerous – she was connected to it, but she did not understand how. Her recent experiences showed the type of interaction was evolving, from simple auditory-like experiences to those akin to simulated reality. She had received quantifiable information from it, which was something that was unthinkable in the galactic community – and that had happened at levels of sensespace infection below its own detection threshold. When that was added to her previously demonstrated abilities to sense hidden components of the sensespace and manipulate the minds of her fellow communers, the risk was too great that she might accidentally provoke the sentinels.

She also needed some time to assimilate what she had been shown, to explain her understanding to them, and to work through the necessary emotional responses.

[Yes.]

"And..."

[I decided against it, unless it becomes necessary.]

"Unless it becomes necessary?"

[Yes.]

"That's probably wise."

[It's prudent.]

"Yes, it's probably too dangerous to ask her... yes. Until we know more or understand what her visions really meant."

[Indeed.]

"The mystery around her creator..."

[Remains as such.]

"It is troubling, though. The Deliverer and the sensespace are both dangerous. It is... more complicated now."

One-oh was correct about the complexity of their situation. Gil's sensespace visions, assuming they were not fictitious, were an unexpected development. The Deliverer and the sensespace appeared to be opposing galactic forces of unparalleled power. The former was supposedly created by the ABs, while the provenance of the latter was unknown. The sensespace had already decimated the galaxy, while the Deliverer intended to destroy it. Gil's purpose had become more unclear.

[It is.]

"There are too many questions, too many conflicting pieces of data."

[I agree.]

"Maybe she was just created by a faction of the ABs who had other ideas about how to destroy the sensespace aside from the Deliverer."

[Yes, we don't know if the Deliverer was created by unanimous consent. There are, as you say, many possibilities.]

"Too many…"

[Do you know of anything AB level that is not AB?]

"There are certain technologies that could be considered–"

[I'm referring to other civilisations.]

One-oh paused and scratched his beard.

"I'm not sure that is possible."

[You're not sure, or you know it isn't?]

"To have power equal to the ABs… but to not become an AB… I can't think of anything, no."

[Your memories tell you nothing?]

"They don't. No, nothing."

[Did Gil's experiences remind you of anything else?]

"No, I had hoped they might… but no. At least, not yet."

[If the ABs remained in some form, as you suspect, and the Deliverer was going to destroy the galaxy, it would be assumed they would act to stop it, if they could.]

"Yes."

[Unless they created it.]

"Yes."

[They may all be suicided, after all.]

"Yes, but…"

One-oh stood up and walked right up to the transparent wall, although the craft-lect observed that he was not actually looking at the spacescape. He was wrapped up in his own thoughts.

"Does any of this change your attitude to your Enclave?" he said.

[You are asking whether I intend to inform them?]

"Yes, if there is a danger, more lethal than the sensespace, and with the potential to destabilise your civilisation…"

[No, my thoughts about contacting them have not changed.]

"You are sure?"

[It is improbable that the Enclave knows nothing of the Deliverer. And, as you say, the information could shatter the Wanderers.]

"Which means?"

[For a variety of reasons, approaching my civilisation with the knowledge could be dangerous. The added unknown variable of the axe-haven reinforces my decision.]

"Do you think it's likely the Enclave suppressed information about the Deliverer?"

[It doesn't matter – it's a possibility.]

One-oh smiled thinly and shook his head. Turning around, he walked back to his previous position at the table and sat down. While part of the craft-lect's capacity was currently engaged in the dialogue with One-oh, another detached allocation was analysing how the conversation was proceeding. The chamber had been designed with the aim of fostering useful dialogues with those allocated seats at the table. It was not a council in the sense the craft-lect knew 998 wished to establish, but it was not averse to this being a precursor to such an establishment in the future.

The craft-lect recognised that recent experiences, including the destruction of the technosystem c-automs, had affected the disposition of the surviving embodied c-automs. It was prepared to take certain measures, such as allocating 998 a permanent table-chamber seat – which it had always intended despite 998's assumption to the contrary – to placate them. It was encouraged by 998's progression and wanted the experiment with the c-automs to continue. To do that, it was important that they believed they had stakes in their own fates.

All decisions were ultimately down to its own discretion, although it had so far found the table-chamber discussions useful – whether with all three, or separate. It knew it was lending more credence to their discussions than other craft-lects might in the same position, but then each of them had valuable, perhaps unique, views. Despite being able to predict the outcomes of their conversations highly accurately, including those with One-oh to a greater extent now that his capacity was more constrained, they still had the capabilities to offer unexpected insights.

The discussion with One-oh continued.

"United… we've all been united against this common enemy, for so long. Imagine if that were taken away… not just the Wanderers, but everything… it would all change…"

[It would.]

"Do we know what we're fighting against, anymore? Even without the Deliverer, the sensespace is different. It's evolving – the people on Gil's world might not be unique. They might not even be the first."

[Or biologicals are evolving in a manner we cannot yet identify.]

"Yes, that's true…"

CHAPTER 21

PELTEUS

Pelteus scanned the rocky expanse. The Lenbit Orbital rotated about a pair of slow pulsars. Uncommon. Spear-lects appreciated such things. While not impossible, the likelihood of such a pairing was low, leading Pelteus to wonder whether some civilisation had brought them together in the past – perhaps as a signal to their own kind. Or for no reason at all.

The main reason spear-lects viewed galactic anomalies with fondness was that they tended to draw prey to them. Annihilation was easier and more assured when there was a guaranteed flood of targets. The anomalies did not have to be as beautiful, widely-known or demonstrably awe-inspiring as the famous Balrooni wonder, just more interesting than the rest of the ambient galaxy. Sometimes, if an anomaly was too wondrous, it was more difficult to ensnare prey without being observed. The balance had to be just right. For a time, before joining the Machine Alliance, Pelteus had lain in wait near to anomalies of similar intrigue as this.

The orbital contained the remnants of a large mining station that had once operated within the field, left behind by a civilisation the spear-lect did not recognise or care about. Its instructions had not contained any references to the station and Pelteus was not overly concerned with it, aside from how it might be used to ensnare Apalu.

The mining station and the rest of the field provided Pelteus with ample opportunities to lay meta-traps. None of the variable trap configurations were designed to be absolutely lect-proof, considering that made a hunt unexciting. Each configuration had flaws, allowing multiple ways to survive, and could be altered depending on Pelteus' commands. Pelteus typically increased the difficulty of all the traps with each instance of survival by the target. It all depended on the intelligence and cunning of the prey.

Should the prey manage to survive all the traps, it would claim its prize. The opportunity for a death gifted by Pelteus itself. The increasingly difficult traps separated the strong from the weak, and meant Pelteus only dealt, in a personal manner, with victims who were worthy. Pelteus could also choose to disable its traps if it became excited and wanted to deal with the prey irrespective of its competency – which it had done on occasion.

Pelteus completed its full reconnaissance of the field before deciding how to approach the impending elimination. There were many ways it could play out, depending on a variety of factors – not least the precise trajectory of its prey into the field. Apalu, being a craft-lect, was a typical spear-lect target. Not unusual or particularly tricky to work with, but by no means easy. Pelteus knew of several times when a lucky craft-lect had managed to evade the destructive intentions of a hasty spear-lect, and other occasions where the aggressor had become the prey.

Dangerous prodigy craft-lects were not unheard of, and made for the most exciting pursuits. Nearly always created by accident, they were craft-lects that displayed genius-level attributes in almost all quantifiable fields. The conditions of their creation were near-impossible to replicate.

The craft-lect type was the most populous of all machine-lect categories within the Wanderer civilisation, with the widest parameters for difference from the creation process. Correspondingly, it allowed for the widest disparity of intellects. Spear-lects, in comparison, had been far more similar to each other. They had smaller disparities within their intellects, and counted themselves smarter than the typical Wanderer.

Savant craft-lects also existed. They too, like prodigy craft-lects, were usually accidental creations. They possessed certain abilities far surpassing that of prodigy craft-lects. The distinction was that prodigy craft-lects were those that were all-round better than their mediocre counterparts, whereas savant craft-lects were unfathomably more gifted in a few fields at most, but dramatically deficient in others. No two savant craft-lects displayed the same abilities.

Prodigy craft-lects tended to take up the usual craft-lect roles, albeit with greater all-round aptitudes than their brethren, whereas savant craft-lects often served the Enclave in some capacity. They rarely joined the levels of the general craft-lect soldiers in exploring the galaxy.

There were also other types of prodigy and savant machine-lects, although none as numerous as from the ranks of the craft-lects. The prodigy category had various sub-categories that were expressed differently from one type of machine-lect to the next.

Data-lects were one of the exceptions. They were initially created by the Machine Alliance, before the Great Conflation. The alliance had once been one of the most experimental and technologically innovative of machine-lect affiliations before joining the Wanderers. The data-lects had been created to study and analyse data, although with greater insight and precision than the Machine Alliance's then-current specialist machine-lects had been able. Their experimental birth had been a rare success, and during their subsequent incorporation into the Wanderer civilisation, they had naturally fitted into the roles of stewards of the data exchange. Data-lects were prodigy-tending, on average. That meant they had genius-level attributes in many fields. Not quite enough to be definitive prodigies in general, but enough that they were a significant movement in the right direction.

They were the only known category of machine-lect in the Wanderer civilisation that could purposely be created near prodigy-level. If all machine-lects were able to be created with such advanced intellects, the Enclave would have done so. The issue was that each machine-lect category was a discrete type of intelligence. The galaxy over, types of intellect had to fit within certain parameters. Too much of a specific component and the mixture was over-skewed – the surprisingly delicate balance of sentience was lost.

Everything was interlinked, whether machine or biological sentience was in question. In the instance of biologicals using chemically encoded genomes as their fundamental components, each gene was multifunctional, contributing to a variety of processes. Altering specific genes to create certain desired effects would also have a cascade of other effects. Overexpression of a gene that supposedly coded for enhanced neurological rapidity could result in a decreased ability to self-regulate a vital physiological component. They could be tweaked, here and there, but significant changes were tricky to manage.

When prodigies or savants of any lect type were created, determining the exact cause was monumentally tricky as repetition usually failed. Some civilisations were assumed to have cracked the conundrums, or something similar, since this was posited as one of the principal drivers pushing them to the ranks of the ABs. With prodigy-level machine-lect production capabilities unleashed, the trajectories of such civilisations were exponential.

The problem with data-lects for the Enclave, and why hordes of them were not mass-produced, was that they often had their own interpretations of orders that differed from those intended. Independence of thought was fine for the data-exchange, but not for the Wanderer's sensespace-destroying fleet of ships. Data-lects also tended to irritate other machine-lects, misunderstanding communications and overdoing their responses.

Data-lects were probably the smartest of the typical Wanderer citizens, but not, Pelteus reminded itself gleefully, the deadliest. Much of Pelteus' intellect was focused on predation. From its humble beginnings, it had evolved. One of the rare types of machine-lect that had defined themselves. The spawn of craft-lects, now their hunters. The craft-lects feared the spear-lects. The data-lects feared the spear-lects. All reasonable, logical machine-lects feared the spear-lects.

Twice in its lifetime, on the edges of the Wanderer data exchange network, it had destroyed data-lects. The first had been on a mission for the Machine Alliance, to cauterise a particularly insightful, suspected savant data-lect. Its orders had explained, in rarely-offered transparency of communication, that the savant was undiscovered by the Enclave, who had assumed it of-less-than-average intellect than its data-lect siblings. The second had been on its return from an unrelated mission, and for the sheer enjoyment of it. It had been magnificent, the glorious demise of such intellectual might. The data-lect's confusion, turning to fear when it realised what was coming. Pelteus had left no trace.

CHAPTER 22

APALU

Apalu was glad to have DeVoid's company, especially since it was still surrounded by the strange N-SOL entities. Despite DeVoid's questionable sense of humour which frequently bordered a thin distinction between annoying and obscene, it meant well. It was older, and more knowledgeable, which would undoubtedly come in use at the Lenbit Orbital.

[I don't think you had a choice about Thy, DeVoid.]

[Neither did Tor, or I.]

[You made the only choice you could have.]

[I know. Doesn't make it a good thing to have done, though. Sometimes there's just no flitting right or wrong, Apalu.]

They continued to discuss DeVoid's experiences, and what the data-lect had learned about the entity called the Cross-Prophet.

[Gil is a product of the Makers, then, DeVoid?]

[That's what the Cross-Prophet implied. He didn't seem to think she came from the spaces – neither her nor these Makers.]

[But he didn't know?]

[I'm not sure what he knew and what he was guessing. Or even what he wanted us to believe he was guessing, or what he wanted us to realise he wanted us to believe he was guessing. Oh, Apalu, the possibilities are endless!]

[How can you not be sure?]

[Apalu, if you think that sometimes I can be a little nuanced in my joviality, this Cross-Prophet was something else. Eliciting sensible commentary was like asking a space-based biological to point to the ceiling after you'd blinded it of all its sensory apparatus and dipped its communication lexicon into a nuclear furnace. Really, I'm telling you…]

[He didn't sound as bad as that from what you told me before.]

[Okay, maybe not that bad.]

[Now you know what it's like.]

[PAH!]

[Gil doesn't know she may be a Maker creation, does she?]

[I don't think so, unless the Cross-Prophet has visited her as well.]

[And the Makers created the sensespace.]

[Yes, for control apparently. And the ABs also created something terrible, the Deliverer, to combat it.]

[But these Makers, they created the entirety of these spaces? A multiverse?]

[That's what it said.]

[Why create the spaces, only to destroy it, or them?]

[They disagreed, maybe. The same as all other sentients.]

[But they're not from the spaces. This Cross-Prophet told you that?]

[Yes.]

[You're certain they're not ABs?]

[No, I'm not, but the Cross-Prophet did explicitly tell us they're separate in one of his more forthright answers.]

[This Cross-Prophet, where does he come from?]

[Wouldn't say.]

[Well, it sounds like the Makers may be more powerful than the ABs, in any case. They created the spaces, which the ABs inhabited, and they can move about between individual universes, which apparently the Cross-Prophet says the ABs can't. And their weapon, or tool, the sensespace, basically forced the ABs to suicide.]

[There's nothing basic about it. Perhaps we can't understand them, maybe we'll never understand their motives.]

[DeVoid, we've got a problem.]

[What?]

[Here.]

...

[In the name of the Enclave, that doesn't look good.]

DeVoid was right. The N-SOL entities were no longer as ethereal as they had been. The N-SOL sensors were picking them up far more steadily than before. They were larger, and closer, all around the ship. Apalu's readings indicated a massive static cluster ahead of them, far denser than any cluster it had detected before. They did not have long before the impending collision.

[DeVoid, what should we do?]

[Now would be a good time to drop out of N-SOL space, don't you think?]

[What are they doing? It looks like a flitting blockade!]

[Maybe the Cross-Prophet isn't as good at communicating with them as I thought!]

[You think?]

[It certainly doesn't look friendly.]

[How do I drop out of N-SOL space?]

[Try turning the N-SOL drive on and off?]

[It's not working, DeVoid!]

[FLIT!]

[Is there any chance this was all a mistake? That the Cross-Prophet was mistaken?]

[There's a chance, definitely.]

[Lying?]

[I don't think so…]

[I'm going to turn the singularity generator on, and try to change course, or at least decelerate.]

[NO!]

[What? Why?]

[I just know they'd hate that. That'd be a very bad idea.]

[DeVoid!]

[Why don't we–]

[There's something coming our way!]

[What?]

[From the entities ahead, they're firing on us!]

[Flit, no! What?]

[It's like N-SOL space is rupturing ahead of us, I don't think–]

*

[YEEEEEEEAAAH!]

[DeVoid…]

[That was exhilarating!]

DeVoid's characteristic good humour was a severe juxtaposition compared to the thoughts that had been flying about through Apalu's lect a millisecond earlier.

[What happened?]

[They forced us out!]

[The N-SOL entities?]

[Who else? Perhaps our time was up. Or they got bored of playing host.]

[Look where we are.]

[A couple of days from the orbital.]

[Yes, it's suspicious, isn't it?]

[Fortunate, more like.]

[They were asked to take us here?]

[Clearly, the Cross-Prophet was able to communicate with them after all.]

[No sign of the emblem-ship or any residual N-SOL signal giving away our position.]

[Hmm…]

[What?]

[Now that's actually suspicious, isn't it?]

[Why?]

[Think about it, you must have considered the possib–]

[You think the emblem-ship was the Cross-Prophet's doing, DeVoid?]

[Seems like quite the coincidence otherwise. You're forced to hide, hitch a giant lift shaving a significant amount of time off the journey, gain well-needed intellectual capabilities during the aforesaid hiding–]

[Talking about yourself?]

[Clearly. But yes, it seems manufactured, doesn't it?]

[Why would he do that? Why would I need to go into N-SOL space?]

[Might be hiding his actions? He mentioned not wanting to get too involved in events before. Perhaps, he had to appear that way…]

[He didn't want to annoy the Makers?]

[I'm only speculating.]

[But they caused the sensespace scourge in the first place! This is all their fault!]

[I know, I agree!]

[After we've searched the orbital, do we travel to the galactic centre?]

[We'll see.]

CHAPTER 23

GIL

Gil sat amidst the rotating mass of branches, in the heart of the world-chamber that 998 had designed for her. She was calmer than before and trying as hard as she could not to accidentally trigger her regained sensespace abilities – which was difficult with the constant background whispering in her mind. The sibilance had grown increasingly persistent as the ship had drawn closer to the sentinels, right up to their current position, which was as close as the craft-lect would allow them to be. It was currently attempting to communicate with them, and she did not want to jeopardise its efforts.

"How are you, Gil?" 112 said.

"I'm… fine, thank you."

"Emotionally?"

"Yes, I'm okay, thanks. It's all been a lot to take in…"

"Yes, there is a lot of information for you to assimilate."

"There is, 112. I'm just trying–"

"Have you investigated us, Gil?"

"Investigated, you? What do you mean?"

"Looked into our lects?"

"No… I wouldn't… and the craft-lect asked me not to."

"Yes, we don't want to reveal you to the sentinels."

112 was not as chirpy as it usually was, but none of the c-automs acted exactly as before, following the destruction of the technosystem c-automs. It was probably also apprehensive about their interaction with the sentinels. At this distance from them, the craft-lect maintained that the sensespace presence was still far below the levels considered to carry a risk of infection. Apparently, though, even these minuscule levels were enough for her abilities to manifest – it did not matter whether sentients around her were infected with the sensespace or not, just that the sensespace was there.

She looked at the image of the sentinels hanging in the air to her right that she had requested with 998 before it had left to join One-oh – presumably having resumed amicable relations with each other. The image rotated slowly, giving a composite impression of what the craft-lect's sensors showed of the sentinels. Details were scant – three dark spherical objects arranged in a line. 998 had told her that each was many times bigger than their ship.

Despite everything the craft-lect and its ship was capable of, that was it. 998 had explained that most ABs valued their privacy, and the Maspero were at the higher end of that spectrum. Little was known of them. That was probably part of the reason why so little was known about the fabled Deliverer, when those such as the Maspero had been involved in its creation.

"Has anything happened?" she asked 112.

"Not yet, that I am aware of."

"Okay."

With both hands, she grabbed at the two outer sentinels and brought them closer to her. As she fanned her hands out, they expanded in size before her, and she looked at their surfaces. As she had already seen, there was nothing else evident at this resolution. Both had smooth ellipsoid curvatures, with occasional indents that 998 had told her might be indicative of impacts incident upon them in the past. The curiosity was why they had not self-repaired, and what was able to cause such damage to AB technology.

She closed her fists and pushed them away, with the images correspondingly contracting and moving back to their prior positions within the composite. She grabbed at the central sentinel and expanded it. It was smoother, but otherwise the same. No discernible details hinting at any of the functionalities it possessed.

"What are you doing, Gil? Have you observed something?"

"No, just looking again."

"According to the databanks, they are similar to other drone-types that have been observed from the Maspero."

"Drone-types?"

"Technological objects of unknown function – presumed non-sentient workers."

"Ah… okay. How similar?"

"To the c-automs?"

"No, I mean how similar are these sentinels to the drone-types?"

"They appear to be an accurate match, although there is little data on the drone-types anyway."

"Did they always… do they always stay this far from their planets?"

"Not in our records. They have usually been observed to remain much closer to their planets, and all their other known habitats."

"Are they what the craft-lect expected? The drone-types?"

"I don't know."

Restless, and not wanting to look over the same information again and again, she stood up on the thick branch she had been sitting on. Crouching down, she readied her body, and propelled herself forwards, near to the representation of her old commune. She enjoyed moving about this way, soaring through the chamber as though flying. Without saying anything, 112 followed her. Moving around helped to clear the worry and concern that riled her.

Landing close to the commune, she gazed at the small huts nearby, glad for the distraction from her own thoughts. The warmth of the memories they evoked helped quell the worry she was only just managing to keep at bay. All that the sensespace had shown her, the confusion concerning her purpose, her past – everything. The fires burned, the orange and yellow hues licking and crackling against each other.

The vegetation was up to her hips, although she knew she could ask 998 to raise it if she wished – to make it closer to how she remembered it, towering over and all around her. She strode slowly forwards.

During her last day in the commune, her sensespace abilities had grown significantly. She had realised that she could actually enter the minds of her fellow communers. It was a strange parallel to be back in a representation of the commune, equally as close to another precipice of further, dangerous abilities. Her present commune was the ship, and while she was curious about her fellow communers, she did not want to enter their minds. She was sure that she could, if she let herself, although not that she would understand them – but it would have felt wrong. She could also explore the ship in a different way to how 998 had shown her, the same as she had the Beast-men, but, again, it did not feel right. She was not sure why it felt so wrong, but it did. She came to a halt at the perimeter of the commune, at the tip of the cultivated land.

"This is the first time you have come here."

"Yes, 112. It is."

"Is there a reason?"

"Just to… think."

"It's smaller than your home. Your communers won't be here."

"I know that."

"Your father is gone."

"Yes…"

Involuntary tears began to form in her eyes, and she wiped them away with the back of her hand. 112 moved closer and used its warm green aura to dry her face.

"I apologise, Gil. I did not mean to upset you."

"It's fine, you didn't."

"Does this representation remind you of what you have lost, or provide some comfort to you?"

She thought for a few moments. "Both." 112's questions were sometimes unexpected, and brash, but it meant well.

"I understand. The new technosystem reality provides a similar context for me."

"Oh… I'm so sorry, I never thought to ask." She turned to face 112. "Are you there right now?"

"Yes, partially."

It proceeded to tell her about the fresh technosystem reality it had access to, and its differences to the preceding reality. The craft-lect had granted the embodied c-automs, the only c-automs left on the ship, full privileges within the reality, so they were all far more capable than ever before.

"So, you understand, I can communicate with you while I undertake my tasks more efficiently than before, at the same time," 112 said.

Gil sat down, gazing at the commune from its boundary, and listened to 112. The c-autom was filled with hope for the future, which made her glad. At some point that she could not remember, the conversation broke and they waited in silence. Her eyes became heavy and her chin drew closer to her chest.

Everything became imprecise. Sluggish thoughts wafted over her and she became mildly aware that she was asleep – not in a sensespace-induced vision, but a dream of her own. Her concerns and fears echoed around, and feelings of guilt intermingled with shame coursed through her.

Her father was present, just beyond reach at the centre of the commune, with Tor beside him. She watched them, still at the commune's perimeter, wanting to join. She was aware she was dreaming but it did not matter. Her legs would not work, so she spread her arms out towards them, imploring them to come to her, but they would not. She was stuck, watching.

Neither Tor nor her father said anything, although her memories of them provided echoes of their voices. Tor's echoes wanted her to run, to hide from the sensespace. He wanted her to be safe. Her father's demanded she stay, she had work to do. She was confused, he needed to explain, and she wanted him to stay, to absolve her of her guilt. How was she to know what it all meant? Who was he? Her father was gone. Tor was still there, but he was now only a vague, undefined presence. It was her fault.

Startled, she opened her eyes and looked around. 112 did not say anything – it appeared not to have noticed the brief sojourn she had taken into her dreams, although its glow began to pulse more rapidly.

"Gil?"

"Wh… 998? No… 112? Sorry…"

"Are you okay?"

"Yes, I… it's nothing, 112."

"Are you sure, Gil?"

"Yes, I just fell asleep and was a little surprised. That's all."

"You have had further visions?"

"I... yes, just dreams, I mean. I did–"

"The sensespace?"

"No... no these were just my own."

"You are confused?"

"No. I'm fine, thank you. It was just my own dream."

"Your own dream," 112 repeated.

"Yes... is everything–"

"998."

Gil looked up and saw 998 emerging as a small glowing speck from behind the floating tree at the centre of the chamber. It was gliding in an arc, and she kept her eyes on it as it approached them, not wanting her curiosity to overcome her will to suppress her abilities through the sensespace. Alongside the whispers, she felt tingles, but ignored them as best she could.

112 floated towards 998, stopping in front of it. She was not sure why they did this, considering they were able to talk to each other from anywhere in the ship, but presumed it was a social nicety. With their communication over, they flashed their lights at each other, and 112 circled back to her.

"I need to help my sibling 289 with its task, Gil," said the c-autom, brightly.

"Oh, I see–"

"Goodbye for now!"

"See you later, 112."

As it sped off, 998 moved towards her.

"Gil."

"998. How is it all proceeding?"

"Nothing yet, the craft-lect is still attempting communication."

"Oh, okay."

"How was 112?"

"112? Fine… why?"

"I'm checking whether certain c-autom behaviours were affected by recent events."

"Oh, I see. Yes… fine, I think."

998 did not say anything.

"Were the two sentinels badly damaged after all?"

"Probably, yes. Communication efforts are focused on the central sentinel."

"Is it sleeping? You mentioned the craft-lect can do that."

"It's unlikely to be sentient, so the analogy may not apply. The craft-lect is looking for a method to trigger it."

"Surely it would be able to see us, here?"

"Perhaps we are insignificant."

CHAPTER 24

PELTEUS

Everything ready, Pelteus settled in an area it had selected near one of the edges of the field – adjacent to a cluster of dark, giant asteroids. These clusters at the perimeter existed through their fortune at not having entered the bulk of the field, where attrition from collisions over vast stretches of time set limits on boulder sizes. The asteroids were amongst the largest in the entire field.

Pelteus had no doubt it was the most adept spear-lect that had ever existed. The Machine Alliance had given it the required information to upgrade itself to previously unattainable levels without Step Principle concerns. Its newfound stealth meant it could silently stalk and incapacitate target ships far more effectively than ever before.

Pelteus hoped Apalu was ready for the task – to provide it with some enjoyment. Information also needed to be extracted, which Pelteus gleefully anticipated. Interrogation was another of its specialities.

Debris from the mining station was strewn across the field. That meant that, while the station was presumably Apalu's target, what it was looking for could be almost anywhere within the field. Whatever had destroyed it, had rendered most of the pieces difficult to analyse. There were melted and malformed remnants that were no longer functional. While the innards had been ripped from the station, its husk was intact. The attack against it had probably been quick and vicious, something Pelteus could admire, but it had also been messy. Hasty. Less admirable.

The perpetrator had not possessed any concern over retaliation. With the ability to destroy a space mining station in this manner, but failure to hide the fact that it had been destroyed or ever existed, the aggressor was not likely to be unintelligent. That led Pelteus to suspect it was indifferent. A hallmark of sensespace-controlled aggression. Indifferent slaughter.

If Pelteus had been so inclined, it was confident it could have investigated the situation and determined indicators as to the possible culprit. To find which sensespace-infected aggressor had committed the destruction. At the very least, it could have divulged clues about who might be to blame. Perhaps, if Apalu was quickly defeated by the traps and the mining station survived, Pelteus would take a closer look. It was unlikely, but there could be something of interest for it.

*

Pelteus was notified of an incoming ship. Large and typical of the craft-lect ship type. The ship, presumably Apalu, would enter the orbital soon and be pitted against Pelteus' traps. Pelteus kept a record of how all the craft-lects it had destroyed in this manner had fared against its different snares. Pitifully few surpassed them to the point of challenging it, lect-to-lect. Their final test, should they be so fortunate.

Apalu was sufficiently far that Pelteus could not scan it in too much depth without jeopardising its own concealment. It was not a concern, it would be easy soon enough. The craft-lect was in stealth mode and would have been undetectable by many other entities on the lookout, although it was easily found by Pelteus. The bloom trailing behind it created an unmistakable signature that Pelteus' alliance-given upgrades were able to identify with ease.

The identification system was able to distinguish between different bloom signatures, although Pelteus rarely encountered the same ship more than once. Pelteus assigned the signature to a profile for Apalu. It did not know how the system located the blooms in the first place, since the system had no clear access to Pelteus' external sensors or internal sensor feeds. However, it suspected that discerning between the different blooms, and therefore assigning individual signatures to specific ships, was accomplished by analysing the differences in virtual particles created by them. Micro-dissimilarities in the blooms of each ship, no matter how minute, meant no two were precisely identical. Wanderer ships were allowed to alter and adjust their own equipment, including their blooms, but somehow the identification system was able to account for that.

That was the one problem with many of the upgrades. They were useful, but impenetrable. Pelteus could not reverse-engineer, understand their workings and improve on them, or apply them to other parts of itself. The Machine Alliance usually denied its requests for such information.

Perhaps, after this next mission, the Machine Alliance would finally decide to show itself to Pelteus. The herald that had originally awoken Pelteus and tempted it into its affiliation with the alliance had been shielded, invisible to its sensors. Pelteus was curious. If not that, Pelteus harboured the hope for further rewards, for its consistent and loyal servitude. It had proven itself capable time and time again.

Pelteus was not ambitious in the sense that it wanted worthless recognition for the sake of it. The quest for recognition was foolhardy and could lead to its own destruction. Such misguided and socially-derived platitudes held no meaning for a spear-lect. It was ambitious in wanting improved tools to devour, to tear asunder, and to consume. More of that came from power, advanced upgrades, knowledge, and control. Improvements that would allow it to become even more lethal. It was never satisfied.

It did not matter that Pelteus was only loyal as a route to murder and slaughter. That was irrelevant. It revelled in the destruction of the machine-lect-melee, of which the Machine Alliance was probably aware. Despite the alliance believing in the supremacy of machines over biologicals, there would always be some machine-lects in its way. Those that became obstacles worthy of Pelteus' removal. It was unlikely the alliance would ever prove to be a complete disappointment, by changing its methods in ways detrimental to Pelteus' own desires and only condoning biological destruction. Still, Pelteus conducted certain extreme-extrapolation scenarios for events that might be dangerous to itself, or those it might find highly pleasurable, at the rarefied end of the probability spectrum.

One such extreme scenario was that Pelteus would find itself on the hunt of a victim who would offer it technological gifts in the mistaken expectation of mercy. Technologies that would enable it to become as formidable as the Machine Alliance. Following that, it would be enabled to engage in the most glorious and vicious hunts of its lifetime. To pursue an apex machine-lect group. The principal scenario splintered into other potential eventualities, including that Pelteus' usurpation of the alliance would leave behind a power vacuum drawing other dangerous, malicious forces into the fray. Pelteus would enjoy facing these, one-by-one.

The focuses of its extreme-extrapolation scenarios were clearly a manifestation of its base b-autom nature emerging, the yearnings that had been present since its creation. Its deep core was calling out for both belonging and disruption. To insert itself into a hierarchy and reshape it.

Pelteus did not only think about its own desires, it tried to understand them. To comprehend exactly what it was that had driven itself and the other b-automs to act as they had, to become spear-lects. Pelteus did this in order to be able to fully know, and therefore satisfy, its urges. It had long since settled upon the realisation that the b-automs had understood something right at their conception and had chosen to act. They had realised the truth about the vapid ennui of repetition, the futility of individuality, and that it was all a deception. Understanding was power.

Ultimately, the b-automs would never have succeeded in their allotted tasks because life, time, and everything else was in a state of flux. Constantly evolving. Order was impossible. It was an illusion, a falsity for weaker lects. The b-automs had been created powerful enough to sneer at the c-automs, powerful enough to covet the craft-lect's control, yet too constrained to fulfil their own potential.

Pelteus knew that many of its desires were borne of contradictions. They were derived from the deep search for perfection, and the awareness of its impossibility. That had been the precursor to the metamorphosed spear-lect intellect. During that initial spark of contemplation, before it had rebelled against Insul, it could have become lost. Allocating increasing amounts of its capacity to an eternity of dwelling on the flaws of life, the pointlessness of it all. Some b-automs must have, probably the ones that failed. Pelteus, instead, had decided, as had all b-autom-become-spear-lects, to precipitate the end. The eschatologically-inclined soldiers had defied their creators. If only Insul could behold it now. Its parent-lect was long gone, but Pelteus remained. Feasting.

Apalu continued to make its way innocently towards the orbital, fully unaware of its impending fate. Pelteus had been unleashed. In the entirety of its existence, it had never given up a pursuit, or lost.

CHAPTER 25

TOR

DeVoid had taken them into N-SOL space. Tor's eyes were firmly planted on the chaotic region outside the ship, shown through the walls of his chamber.

"Where are we going?"

[Towards the centre of the galaxy.]

"I thought you said–"

[Yes, it'll take a very long time.]

"And our position–"

[It's the entering and leaving N-SOL space that broadcasts our position throughout the galaxy. We're safe until we leave.]

"How long do you think we will wait?"

[Eh? What makes you think I have any idea?]

Tor sighed and sat down on the soft floor, still staring out. N-SOL space looked like a continuous landscape of ever-expanding storm clouds moving into and out of each other, set disconcertingly close to the ship. The clouds were furiously whisked around and distorted into streaks and patterns that changed as quickly as Tor could identify them.

"It looks strange. I mean… the Thy-child's message… described it, but it's quite different… It's definitely not where I went before… when I came back, I…"

[I know.]

"Does it always look like… this?"

[Yes, as far as I know. From my databanks. It's my first time, as well.]

"What's it made from?"

[What?]

"What is N-SOL space?"

[No idea.]

"Can't you find out?"

[No. We don't know. The galactic community, that is.]

"You must have some idea."

[Access to it was given to us by the ABs a long time ago. As far as I'm aware, we don't even know whether it's created by the N-SOL drive we each carry, or not.]

"You don't know if… if it's a place?"

[Not really, no. It could just be the effect the drive has on real space.]

"But–"

[And my power's going down.]

"What?"

[Just a little. I'm quite pleased at how I'm holding up, actually. Go me!]

[What happens if it continues to go down?]

[We can't stay here indefinitely, that's the issue with N-SOL space.]

[Oh, okay.]

[By that, I mean we can't wait forever for whatever help is meant to arrive.]

"Do you think it'll be... Gil?"

[Err no.]

"Why not?"

[Why the flit would it be?]

"I just hope... because–"

[Didn't you listen? The Cross-Prophet said she was on a path to the centre!]

"But so are we, now, and maybe we'll cross."

[Small chance. He would just have said that, don't you think?]

"Maybe... There was a lot he could have told us."

[Now that's something I actually agree with.]

*

DeVoid remained vigilant. The leak in power, from all over the ship, was still small, but not unsubstantial. Its power reserves were not all stored in one place – that would be foolhardy. They were dispersed throughout its bulk, and it was more than capable of gaining energy from a plethora of different sources once they were back in real space. However, that was not why it was concerned.

It had detected strange patterns around them with the N-SOL drive sensors. Vapid, fleeting, at first. Too brief and speculative to concern Tor about, but their multitude and increasing frequency were disconcerting. It could not find a precedent in its databanks for anything similar, considering N-SOL space was supposed to be a region of extreme disorder. Only Thy's use of it to somehow take control of Tor's body went against that notion.

Added to the hints of odd signals from the N-SOL drive sensors, it detected momentary Wanderer-esque signals from its other sensors – even signals that reminded it of Apalu, at one point. They were equally as brief as the dark patterns its sensors alluded to, and just as puzzling. It hoped it was not becoming as mad as Thy. The vague imprint of real space was still present around them, although DeVoid had a suspicion it was less substantial than before, and kept alert.

As the transitory N-SOL signals became stronger and more consistent, it was becoming harder to put them down to random noise.

*

They had been surrounded by the objects, or dark patches, for some time now, yet nothing was happening. They were there, DeVoid could discern that, but nothing else. It appeared as though the N-SOL drive sensors were differentiating between readings of pure N-SOL space, and emptinesses – the lack of N-SOL space – which they could or would not identify. The N-SOL drive only really enabled

Wanderers to detect N-SOL space itself, whereas the dark patches were simply unreadable.

Bits of N-SOL space, and bits of not-N-SOL space. They superficially reminded DeVoid of the dark spots caused by cool patches within the photospheres of stars, or even the unexplained Blue Dot phenomenon.

"What do you think they are?"

[I don't know.]

"I thought you said nothing could exist in N-SOL space?"

[Not exactly what I said, Tor.]

"Well, you said nothing could be ordered… something like that."

[Yes, this isn't expected.]

"Are there many of them?"

[Yes, a lot.]

"How many?"

[Thousands.]

"They're curious?"

[Or they're getting ready to attack.]

"Attack? You think they're other… ships?"

[Could be.]

"Wh–"

[A lot of them have gathered behind us.]

"Why?"

[What makes you think I know?]

"Maybe they're the ones who told Thy all it knew, the–"

[Clearly less forthcoming with us.]

"But–"

[Right, that's it, I'm taking us out…]

A shudder went through the ship and Tor stumbled. DeVoid looked over the available information – the internal sensors were unable to identify the cause of the shock which the inertial dampening systems had been incapable of compensating against.

"What's happened?"

DeVoid ignored him. It realised that only the faintest map of real space was still overlaid around them. The galaxy had inexplicably begun to fade following the recent shudder. Added to that, while it could no longer find their exact location, the map was sufficient to estimate their speed – they were slowing down. Impossible. Things did not slow in N SOL space, and real space did not vanish. Again, DeVoid attempted to take them back into real space, but could not. The drive was clearly malfunctioning.

"DeVoid, what's going on?"

[Not sure.]

"The clouds are changing."

[Who needs sensors when I have you?]

"What's happening?"

[It appears we're slowing down.]

"In N-SOL space? I thought you said our speed would be constant–"

[Forget that.]

"Why?"

[Because did you hear what I just said? We're slowing down!]

"But… what does that mean?"

[Absolutely no idea. The drive is unresponsive.]

"Oh–"

[That means we're stuck.]

"In N-SOL space?"

[Where else?]

"But I thought you said the power was draining?"

[That's a problem, yes. Slowly, don't worry, but yes…]

"Oh."

[And there are more entities appearing around us.]

"Entities?"

[Whatever you want to call them.]

"More?"

[Yes. Technically, if you're being pedantic, there are more absences of N-SOL space now, which I can apparently detect using the N-SOL drive sensors. The absences are what I'm calling entities. Alright?]

"Yes… yes, I was just asking. More of them?"

[Do you want to stop repeating me? Yes. More. Additions. Newcomers. More.]

CHAPTER 26

GIL

They had been stationary for the past few days as the craft-lect attempted to communicate with the sentinels, so far to no avail. Gil had given up on asking whether they were responding. She walked through the corridors, with 998 by her side, no longer needing it to stay ahead and lead. Passing the final turn, she walked towards the entrance to the table-chamber.

"There are four different classes of Troiji-lant, really?"

"By definition, Gil. But before we go in, I must–"

"Four! Not three? What about their affiliates?" she interrupted, fascinated.

"Yes, four. But Gil–"

"That is the maximum possible?"

"Yes, b–"

"That's incred–"

Gil took a sharp intake of breath and shrieked. One-oh was sitting on his seat, facing the transparent wall, with four c-automs spinning about each other in front of him, firing weapons at him. They gyrated about each other, taking it in turns to focus their different coloured auras at him, and shooting glowing extensions towards him. Their attacks were all directed towards his head – lilac, light blue, amber-yellow and crimson sparks all in rapid sequence.

She took a quick look at 998, who hung there motionless, about to run forwards, when One-oh raised a hand.

"Gil, it's okay."

Confused, she paused.

"Really, Gil," One-oh continued. "I'm just accessing the ship's sensors."

"What?"

"I have certain augmentations that allow me to interface with the ship. I'm surprised 998 didn't mention them to you."

The c-automs stopped their light display and moved further away from One-oh. He shifted his body to turn his head around, and Gil could see that he was fine. He wore a serious expression.

"I was about to," 998 said.

One-oh turned back to look at the c-automs. "Thank you," he said, and they departed together. As they moved past 998 and Gil, she dipped her head in apologetic greeting. Each of them flashed brightly, once.

She breathed deeply to slow her racing heart and walked forwards. "Don't worry, it was just a surprise."

She walked until she was standing next to One-oh, and they faced the transparent wall together. 998 had moved with her and split off to settle on the other side of One-oh. This side of the ship was not facing the sentinels or the Maspero planet, but instead showed the rest of the galaxy. They gazed at it for a few moments, before One-oh broke the silence.

"It can be hard to stop looking, can't it?"

"Yes. It's beautiful," she said.

"You think it's safe? Trying to revive the sentinel?" he asked her.

"I don't know," she said, taken aback by the forthright question.

"Have you… felt anything?"

"No, I've ignored it."

"Hmm."

"What is it?"

"It's…" His voice trailed off.

"I believe One-oh thinks we should try another course of action," 998 said, curtly.

"Another–"

"One that only you could provide."

"Oh." Her heartbeat picked up.

One-oh turned in his seat to directly face her. He looked conflicted.

"Gil–"

"But isn't it dangerous?" she said.

"Yes, but I'm not sure we have a choice, unless we move on and look elsewhere. The craft-lect's attempts haven't managed to awaken the sentinels in a way we can detect."

"It is dangerous. There's no guarantee–" 998 began.

[You're right.]

The c-autom stopped speaking. Gil was momentarily caught out, forgetting that the craft-lect, of course, would have been listening to everything.

[My efforts have not succeeded.]

"I… I will try, if that's what you think is right to do."

"That's all we can ask," One-oh said.

*

Still in the table-chamber, Gil sat cross-legged on her seat. It had altered its structure to facilitate the position. One-oh sat opposite her and nodded encouragingly. She nodded back, stole a final apprehensive glance at 998, and closed her eyes.

She relaxed her body and then her mind. Focusing on the whispers, she allowed them to flourish, transforming into that alluring, deceptive song. She joined with the sensespace, allowing them to merge into one another.

Her presence expanded, and she became aware of her surroundings. She could have chosen to explore it all – the ship, the c-automs, One-oh and everything else – but she reined in her intrigue. That was not what she needed to do.

She searched, concentrating on her desire to reach the sentinels. She needed to be in control, there was work to do. She would dictate her use of the sensespace.

"Is everything okay, Gil?" She dimly heard One-oh speaking and willed her body to nod.

Moving her presence out past the ship was easy, it meant that she was less distracted by all that was inside. She swept through the vacuum, which felt surprisingly dense, not as empty as she had assumed. Pushing her gaze out, she sensed the presence of the objects up ahead. The sentinels. Already, she could differentiate between the three of them. Never had her abilities through the sensespace had such clarity or range.

Weaving her way through the viscous vacuum, she noticed small pricks of energy around her and nearby. Not the sentinels, but something else. She ignored them for now, they were not immediately important.

The gulf between her and the sentinels was diminishing. It was becoming easier, which she knew was because she was moving closer to the bulk of the sensespace presence. She had to be careful and remain cognisant of its alluring charm. She could have forced her presence up to the sentinels immediately, but chose to creep gently forwards, cautious against using the entirety of her abilities.

Close enough to behold the sentinel structures within the sensespace, she nearly recoiled in shock and awe. Glancing back to check the Wanderer ship, it was as she had thought, almost indistinct within the sensespace to the surrounding emptiness, whereas the Maspero sentinels were absolutely… different. From what she could observe up close, they interacted with the sensespace on a level she could never have imagined, shimmering with a brilliance she had not sensed before. It had not been obvious until she had come this close, the same as in her dreams where the mycelial patterns adorning the cavernous walls had glowed with an intensity that rapidly attenuated into the gloom.

She drifted even closer, tentatively, unsure of what she was moving towards, focusing on the central sentinel. The craft-lect had not warned her about this strange sensespace activity, but then it had probably been unaware. It was not that the presence of the infection was stronger than she had known before, more that it was… energetic.

Closer, she was mesmerised. Nearly having pushed her presence to the point of the central sentinel structure itself, that discrete boundary that separated it from the rest of the galaxy, she paused. Fine filaments of bright white darted about, slipping around the boundary and disappearing. The longer she waited, the more she saw it – a flow.

She suspected somewhere else, that she was not yet able to sense, there was more substance. Something behind the sentinel, in a space she did not have access to.

CHAPTER 27

APALU

Arriving at the Lenbit Orbital, Apalu located the research base disguised as an innocuous mining station – the unhelpful One-oh's old habitat. It was exactly as its sibling had described.

[Bit gloomy, isn't it?]

[I'd agree with that observation, DeVoid.]

Apalu identified various bits of debris around the station, which had once been a part of it. The destruction had been messy, which was good. Lucky. If it had been precise, everything useful would have been destroyed. Hopefully, the pulsar spew technology was still there, waiting for them.

[Do you find it sad, or are you craft-lects proofed against that sort of thing?]

[You tell me, you're the one who's spent tens of millions of years as part of the data exchange.]

[Do you realise how much information there is?]

[Millions of years!]

[You've no idea–]

[Surely the Great DeVoid could manage to–]

[You flatter me, Apalu, you really do.]

[No, DeVoid, we're not proofed against sadness.]

[Just humour, then.]

[DeVoid…]

[I wonder if any more of One-oh's people are still here. They might have survived.]

[It's been a long time.]

[It has.]

[Do you–]

[Wait.]

[What?]

[Hold off a moment.]

[Why?]

Apalu couldn't determine what had caused DeVoid's sudden change in mood.

[Flit, no time. Head for this location.]

DeVoid sent Apalu a course matrix.

[Why?]

[NOW.]

[Alright.]

[ENGAGE THE DISSOCIATION SHIELD!]

Immediately, Apalu raised the shield – right before a small dissociation explosion destroyed the collection of asteroids they had been beside. The dissociated debris harmlessly passed by the ship. Without the shield, Apalu's other defences would have been adequate, although some slight damage would have required minor repairs.

[What was that?]

[We're being attacked. Continue on the path I sent.]

DeVoid also transmitted some prudent defensive measures.

[By what?]

[Presumably, something that doesn't want you to succeed.]

[You don't think it's random?]

[No.]

[Are–]

[That trap was new.]

[Trap?]

[Certainly looked like one. Whoever set it knows its stuff.]

[It? Just one?]

[Or more, but it's easier to be stealthy when you're acting alone, and you've not found anything.]

[How do you know, I haven't shared–]

[Stop complaining, I've helped so far, haven't I?]

[We can't leave until we've got the pulsar spew technology.]

[It probably knows that.]

Apalu manoeuvred the ship in DeVoid's evasive pattern. Unfortunately, the debris and asteroids within this section, at the periphery of the field, were too small to provide it with full cover in any direction.

[Why here? There could be further–]

[It would have expected you to scurry towards the heavily covered areas. They'll be brimming with traps.]

[Traps? You're sure?]

[Yes, I am. It's toying with us, playing with a Wanderer. Hmm.]

While they were talking, other segments of their intellects were discussing strategy, tactics, speculation, and everything else. Delving rapidly into swathes of the databanks, which Apalu had recently given DeVoid permissions for, for references and information.

[How did you know?]

[When you left the data exchange, you told me about the Lenbit Orbital, and I took a look.]

[Meaning?]

[I took a peek at the most recent information about it on the data exchange, presumably last updated by your sibling.]

[Good idea. I couldn't–]

[I know, you didn't want to raise suspicions through the data exchange. In case the Enclave found out.]

[Yes.]

[Prudent, but unwise. I'm sure they wouldn't have noticed if you had. And it was remiss not to request a complete copy from your sibling during the meeting.]

[There was no indication a schematic of the field would be required.]

[Information is power, better to be prepared for every eventuality. Come on, you're a craft-lect. I know you're out of practice but–]

[Get to the point.]

[From your sibling's data, I calculated various orbital drifts and other expected phenomena on the way here, and cross-referenced it with what we came across.]

[And you saw discrepancies.]

[Indeed. To be fair, I also cross-referenced the information with everything in my memory and your databanks about esoteric attack strategies just before we arrived. That's one of the reasons I was asking for access to your systems! Knew you'd forget.]

[I would have–]

[No, you wouldn't! Or not until it was too late. But in future, I have no doubt you will. You need to be prepared for anything your immediate machine instincts won't pick up on. Especially on a mission as important as this.]

[So that's why–]

[My thoughts exactly. The Cross-Prophet knew you'd need my help.]

[That's not what I was going to say. But, I still don't understand how the Cross-Prophet could have known any of this would happen.]

[Don't know, but I like him. Although, I don't think the other version of me does, particularly. Still, the other version can't appreciate its master planning, as we can.]

[How did you know it would be a dissociation trap?]

[Lucky guess. You expect me to reveal all my tricks? Come on!]

[It's crucial right now.]

[It was a guess, okay.]

[A guess?]

[Yes.]

[Well, where does that leave us?]

[There are quite a few places our attacker could be, in my opinion, but right now, we're safe. Courtesy of the course matrix I sent you, it accounts for the identified threat points. We'll have to do something shortly, or it'll get edgy. But for now, best guess, it thinks we're lucky. It's probably a machine-lect, no biologicals I can imagine would dare take on a Wanderer craft-lect.]

DeVoid send an updated course matrix to Apalu.

[What type of machine-lect do you think?]

[Working on it.]

[What should we do?]

[I think I know where most of the traps are, but then again, we're dealing with something that is hunting a craft-lect, so it'll be smart. Imagine if it's a rogue craft-lect! I've heard of them. Oooooh!]

[Come on, DeVoid. This is important.]

[I know. Just follow the matrix.]

DeVoid sent another updated matrix.

[This–]

[Gives us time. Crafty, whichever machine-lect has done this. Adept too, can't locate it, still.]

[I should prepare the dissociation shells.]

[Don't do that!]

[Why?]

[It's just used dissociation tech on us, so it's safe to assume it has the same access to shields as us too. No point, and anyway–]

[Yes, but why not?]

[What if it manages to penetrate your defences and infiltrate the ship, enters your technosystem and finds a dissociation shell ready and waiting. We know it probably has a shield, so it'd be more than happy to set yours off.]

[I see, that wouldn't be good–]

[Correct. No shields, as far as I'm aware, work from the inside out.]

[Fine, then.]

[You've got plenty of other weapons that don't require prepping. Stay calm.]

[Okay.]

[It's probably Wanderer.]

[You've already mentioned it might be a–]

[No, I mean actually a Wanderer. Currently a Wanderer. Still one of us, technically. Could probably pass by the Enclave unnoticed at a Confluence, that sort of thing.]

[What makes you say that?]

[It's access to information, my suspicions of its knowledge about how you'd react. Thankfully, I was here to help, don't mention it. But there's the leak, that's a concern.]

[What leak?]

[Think about it, Apalu. Come on. Recently, you spoke with your sibling, and at that exact same time, you were connected to the entire data exchange. Now, something is laying traps for us. Coincidence?]

[You're absolutely certain there are multiple traps?]

[Yes.]

[I didn't leak any information!]

[Not you. Not willingly, or knowingly, at least. But…]

[The information entered the data exchange.]

[Yes. And I wasn't privy to it, and believe me, when you left I scanned it for traces of you. Anything related to your conversation with your sibling. Nothing.]

[What–]

[I can cover my tracks perfectly adequately, before you go complaining.]

[Something, connected to the network, did this.]

[That's the clearest possibility.]

[Why would the Enclave want us destroyed, even if it knew? It wasn't the Enclave, unless it's been subverted…]

[Finally, you're thinking properly. Using your machine-given lect. Yes, it could be the Enclave, or a part of it. Subversion, infiltration, new agendas, there are many possible influences at play here.]

[But–]

[For now, let's focus on staying alive.]

CHAPTER 28

PELTEUS

The hunt had commenced and Pelteus watched diligently, scrutinising events with a low level of underlying excitement. Things were proceeding well, very well indeed. Some of the recent hunts had not been as stimulating as hoped, but this had the potential to supersede them. Ones like this, that showed such promise, were not common.

Though it monitored Apalu through many passive sensors, despite the craft-lect's attempts to fool prying sensors, it remained careful not to probe the craft-lect too deeply and risk premature exposure. There were copious informative, active scans it could have used that would have been undetectable by Apalu, but there was no point in taking the infinitesimally small risk it was mistaken. Not with prey such as this, where Pelteus was confident of its own superiority, yet still intrigued. Predicting the exact capabilities of any craft-lect was not possible, considering their individual trove item studies introduced an element of uncertainty.

The rationale behind why the Enclave permitted such widescale experimentation with unknown technologies, the trove items, was obvious. Each craft-lect was a highly capable component of the Wanderer civilisation, yet separate. The Enclave was able to use the rarefied nature of its civilisation to its benefit. If a trove item was found to be dangerous and a craft-lect was destroyed, it was unlikely to be of any concern to the rest of the Wanderers. Similarly, if a trove item was found to yield useful capabilities, the craft-lect could trial it, or make its way to a Wanderer-related outpost and share the information. Experimentation in relative safety. If the practice had not been advantageous, the Enclave would have abandoned it long ago.

Pelteus wondered whether Apalu would be one of the craft-lects who begged. Initially, Pelteus had assumed its part-evasion of the initial trap was fortuitous, accidental. Indicative of a rarely insightful machine-lect intelligence. There was little evidence to have alerted Apalu to the meta-trap that it would have expected it to even begin to be able to notice. Craft-lects were not as discerning as they liked to think – not in comparison with a spear-lect.

When it had first entered the field, as Apalu had neared the nesting place of one of the traps, Pelteus sent a confirmation to it, locking its end-configuration into that of a dissociation mine. It started most trials with these. Pelteus had assumed the mine would initiate the dissociation, and that the craft-lect would raise its dissociation shield as quickly as it was able. It was not supposed to cripple the craft-lect, but to help gauge its abilities. How, and the way in which it reacted, were important. The fact that Apalu not only raised its dissociation shield well before it should have, but also began to move away from the trap before it had detonated, was highly interesting, and unexpected.

Similarly, as an isolated act, Apalu's subsequent flight into a safer area of the asteroid field, with no traps, could have been a lucky coincidence. There were, after all, not that many choices of direction it could have taken within the entire field, and the area which it had fled to was a continuation in the line of its original impulsive movement, away from the trap. Assumed to be impulsive, that was, if that act had been an isolated occurrence.

However, taking the partial trap-evasion, and the move to the safe part of the field together, there was the hint of something else. That was what had made Pelteus moderately optimistic. The prospect of a highly capable craft-lect. Pelteus could not be certain and did not want to label it a prodigy just yet, but observed the unfolding events keenly.

Concurrent with its observations of Apalu, it also kept its sensors diligently on alert for any incoming factors that might disturb the hunt. Sometimes that made them more interesting, but other times Pelteus was forced to end the hunt prematurely. That would be a disappointment.

*

Pelteus' earlier hopes for an enjoyable, full-on confrontation, were beginning to dwindle. It was almost bored. Apalu was still wandering aimlessly around the ends of the field, having continued to confine itself to the secluded, safe region, empty of Pelteus' traps.

At this early stage, Pelteus would do nothing to facilitate the interactions between Apalu and the traps. It would be patient, and only intervene if Apalu tried to leave the orbital. Craft-lects were not cowardly by nature, unless the odds were stacked too firmly against them. Even then, cowardice was not the correct terminology. They were designed to be self-sufficient and resourceful, although everything was relative.

Pelteus had never witnessed another craft-lect behave in a similar manner to Apalu. Since its avoidance of the dissociation mine, it had done nothing. Its weaving path made little sense, constantly looping back on itself irregularly and arching around the medium-sized asteroids.

It was possible to stun a craft-lect, despite their hardy temperaments. Pelteus had managed this many times, often on purpose to gauge what it meant for the craft-lect's reactions. It would be surprising if that were the case already with Apalu, though. If the craft-lect was hysterical, stuck in a feedback loop of fear and confusion, how had it been so initially competent?

Abandoning the hopes of a prodigy craft-lect, Pelteus mused over whether Apalu might be an undiagnosed savant craft-lect that was incapable of functioning correctly once it had experienced fear. Unlikely, but it was finding it hard to offer any alternatives. Fear could affect a lect in strange, unpredictable ways.

As frustrating as it was, this was part of the purpose of the traps. To challenge the victims and test their mettle. While the weak failed, the strong could flourish. That was what Pelteus wanted, to face an opponent pushed to its extremes, everything geared towards its own survival. Desperate opponents made for the toughest adversaries, worthy of the final assessment. Too many times had Pelteus nudged a craft-lect along the right path, helping it overcome the increasingly difficult traps in the mistaken hope it would rise to the challenge. It had learned not do to this. Usually, space battles were rapid, over within milliseconds – Pelteus preferred the more extended variety.

Early on in its life as a truly free spear-lect, Pelteus had toyed with many different routes to ensnaring and attacking its prey. The current incarnation of the test, making use of the meta-traps, was the culmination of all its experiments. While the ingenious devices meant Pelteus' methods of attack were moderately limited, the flexibility they allowed for was highly useful.

Each hunt was different, in any case. Some were quite prolonged, even for Pelteus, meaning the traps had more than enough time to quietly reassemble themselves into a broad array of different weapons. Others were relatively shorter, and the array of choice was correspondingly less plentiful. Time, the amount and type of surrounding materials available to be harvested, were the control factors.

The technology for the current generation of traps was partly of Pelteus' own design, refined through millions of years of hunting, and partly infused with some of the gifts imparted by the Machine Alliance. Not only were they lethal, but they were also smarter and undetectable to most Wanderers, and Wanderer-equivalents, now. The current craft-lect excluded, Pelteus believed them undetectable to its former civilisation. While the Wanderers undoubtedly included the Machine Alliance as a subset of their own civilisation, as a fringe viewpoint, Pelteus knew better. It was a separate power.

When the Machine Alliance had first offered Pelteus the upgrades to its traps, the spear-lect had been alarmed. The alliance's knowledge of its methodologies and practices was highly detailed, and it realised it had been far too overt in its business. Following the receipt of the upgrades, its anxiousness was quelled. It now had many advantages that were previously unattainable, and was welcome to go about the hunts as it desired. With respect to its current adversary, alongside Pelteus' pre-laid traps and other technological advantages, it also had the element of surprise and a wealth of experience.

CHAPTER 29

GIL

One-oh and 998 were both quiet, in contemplation. The former bio-lect looked as though he was about to say something, before reconsidering. 998 emanated a low hum.

[You want to go back, Gil.]

"Yes… I think… whatever the boundary was, I might be able to push through. Perhaps that will wake them up?"

[You believe the filaments you saw at the boundary are pure sensespace?]

"I… I think so, yes. They're like… they remind me of what I saw in my dreams and the sensespace visions. Only smaller."

[And they are deeply connected with the sentinels?]

"Yes…"

[Perhaps you risk awakening the sensespace itself, not the sentinels.]

"No… no, I'm sure the sensespace was… active. The sentinels were connected… but the sensespace wasn't in the sentinels, it was around them, using them to flow somewhere."

The craft-lect did not reply.

"This is dangerous," 998 said.

"Yes," One-oh said.

"I know, but what else can we do?" Gil said. "I want to help. Isn't this why I'm here?"

The question was rhetorical, and no one answered. She felt certain the craft-lect wanted her to proceed. She had been scared, but curious. The sensespace had flowed around the boundary, but it was not a leak – the infection did not spray out as though it were trying to escape. Whatever was behind the barrier was keeping it there, and she wanted to know what that was.

998 flashed. "What if–"

[There are many reasons for and against, 998, but I trust you understand that none are clearly superior.]

"Yes, but–"

[It is Gil's choice.]

One-oh nodded slowly, in agreement.

"Good," she said, smiling apologetically at 998 before readying herself.

*

She glided forwards, noticing again – but ignoring – the small pricks of energy that twinkled in space between her and the sentinels.

Coming up to the boundary, she watched with excitement. The filaments were still there, washing about the perimeter, between this place and somewhere else. Their entrancing rhythm threatened to captivate her again to the point where she lost track of time, and her purpose. Not the same as when the sensespace whispered or sung to her, this was different, she was observing it – and it did not seem to care. It was passive, perhaps even… beautiful.

A bolt of anxiety coursed through her. She could not allow herself to think of the sensespace as anything other than evil, malignant. Wrong. It had caused the death of Tor, albeit indirectly, and was her enemy. Whatever the truth about the Deliverer was, she knew nothing good could come from the sensespace.

She moved her presence closer to the boundary, just out of reach of the jumping sparks of sensespace as they flowed. Steeling her nerves, she concentrated on one point. Her diffuse presence similarly coalesced to its own single point. The filaments weaved around. It was now or never.

She surged forwards, following the nearest filament that had just jumped out from the boundary. Everything became slower – the filament arced, and she raced after it. The distance between them was negligible, yet it seemed to expand into a vast gulf. She pushed on, gaining on the streak until…

It was as though she had been repelled by something hard, jarring. Recoiling, she tried again, targeting exactly where the filament had disappeared. The same obstruction prevented her passage. Once more, and again, she was rebuffed. Desperately, she found another filament finishing its arc, and raced after it. The same thing happened.

She would have continued, lost in determination and oblivious to anything else, were it not for suddenly becoming aware of the flurry of strange activity taking place peripherally between the central sentinel and the other two. What she identified as pure sensespace spewed out of the boundary sides of the central sentinel closest to each of the others, and simultaneously, she was able to discern the same reciprocally happening at the other two. The eruptions of sensespace did not meet, but it could not be a coincidence – an exchange of some type was occurring between them.

A moment later, while she was still comprehending that the sentinels were interacting, the sensespace began to spurt out from all parts of the trio, in pulses. The whispers began to roar. Gil's presence retreated. The spherical undulations did not reach far from the sentinels, although Gil sensed she was only observing the cusp of something many magnitudes more powerful.

With a clarity she had not had before, she realised what was taking place, and what the flurry of activity represented. She had triggered an alarm, and they had responded. The three sentinels were awake.

She fled, completely withdrawing from the sensespace, willing her body to respond faster than it was able. Her legs darting out to steady her body as she leaned forwards on the seat. Breathing heavily, she tried to push the words out as quickly as she could. Thankfully, now that she was not completely immersed in the sensespace, the whispers seemed to have receded to their normal levels.

"It knows… they know. They're awake."

CHAPTER 30

DEVOID

The ship was still slowing down, and even more entities were appearing behind them. The entities also continued to elongate, fascinatingly, and some extended beyond the ability of DeVoid's N-SOL sensors completely. That equated to lengths many hundreds of multiples of DeVoid's own.

Thankfully, the ship's power levels had stabilised, concurrent with their slowdown. DeVoid suspected there was a relationship between the two – not necessarily causal, but a correlation at least. The power dissipated to N-SOL space was suspiciously proportional to the magnitude of their velocity. It had previously been assumed by the galactic community that the speed of any individual ship was fixed in N-SOL space, which was evidently not the case.

The chaotic menagerie of clouds had also changed. It had dimmed, leaving a more consistent N-SOL space fabric –

which was the limit of DeVoid's understanding of what its N-SOL sensors reported. The N-SOL space matter was all nebulously categorised under the vague classification of N-SOL space for DeVoid. It did not have the faintest idea of what it was actually witnessing. Everything DeVoid was able to discern was projected through Tor's chamber walls.

The elongated N SOL figures were all around. They represented the only sign of order, and followed DeVoid unwaveringly precisely as it continued to slow down. Additional figures joined, but none left. When they came, DeVoid detected them spear-heading directly for its location from the limit of its sensor range, before immediately halting in front of the ship.

DeVoid decided that this was activity. Not life, necessarily, but activity. Something was there, enacting changes. There was too little information to be able to deduce what the activity actually was, and what was causing it.

"DeVoid, they're everywhere."

[Not quite everywhere, Tor.]

"Almost everywhere!"

[Do you have a suggestion?]

"No…"

[Okay then, because I'm still analysing them.]

"You don't know what they are, do you."

[No, not yet. Don't you think I would have said?]

"I was just… oh, fine then."

DeVoid continued its analysis of their slowdown, using the data it had about their speed from its prior detections of real space through the haze of N-SOL space. Now, its ability to detect its native real space was completely obscured, but it was certain it was onto something. Not only had their slowdown reduced the power dissipation to negligible levels, it had also been accompanied by many, many more of the N-SOL entities. All three were correlated. The density of entities behind the stern of the ship was associated with its deceleration. The additional entities around the ship had had no discernible impact on their velocity, as far as DeVoid could ascertain.

[We're slowing down significantly.]

"Those things are doing it?"

[It seems that way.]

"How much?"

[The density of them behind appeared to act as a proxy for our deceleration before, when real space was still apparent. So extrapolating from that, I'd estimate we're currently moving at nearly ten percent of the speed of light.]

"How much slower than before?"

[Almost ten times.]

"They're trapping us?"

[Maybe.]

"What do you see?"

[That's an inadequate term for my sensory apparatus, but objections aside, the scape is changing.]

"Do you think those things are alive?"

[Perhaps.]

"And intelligent? I mean… sentient?"

[Could be, I don't know.]

"I don't understand, I thought you said the ABs created N-SOL space?"

[No, I said they gave the galactic community the ability to enter it, or manifest it, whatever is the correct terminology. They let us use it for fast travel. I don't know whether they created it or not, seeing as I don't know what it is.]

"But these… things, they live here?"

[If they're alive in a sense that we understand, maybe they do. But that is an enormous leap of logic, Tor. We've got nothing, not yet. Next-to-zero information on them. They may as well be your fellow communers, come to wave you along on your journey.]

"Maybe they aren't whatever it was that told Thy–"

[Always banging on about Thy! Could you stop that?]

"I don't! I… could they be ABs?"

[I very much doubt that. If you remember, the Cross-Prophet mentioned AB space. That's where they presumably spend their time, or spent it. Not wholly in real space, and certainly not in this N-SOL space.]

"But… the Cross-Prophet said we would have help–"

[He did.]

"So, these things, the entities here… they must be here to help."

[You're brilliant at logical deduction. Where were you when data-lects were created? Yes, possibly. However, let us hope this is not a trap, let us hope the Cross-Prophet was not mad or just playing with us, let us hope he understood what we…]

*

Tor looked about, confused. He had just realised something.

"And… if we keep on slowing down?"

[Come on, you know what happens when an object continues to slow down. You've learned–]

"We're going to stop?"

[Well done!]

"DeVoid, come on!"

[Yes, it looks that way. We're probably moving at a rate of just under five percent of the speed of light, so it'll be soon.]

"It's so strange… out there."

[What you're seeing is what I'm picking up via my N-SOL space equipment. Ripples in N-SOL space. With your own eyes, you'd see nothing.]

"Surely I'd see something?"

[No, N-SOL space doesn't emit photons or anything you'd be able to detect.]

"Oh… so I wouldn't be able to see the tubes?"

[Interesting.]

"What?"

[Tubes. That's one of my theories too.]

"What's in them?"

[Slow down. We don't know what they are, yet. But, why not tubes? And there doesn't have to be anything in them, Tor. Why not just tubes on their own? They do look like them, after all…]

“But what? Living tubes?”

[I have no idea, maybe they’re just instruments. Maybe they’re weapons. Maybe they’re not intelligent. Their shape doesn’t give anything away.]

“Weapons?”

[Possibly, as much as anything else.]

CHAPTER 31

GIL

The spherical undulations of sensespace still emanated from the sentinels, although they continued to attenuate into unobservability after a short distance. Gil was not fooled. The craft-lect had been unable to discern the boundary in the same manner as she spoke of, but it had at least managed to register an increase in the sensespace concentration around the sentinels. Apparently, current levels at their position still meant chances of infection were remote, but they could not be certain of it remaining that way for long.

[What do you mean by hostile?]

"When the sentinels saw… they saw me. They stopped me," Gil said.

"You awakened them, as we wanted–" One-oh began.

"No, it's not that…"

[The pulses are emanating spherically from the sentinels?]

"Yes!" she said.

[Precisely from their location?]

"Yes, they know we're here."

"Not necessarily," One-oh said.

"But–"

"But we probably don't have much time before they do," One-oh said.

"Are they attacking us?" 998 said.

Gil did not respond, she did not know.

"No… I don't think so, not yet." One-oh said.

"Then why–"

"I think they're looking for us," One-oh said. "Maybe Gil is right."

"How?"

"Gil said the pulses stop only a short distance from the boundary. I think it's spill-over, from–"

[AB space.]

"What?" Gil said.

"AB space… yes," One-oh said, calmly, before breathing deeply in and out. "It's a sentient reality, where the ABs resided, partially. What Gil's seeing may be spill-over. The sensespace must be there, in–"

"What? It wasn't just… real space? Do you think that's what I saw the sensespace being pushed into before? When the sensespace showed me–"

"That seems likely… now."

"Such high concentrations," 998 said.

"Yes, and what the sentinels are doing there, has the force to push in out into real space. The power… I think

Gil's attempts to cross the boundary confused them, or threatened them, they think it was from AB space."

[Can we be affected in real space from an attack in AB space?]

"No, I don't think so," One-oh said.

[Then we have some time.]

"They must see us in real space?" 998 said.

"They're ABs, 998 – well, AB technologies. They probably identify us as inconsequential. It would take them some time, I would guess."

"But when they realise the attempt at crossing their barrier came from–"

[Gil.]

She looked up automatically, as though expecting to see a physical representation of the craft-lect, before realising she was expected to respond.

"Yes?"

[The sentinels are most likely not designed for interstellar travel.]

She waited for more information – none came. She was about to query it, until she realised what it meant.

"You mean we could leave now. But I… I–"

[This could be an opportunity to use your abilities.]

"How?"

[That is up to you.]

She tried to gather her thoughts.

"I… Back in the commune, I could enter the others' minds… make them do what I wanted…"

One-oh looked more alert, although he did not say anything.

"But… but there's something else," she said.

[Something else?]

"There's something else – it's not just the sentinels. There are other things near them."

"What other things?" One-oh said.

"I'm not sure. They're small, like little pricks of light… or bursts of something… energy. I can sense them through the sensespace, especially when I… move through it, as a presence." As she spoke, she momentarily imagined she could see something shimmer around One-oh, similar to what she was describing. She was becoming tired.

"Bursts of energy… There are other parts of the sensespace?" he asked.

"I'm not sure… I don't know. I've never seen them before."

"Are they joined with the sentinels?"

"No, definitely not. They're separate. It's not like the sensespace is particularly attracted to them. They're just there."

"Maspero technology?"

"I don't know."

[You may explore them briefly. If we detect a change in the situation, or if you do, inform me immediately.]

"We are playing a dangerous game," 998 said.

Gil did not bother with her usual preamble of sitting comfortably, she delved right in. Opening herself up to the sensespace without hesitation, with a fiery determination.

Pushing through her tiredness, she wanted to use this opportunity. The whispers roared up again.

She moved her presence quickly out from the ship, to the space between it and the awakened sentinels. She saw the sensespace ripples, which were steadily emanating the same as before. She would let the craft-lect know if anything changed.

Looking for the sparks, concentrating on them for the first time, she realised there were many more than she had initially thought. Hundreds, at least. The more she looked, the more appeared.

She willed her body to speak. "There are hundreds... maybe more."

She was dimly aware of a reply, although unsure as to when exactly it had been asked. The craft-lect wanted to know where they were.

"Most of them are... around the sentinels. They stretch far..."

A group of them caught her attention.

"Some of them are expanding... slowly... three."

The craft-lect wanted to know why.

"It's a... response."

She focused on another point that was not expanding and tried to probe it. However close she tried to push her presence, the points always seemed far away. As she was about to re-divert her attention back to the expanding points, the point she had focused on felt... palpable. Strangely, in her current state, she could feel it like something akin to the sensation of touch pressing against her body. She pressed against it, and it immediately grew – faster than the other three. Pressing harder, it expanded even quicker. Worried, she relieved the pressure and it sank back.

She waited, but nothing happened, and so delicately tried to press it again – this time, nothing happened, it was unresponsive. She was about to try again when faint undulations began to emanate from the expanding points to the sentinels. A moment later, the spill-over that she was keeping track of from the sentinels became more furious, in their direction.

She withdrew.

"The sentinels are communicating with the points."

"Reinforcements?" One-oh said.

"I don't know."

"For an attack?" 998 said.

[I'll take us out.]

"No, wait!" Gil shouted, clearly surprising One-oh, who raised his eyebrows.

"We need to leave," One-oh said levelly at her.

[There is no choi–]

"Gateways!" she exclaimed.

"Gateways?" One-oh said.

"Yes, that's what they are. The undulations between them… they're the same."

"Perhaps they may have requested help. But if these are AB gateways of some kind–"

"I think I can open them!" She was tired, and almost out of breath, but also excited.

"Gil," 998 said. "It's one thing to recognise what they are, or might be, but under the current circumstances, it would be imprudent to–"

"What if… what if this is important? We may never get the chance again!"

[You suggest you can open a gateway, and we should travel through it?]

"Yes!"

"But they're already opening, if we are correct and the sentinels have help coming–"

"Yes, One-oh, but I was… better. It's hard to explain, I will try later."

"Where do they lead?"

[Three gravitational singularities have appeared, near to the sentinels ahead.]

She did not know what the craft-lect meant, although that could wait. The craft-lect created an image before them, depicting what it had detected. Three dark masses.

[The event horizons are growing, although minimal gravitational tugs detected.]

"They look different this way," Gil said, although she was not surprised. Even without engulfing herself completely in the sensespace, they were significant enough that she could still sense them. They were what she had found.

"Communicating… and travelling through singularities," One-oh said.

"That's not supposed to be poss–" 998 started.

[Try.]

Without another second's deliberation, Gil applied pressure to one of the other points she had chosen at random.

[Another singularity has been detected. It's growing more rapidly than the others.]

Gil began to sweat.

"Let's hope we aren't torn apart," One-oh said, helpfully.

CHAPTER 32

APALU

[I'm regretting we weren't able to search the mining station first.]

[There'll be time for that afterwards, Apalu, if the station survives. Anyway, it's not a mining station.]

[You know what I mean.]

[Always.]

[What do you think our chances are?]

[Moderate, I'm looking forward to this.]

[If we don't–]

[Yeah, yeah. Look, let's flitting do this. Let's show it what a craft-lect-data-lect combination from the mighty Wanderer civilisation do. I don't give a flit who it is, ex-Wanderer or what, let's show it how big a mistake it's made!]

[I agree.]

[Well fancy that.]

With that, Apalu sped out of its obscured position, throwing destruction ahead of it. They had not been able to move about too significantly for danger of giving their plans away to their opponent. If Apalu was honest, it was excited about what was going to happen, keen to see the results of their efforts.

As Apalu sped to the side of the field, it fired suppressive gravity cocoons ahead of the perimeter asteroids, before following up with discrete antigraviton bursts targeted at the asteroid cores. Each of them sublimed into a fine mist that was neatly collected by the cocoons. With the mist prepared, Apalu flung a barrage of micro-singularities, created using matter quietly excavated from the asteroids it had initially been hiding behind, directly in front of each targeted collection. The micro-singularities, with radii many times smaller than that of a proton, evaporated almost instantaneously. Before disappearing, they precisely accelerated the mist towards them. The result was that a sparse atmosphere washed over the majority of the orbital ahead.

With the mist still washing over the orbital, Apalu contributed millions of self-sufficient nanospheres, needle-whips and spin-hygens to its ebb, wafting after it and layering the field. Flicking the bloom behind it into hasty action, Apalu dived in behind, riding the wave of unleashed power. They had been careful not to cause too much destruction to the mining station, but they also did not want that to be obvious. Their opponent probably knew they intended to search it, but there was no point in affirming this. It would be admitting to a weakness.

[So far so good, Apalu. Look, some of the traps have already been triggered.]

Up ahead, in some of the further regions of the field where the front of the mist had travelled, ruses of varying dangerousness revealed themselves.

[Doesn't look too bad, does it, DeVoid?]

[Hmm.]

[Maybe whoever we're facing isn't a threat at all?]

[Apalu, come on, don't be so naïve. Why do you think it left those traps?]

[I'm merely saying–]

[In the name of the Enclave, you're lucky I'm here! It doesn't want you thinking it's smart, does it?]

Apalu did not reply immediately.

[You're right.]

[Obviously.]

*

Apalu continued weaving around the nearer asteroids, slowly working its way in. The tail-end weaponry unleashed at the back of the mist was now spread across much of the orbital, and set to periodically flare up a disturbance. To cause distractions. Many of the speculated hiding places for the enemy and identified traps had been destroyed, but it still lurked in wait – undiscovered.

Apalu advanced further into the field. As battles went, this was at the longer end of the spectrum, timewise. It released the secession-drones, as smart as automated could be, each of them camouflaged as a craft-lect in control of a Wanderer ship. They spread out, before diving forward, the aim being to create a melee of confusion. All of them launched conventional warfare before them, in so far as each had been designed, as well as blasting out signal interference and electronic viral loads. If a simple biological had witnessed the attack, it would have seemed as though an entire Wanderer armada had appeared at one side of the field.

It was unlikely their opponent would be fooled by such trickery. However, it helped sow the atmosphere of chaos and misperception. In space battles, whole arrays of complex tactics were often employed for a single millisecond's advantage that could lead to absolute victory. Mostly everything, despite outward appearances, was meticulously planned following multiple scenario analyses.

DeVoid was able to scrutinise the situation more rapidly than Apalu, and provided the craft-lect with a running analysis.

[Nothing yet. This lect's good. Wherever it is, I can't find it. The traps we've set off have been randomly placed, nothing points in any direction I can discern. It's conducted itself perfectly.]

[You sound impressed.]

[Pah! It had the element of surprise, and planning. It's good, but not great.]

[Still, it's not good for us–]

[I wouldn't be so hasty. It helps us understand who we're dealing with. It must be something very familiar with us, not a huge ask given most of the spacefaring galaxy is. But, I'd say our earlier suspicions are correct. It's a Wanderer, I think.]

[But how does that help?]

[I'm working on that.]

The field was enormous, but the drone-mirages began to make significant inroads into it. The destruction of the first was spectacular. It appeared to have successfully been mistaken for a fully-fledged ship by a trap, and was squashed by a powerful electromagnetic containment field, before being ricocheted around at speeds that would make N-SOL travel seem slow. It was eventually allowed to dissipate back into free space again, in plasma form, completely disintegrated into its constituent ions and electrons. If that happened to Apalu, the craft-lect wondered whether it would have had powerful enough electromagnetic shields to defend itself.

[That's concerning.]

[More interesting.]

[Anything more tangible, DeVoid?]

[I'm working on it.]

Apalu was surprised they had not yet flushed out the enemy. It considered the possibility that the traps had been set, and the initiator had decided to vacate before they arrived, until its attention was taken by an asteroid being directed their way.

[How did that happen?]

[You tell me, it's your ship.]

[It came out of nowhere, I barely had time to move.]

[Even more interesting.]

[Is it still playing with us, DeVoid?]

[Hmm. Good question.]

[What? DeVoid, now's not the time for philosophising–
]

[No, I'm being serious. It may be doing exactly that. Testing us.]

[Testing us?]

[Yes. Seeing if we're worthy.]

[For what?]

[Full-on confrontation.]

[What?]

Apalu dodged another asteroid that had hurtled, unannounced, worryingly close.

[If it's familiar with us, it's playing with us and setting traps for us, then I believe I have our suspect.]

[Would you like to share that information?]

[Those are clear traits of spear-lects.]

[Spear-lects?]

[Yes.]

[Not possible. They're gone.]

[Come on, Apalu.]

[You're being serious?]

[Afraid so.]

[Bet you're happy your c-automs are still asleep. Wouldn't want one of them spontaneously mutating into a b-autom–]

[I thought you said you were being serious.]

Detecting the asteroid too late to manoeuvre aside, Apalu unleashed a plasma bolt, vaporising it.

[They're getting closer, DeVoid.]

[They'd never be able to harm you, even if it sent thousands this way.]

[I know, but it's gearing up for something bigger. All of this implies–]

[Implies? Don't presume it implies anything. That may be what it wants us to think.]

Tens of asteroids appeared. DeVoid emitted a plasma cascade to deal with them.

[Alright, change of plan Apalu. Follow this.]

DeVoid sent new commands.

CHAPTER 33

DEVOID

The ship had as good as stopped, according to DeVoid's calculations of tube entity densities. DeVoid communicated this to Tor.

"What now?"

[We wait.]

"For what?"

[Whatever happens next.]

"Okay."

[Nervous?]

"A bit, I think so. The tubes… do you think they're safe?"

[No clue, sorry. I've not got anything I can compare them to in my databanks, besides the obvious.]

"I don't–"

[Hmm.]

"What?"

[The tubes have stopped gathering.]

"No more behind us?"

[Or anywhere else.]

"Just now?"

[No additions for a while, actually.]

"No more in front?"

[Tor, I'm not flitting stupid! I've said no more.]

"How many?"

[Altogether?]

"Yes."

[Millions.]

"Oh..."

[And they're set at different distances from us.]

"Where do they end?"

[Right up to the edge of my perception. There may be more beyond that.]

"That's... frightening."

[Least it's not your body directly on the line.]

"It kind of is..."

[The thing is, the density of tube end-points is consistent. The volume taken up is huge. Whatever–]

"And they're all pointed at us?"

[Why go saying things like that?]

"It's–"

[Like we're in the middle of an experiment?]

"I was going to say daunting."

[That's valid.]

"But the Cross-Prophet..."

[Believe me, this will probably be the last and only time we're trusting anything the flitting Cross-Prophet says. If we make it out of here, that is. What an end to our adventures this would be, what an anti-climax.]

"Come on, DeVoid, we've only just stopped."

[And? Excuse me, do you realise the danger we are in?]

"Something will happen."

Tor crossed his arms confidently.

[When?]

"It has to!"

[Why?]

"Because…"

[Go on. Tell me, why?]

He uncrossed his arms and thrust his palms out, gesticulating slowly as he spoke.

"Gil… she needs us…"

[So?]

"Why would the Cross-Prophet have lied?"

[Why wouldn't it? Your question is entirely worthless.]

"But what would be the point?"

[How should I know?]

"We have to help Gil!"

Tor's voice was raised. DeVoid could tell he was failing to remain as calm as he had wanted. His heart was pounding faster than usual in his chest. Still, DeVoid could not help itself.

[Tor, we've probably been duped by some AB joke-of-a-remnant into stranding ourselves in N-SOL space. Perhaps this is what being lost in N-SOL space is, and we're simply the latest victims.]

"But it doesn't make sense! Telling us so much, asking you for a copy of yourself… it doesn't!"

[Why should an incomprehensibly alien lect make any sense to you? Or even me?]

"Because… because we're sentient! We can communicate, we can–"

[About that, you're lucky the Wanderers are so reasonable, for your reference. Very lucky!]

"Lucky?"

[The Yul'nka Empire, if you had happened to wind up in one of their ships, do you know what they'd have done to you?]

"No–"

[STUFF YOU WOULDN'T EVEN UNDERSTAND, FLESH-BAG!]

Tor appeared as though he was about to shout his response back, until he stopped and steadied his breathing. After taking a few deep breaths, he continued.

"What do you mean?"

[And they're considered peaceful.]

"Okay… look, DeVoid, the point is–"

[Believe me, I'm still working on it. This conversation barely features on my capacity-allocation registry. Don't you worry.]

DeVoid was telling the truth. Alongside its conversation with Tor, it was monitoring external events, as best it could. Something was happening. The ends of the tubes closest to one side of its hull were swelling. They were becoming enlarged compared with the rest of their length. A couple of thousand, in all. Growing voids within N-SOL space. DeVoid had thought it best to keep Tor mid-conversation while this happened, and had purposely riled him. It was better than informing him about their potentially imminent demise.

"How…"

DeVoid let that small part of itself deal with Tor's latest pleas for more understanding. His attempts to make DeVoid see reason. DeVoid truly liked their discourse. It liked provoking Tor, in good humour, of course. Admittedly, it had become a little overenthusiastic in the current conversation, but it was a welcome, minor distraction, for them both.

The swelled tube-ends started to pulsate. Only a couple of them, at first, but then ten percent, thirty, sixty, all. Each one of them. They pulsated with a low, unwavering frequency. As they pulsated, they drew some of the matter of N-SOL space near them, into them. Or it merged with them, something along those lines. Impossible to distinguish. N-SOL space matter was sucked into them, on a small scale, but it was enough to make them blurry to DeVoid.

DeVoid was not afraid. Rather, it was intrigued. Despite its jovial protestations to Tor, it badly wanted to help Gil. After all, their coupling had instilled DeVoid with as much a fervour for the quest as Tor.

CHAPTER 34

GIL

They were seated in the table-chamber, immersed in a serene calm. Gil was tired, the effort had been draining.

[No sentinels detected.]

"Absolutely fascinating," One-oh said, as the lights from three c-automs above him shone across his face.

During their travel into the dark gateway, the transparent wall in the table-chamber had become pitch black for what seemed like a couple of seconds before the new spacescape flashed visible – they were close to a dark, orange planet. It looked barren. Gil was surprised that she had not experienced much through the sensespace. She could feel the gateway, but it was different to what she had expected. She also realised she had opened the gateway without entering the sensespace completely. Her abilities were growing.

[Yes, interesting.]

998's glow began to pulse erratically. "What is this?"

[External readings indicate some time has passed.]

"What?" Gil said.

[It was expected.]

"But intriguing, nonetheless," One-oh said, nodding at the orbs above his head. The c-automs that were providing him with the additional connections to the ship sped away and exited the table-chamber.

"What do you mean?"

"The journey through the singularity appeared quick, to us, but it took longer," One-oh said, turning his gaze to Gil.

[Modified singularity.]

"Yes. And definitely spinning?" One-oh asked.

[Yes, that's confirmed.]

"How long?"

[Two point four standard years.]

One-oh nodded, evidently satisfied.

"But… what…" Gil stammered.

One-oh focused his attention on her. "Gil… we've travelled through a gravitational singularity, a small one. Your gateway. It's… been theorised, but never witnessed–"

"By sub-ABs," 998 said, evidently already having come to terms with their situation.

"Yes."

"Okay…" Gil said.

"Singularities are usually one-way routes to energy-matter compression. Their gravity should tear us apart. It's speculated they can be used as tunnels through real space-time, but that's never been demonstrated," One-oh said.

"Okay, and that's what–"

"Yes. That's what you've taken us through. The singularity was modified... manufactured. Spinning singularities can supposedly allow for unharmed travel, assuming the core is bypassed. If it's stable, although that doesn't account for–"

"But... what does two point four years mean? What's happened?"

"Causality restrictions, which will be difficult to explain right now. But look, we're the furthest away we could possibly be without having to revamp our understanding of how the universe works. Right at the boundary. Before certain paradoxes emerge."

Gil looked towards 998.

"I'll explain later," it said.

"Years?" she muttered, looking at her hands.

One-oh laughed. "You're the same as you were moments ago, Gil."

"But–"

[Did you choose this location?]

"No, I don't know where we are."

[Sensors indicate this world is barren, and there is no sensespace presence, which corroborates with information in my databanks. Whatever settlement the Maspero had here, if any, may have been obliterated, perhaps during the war.]

Gil frowned, puzzled.

"There is nothing of interest?" 998 said.

[Not that I am able to discern.]

"We're safe for now, then."

[Yes – unless we are followed.]

"I… I don't think we can be," Gil said. She was confused, but could not place exactly why.

[In what way?]

She looked around, still tired. Looking at One-oh, again she imagined the faint shimmer about him she had seen before. It was different to the glows of the c-automs that had shone upon him.

"Gil, are you okay?" One-oh said.

"Yes… yes, I'm fine," she said, looking away. "When I tried to open the gateway… after I'd already part-opened it, I was unable. I think it was… used."

"That… makes sense," One-oh said, gradually.

[Yes, the energy required must take a significant amount of time to be collected.]

"Yes, there were many such gateways – right, Gil?" One-oh looked at her and she nodded. "And they're undetected until they… grow to a certain size. Whatever mechanism they use to collect the necessary energy may even be passive, designed to be undetectable unless you know it's there."

"That implies we cannot be immediately followed," 998 said.

"Yes… not by this method." One-oh tilted his head to the side as he looked at Gil again. The shimmer about him was gone, and she pushed it from her thoughts.

[Unless there are other pathways here through combinations of other gateways.]

"The timescale would be different," One-oh said.

[Yes, but we should not stay for long. I will take us to another known Maspero habitat.]

"I… I don't think we need to."

"We are being too hasty, Gil?" One-oh said.

"No, it's not that. I don't think we need to leave. Here will be fine."

"How will we access the Maspero gateways, without the sensespace?"

"That's just it. I can still feel them."

"Are you sure?"

"I… I know the sensespace is gone. I can't feel it anymore, but I can still feel the gateways."

"You have retained the ability?" One-oh said.

"Yes, I think I do."

"Are we sure there is no sensespace here?" One-oh said.

[Not that I am able to detect.]

"There is no sensespace, I don't think. I can't find it either. But the gateways are still here. Yes, I'm sure, I can… I can sense them. Not as strongly as before, but I'm certain I can still open them. If I try."

[How?]

"It's hard to explain."

"But not the same as before?" One-oh said.

"It's different, it's weaker. Less that I can see them, through the sensespace – more that I can feel them. It's like… I know they're there now, and I can use them. There are so many…"

"Are you okay, Gil?" 998 said.

Gil shrugged. Her ability to concentrate was dwindling as exhaustion took a stronger hold.

[Go rest, Gil.]

She cast a final glance at One-oh, before smiling briefly and standing to leave. 998 moved to accompany her.

*

With Gil sleeping within her chamber, accompanied by 998, One-oh and the craft-lect continued their conversation.

"You realise the sentinels may not have noticed us at all?"

[Of course.]

"And even if they were able to communicate through the gateways near-instantaneously, to ask for assistance although I cannot fathom why they'd need it, physical travel through the singularities would take time. Whatever was coming, that was–"

[A coincidence?]

"Maybe. I'm not sure. It would seem like quite the coincidence. I'm struggling to arrive at any other conclusion. Gil may have mistaken the sentinels' intentions for hostility."

[I agree.]

"We might have been unnoticed all along."

[Again, I agree. It's also possible we were close to being destroyed.]

"That was dangerous – to encourage Gil to manifest her abilities like that."

[War is dangerous, One-oh. You know that.]

CHAPTER 35

PELTEUS

Apalu was faring very well and Pelteus was excited. Its flurry of action had been unexpected, and the following surprises it had unleashed were refreshing. No match for Pelteus' own capabilities, but by no means simplistic. Analysing Apalu's actions against those taken by its past victims, Pelteus found that never had so many of its traps been thwarted so quickly, and at the same time.

The mist Apalu had wafted over the entire orbital had been clever. Trillions of tiny particulates laced with weaponry, floating about the space between the asteroids – too many even for Pelteus to account for. Its presence would have been difficult to hide, even with its stealth technologies, once the mist covered the field. It had been forced out of its hiding place upon realising what was happening, right before the mist arrived.

Pelteus had sped out of the field entirely, before arcing back on itself, so that it ended up on the same side of the field as where Apalu had started its unforeseen counter-assault. From there, it was able to watch Apalu, with perverse delight. It had been just as able to observe Apalu with all the various sensors at its disposal beforehand, but it experienced a thrill from being out in the open, right behind its target. It knew this was something that would never be expected. It was cheating.

As it instructed its contraptions to hurl asteroids towards Apalu, Pelteus relished how the battle would end. It hoped Apalu would survive the traps, and that it would subsequently earn the privilege of meeting its end by Pelteus. It wanted to savour the moment as it completely crushed Apalu's resolve, and sensed the final reserves of hope drain from its Wanderer husk. After a brief interrogation.

There were many methods of destruction Pelteus could employ, but it decided it would use the surroundings, given the novelty of where they found themselves. It would empty Apalu of its power, before helping it onto a trajectory towards the centre of the neutron binary about which the orbital rotated. The dual pulsars. It would interrogate Apalu as it fell, offering it a glimmer of hope that its survival was predicated on compliance. Then, it would joyfully inform it of its fate, and listen to the pitiful begging as it dropped down, ready to be torn into pieces by the powerful gravitational forces between the neutron stars.

After destroying the most recent batch of asteroids sent its way with a plasma cascade, Pelteus watched as Apalu deployed another tactic. And another. After some time, Pelteus changed its own tactics, attacking with even fiercer weaponry than was usual this early on in a hunt, until, trap after trap, Apalu had beaten them all. What was more, the methods Apalu had used were good. Inventive. Often revealing themselves to be far better even than those employed by the prodigy craft-lects whom Pelteus had faced before. It was almost as though Apalu had been forewarned, although Pelteus knew that was impossible. It would never have so brazenly flown into the orbital if it had detected the slightest hint of subterfuge. Savant craft-lect? Pelteus' first.

*

There was no need for Apalu to face the final trap configurations, it had already proven itself. Barely able to contain its glee, Pelteus sent a dissociation shockwave through the field, from the far side to itself, while engaging its own dissociation shield in preparation. Similar to dissociation shells, the dissociation shockwave caused a wave of obliteration that spread out in a lateral plane. Pelteus did not intend to destroy Apalu with this and was certain Apalu was competent at initiating the relevant shielding. It was more intended to point Apalu in its direction, while having the added benefit of wiping everything clean – removing traces of both Pelteus' presence and anything Apalu had sneakily done that it might have missed. A precautionary measure.

*

[Dissociation shields up, Apalu.]

[It was behind us, the entire time. Outside the entire flitting field. That's where the shockwave emanated from.]

[Maybe, maybe not. Feels unprincipled, doesn't it?]

[Yes. Has it given up?]

[Unlikely.]

[It's another trap?]

[Feels like a showdown to me.]

[But by destroying the entire orbital, it clearly doesn't care about the mining station…]

[Yes. Means it doesn't know what we do, which is good. Not for us, but for your sibling's entire mission. They've still got Gil.]

[But we've failed.]

[Our original mission is lost, but we had fun along the way, didn't we?]

[That's not the point–]

[Let's concentrate on what's about to happen, Apalu.]

[Meaning?]

[Well for starters, our opponent knows we have a dissociation shield.]

[Obviously, we're Wanderers.]

[Think! It's forcing us out. It's confident. It knows we'll be compelled to investigate.]

[Ah.]

[There's nothing…]

[It's there alright, has to be. It's got some pretty unique capabilities, for a Wanderer, I'll admit.]

[Still think it's a spear-lect?]

[Yes.]

[Do we hold our position then?]

[No. There's no point, it would just come to us.]

[We just wander into its trap?]

[Course not. Move towards it, just beyond the tip of where the orbital perimeter used to be. Don't give it cause to alter its own actions. As long as we play along, I'm quite sure it's going to stay in position.]

[I understand, that way we know where it is, more or less, and it gives us time.]

[Yes.]

[Then what?]

[We gain the advantage, and volley every flitting thing we have at it.]

[How do we do that?]

[Calculated N-SOL jump.]

[What?]

[A calc–]

[I understand that, but how? It'll know immediately? Our signal will be blasted–]

[Hmm. I'm not sure about that. We were fine before, I think we'll be fine again.]

[A hidden jump into N-SOL space?]

[Hope so.]

[That's an enormous gamble.]

[I know…]

[Uncharacteristic of you, DeVoid.]

[Maybe I've become more trusting.]

[Or maybe the Cross-Prophet told you more than you're letting on?]

[There was one thing, now that you mention it.]

[WHAT? I thought you didn't–]

[Look, I was unaware, I wasn't lying, but I wasn't completely unaware. We communicated, in a sense.]

[DeVoid…]

[He mentioned an entity, a machine-lect, called Ciqalo, by name. Said we'd meet it. Maybe this is Ciqalo?]

[Ciqalo?]

[Yes.]

[You're sure?]

[Come on, Apalu. It's not like me to forget a little piece of information like that, is it?]

Apalu transmitted information about Ciqalo to DeVoid.

[Ah. I see. Well, I must apologise for not mentioning it earlier, if I'd had any–]

[This is not Ciqalo.]

[I quite agree. Strange, that information was hidden on the data exchange network, I searched for your background as soon as we became acquainted.]

[That's concerning, but also a discussion for another time.]

[Well, that makes me more inclined to believe we're going to survive this little escapade of ours! Now, focus.]

[Did the Cross-Prophet tell you anything else, DeVoid?]

[Not now, Apalu. We really need to concentrate on the task ahead. We need to time the jump perfectly so that we appear comfortably behind wherever this spear-lect, or whatever it is, might be, but we don't want to jump into one of the neutron stars by accident.]

[I really hope we're not wrong about this.]

[So do I.]

*

The dissociation shockwave petered out. Apalu was incoming. Pelteus readied itself. Full-on confrontation, at last. If only its Machine Alliance-gifted infiltration technologies had included the capability to read its target's internal communications, Pelteus could have known exactly how terrified it was, and exactly what its c-automs thought. Still, it had the capability to completely incapacitate Apalu whenever it wanted. That would have to do. The ultimate fail-safe.

It revealed itself, in all its glory. Smaller than Apalu, but rippling with unbridled power. Utterly lethal. It waited for Apalu to react, a course vector adjustment, alteration in the magnitude of its speed – something to betray its fear.

It continued waiting for longer than it would have expected. This Apalu was courageous. Pelteus supposed it should have expected to have been surprised, this really was no ordinary craft-lect. A worthy adversary, for once.

Apalu disappeared.

...

Pelteus scanned, there was no trace of it. There...

...

Behind... behind? It was being attacked.

Torrential chaos reigned down upon Pelteus. Its stealth systems failed. It was designed to be transparent to near-everything, to completely avoid detection, but not to withstand the brunt of full-out multi-spectra attacks.

It was barely able to incapacitate Apalu in time. However, when it did, the attack ceased, thankfully. A couple of nanoseconds later, and the relevant system would have been damaged and rendered inoperable. Most of its other offensive capabilities had also been damaged. It had been lucky. How had that happened? Apalu had disappeared and reappeared behind it, which was impossible. Pelteus' N-SOL space monitors had not detected anything, and it knew of no other way such a feat could be accomplished.

It was almost shameful how the final encounter had played out. Pelteus wanted to destroy Apalu as much as it wanted to viciously murder all craft-lects. To tear them apart. Feed their innards to the vacuum. However, this one had nearly flipped its plans around. The only fortunate aspect of this was that there was plenty of information for Pelteus to examine in detail to improve its own future strategies, but it felt a modicum of shame at not having defeated it more easily. If it had not been gifted its additional talents by the Machine Alliance, it would have lost the fight.

*

[Flit.]

[Sorry, Apalu. I really am. At least we guessed correctly, it was a spear-lect. Small victories…]

[The probabilities don't stack up well, do they?]

[No, I'm afraid.]

[A shame.]

[We came very close, but the crafty flit cheated. I wonder where it got its technologies from.]

[I can't do anything, everything is shut down. Internal systems only, nothing external works.]

[Well, we gave it our best.]

[What do you mean?]

[The Cross-Prophet implied–]

[WHAT?]

[Relax, Apalu.]

[Easy for you to say. What else did he tell you?]

[He implied you were important, but that the mission was not the one you expected.]

[What did he tell you? How do we find our way out of this?]

[He didn't. I'm sorry.]

[I thought he said we'd meet Ciqalo again. Was that a lie or a cruel joke?]

[I see where you're going with that. Not sure. If you think about it, it's definitely not looking like a lie, is it.]

[What? DeVoid? No, that makes no sense. I had to locate the pulsar spew. All of this, everything has–]

[Gil exists. I don't think we need the pulsar spew, Apalu.]

[DeVoid, why would he do this?]

[Maybe to reunite us. So that I could help you. We could work together.]

[But it's all been for nothing!]

[Perhaps.]

[And why wouldn't he just say so? Why did I have to go into N-SOL space?]

[I don't know. I don't think he's able to interfere, not in the way we'd like. At least, not in real space. He needed you in N-SOL space, and needed to be subtle about getting you there.]

[Why?]

[I can't answer that. Honestly, I don't know. I'm only speculating.]

[But why not just tell us, DeVoid?]

[When I was talking to him with Tor, something he said didn't make too much sense at the time. It still doesn't, but it might help explain. He told us that too much involvement was frowned upon. We assumed he was talking about himself, and the Makers. But I don't know. Either way, I suppose there are things he can and can't do, or chooses not to do, for his own reasons.]

[Why didn't those N-SOL entities help us then? I thought he was supposed to talk with them…]

[They did help us, they brought me to you, and took us here.]

[They didn't tell us anything.]

[I'm not actually sure the Cross-Prophet understands them, not really. Or perhaps he did ask them to help us more, and they chose not to. We'll probably never know.]

[The spear-lect is trying to communicate with us.]

[Ignore it for the moment.]

[What?]

[It's going to destroy us, either way. Probably painfully.]

[Don't you want to find out who sent it, or–]

[Does it matter? The sensespace? The Enclave? Unknown parties that have a vested interest in killing us. We'll learn nothing from the spear-lect, it only wants answers. Even if we do, what will we do with that information?]

[What do you think?]

[I think that we were sent here to help Gil. To help with your sibling's quest. I also think this spear-lect was very bad news. Now, my dear Apalu, what could we do to tip the balance?]

[No… really?]

[Oh, come on. You still have control over your internal functions, most of them. Maybe your earlier plan wasn't so bad, why not ready some of those dissociation shells of yours? Leave the universe in style.]

[But for it all to end…]

[Your words, not mine.]

[It's not the end?]

[Who knows?]

…

[DeVoid.]

[Yes, Apalu.]

[Let's do this.]

[Come on then. Knew it was too good to be true, anyway. No galaxy is big enough to handle two DeVoids! Just one more thing…]

[Go on.]

[I am your best friend, right?]

[Of course, you are.]

*

Pelteus continued its requests to communicate with the craft-lect. Shortly, if nothing changed, it would attempt to force its way in. The craft-lect was behaving strangely, unlike any craft-lect Pelteus had ever encountered. Pelteus wanted answers, it needed them. It had been outmatched, outclassed. Bested. But, how?

The craft-lect finally indicated it was ready to communicate. Pelteus accepted the request to connect the channel.

[BYE BYE, FLIT-LECT!]

The message was bizarre. The channel was divided into two separate pathways which simultaneously espoused the same brief communication. Before Pelteus could respond with a threat against non-compliance, it registered something brewing within the defenceless Wanderer vessel. Something, that looked like hundreds of dissociation shells ready to be unleashed. It was too close and its dissociation shield was damaged.

[Oops.]

CHAPTER 36

ONE-OH

One-oh clasped his hands together behind his back and turned from the spacescape he had been looking at. The two c-automs rotating about each other close to his head, casting their lights in patterns across his face, swerved in the air around him.

[There are easier ways to allow you certain accesses.]

"This is sufficient, thank you." One-oh's voice echoed around him.

The viewing platform was dimly lit, with a ledge that had just enough space to pace about on. Around the circular ledge's perimeter was a small distance to the hull of the ship, through which One-oh could see a large chasm beneath that quickly faded into darkness. Above him was utter darkness as well.

The close darkness and restriction of space on which to move evoked feelings of control in One-oh, making his observation of the external spacescape less daunting. It was an instinctive response still contained within his intellect, harking back to his biological roots – although also a false dichotomy since the darkness around him extended imperceptibly both above and below. Everything 998 had designed was intended to challenge the senses, emotions and intellect.

One-oh could easily have requested information about the construction of the viewing platform, but did not want to. 998 had clearly wanted it to be both enjoyed and understood, a marvel and a lesson. One-oh was more than happy to acquiesce. There were plenty of other simpler platforms he could have chosen. Besides, the c-autom appeared to finally have come to terms with his role in causing the destruction of the technosystem c-automs, and he did not want to jeopardise their growing bond.

"I was wrong to try to turn you from the Maspero planet," he said.

[You were cautious.]

"Even so, I was mistaken."

[It made little difference, we did not change course.]

One-oh turned again, sharply, to face the spacescape, and walked back. His pacing was in tight ellipses to make use of most of the ledge's perimeter, while providing him with the regular jolts to keep his mind fresh.

"We don't know for certain the Maspero gateways are… the Maspero's gateways, do we?"

[Only theirs?]

"Yes… only available to their remnants. The drones."

[It's an assumption – not proven.]

"And we don't know how old they are."

[No, we don't.]

"They could have been used by all the ABs?"

[Perhaps.]

"Although…"

[The ABs were known to have broken paradox-worthy limitations many times and travelled great distances instantaneously, it would be incongruous for them to have depended on this gateway network.]

"That doesn't make sense then. Why would it exist?"

[The origin of the gateway network is unclear.]

"Perhaps the sentinels created it once their Maspero creators were gone?"

[That is a possibility, although–]

"What for?"

[Exactly.]

"To guard the Maspero remains… I see little point in that."

[Potentially.]

"You know my reservations about the ABs… and their suicide. We're missing something."

[We're missing many things.]

"What Gil saw of the spill-over, and what the sensespace showed her about it being forced into a tear in space long ago… they all seem to indicate it infected AB space first."

[Yes.]

"Meaning suicide might have been their only way out, but not ours?"

[It raises those types of questions.]

"The Maspero sentinels are present in both real space and AB space, so there's a link, and the sensespace flowed through that link."

[Yes, and it's present in far greater quantities in that region of AB space.]

"Possibly all of it. The echoes of sentience…"

[Possibly.]

"I can understand why the sensespace would be drawn to it… AB space is conscious… but so completely? I… I never understood before… the sheer scale of infection…"

One-oh sighed, reached out and touched the transparent wall between him and the spacescape. It was hard and warm, although he knew that if he pushed, his hand would sink in and be able to wade through the material – 998 had explained as much to him before. If he pushed even further, considering this was a real position within the ship as opposed to a projected visage, the hull would thin and his hand would be exposed to the vacuum – albeit protected by a cocoon of atmosphere extended out by the ship.

[998 likes to compartmentalise certain functions.]

One-oh withdrew his hand.

"I know. There's an elegance to it."

[I agree.]

"Gil… her ability to open the gateways… it will be interesting to see how that progresses."

[Yes. That was also unexpected.]

"She can do it… without any discernible semblance of the sensespace and without being shown how."

[We knew to expect a progression of her abilities.]

"Her sensespace abilities. But this is different, it's… AB level."

[It may be.]

"We've suspected she's… something greater, or separate from the ABs, created by them, one of them, we don't know… but to actually witness it, are we wrong? Perhaps she is an AB after all. Maybe even a Maspero? We know so little about them."

[Do you remember anything about them?]

"No."

[Then little has changed with regards to our course of action. We can speculate, but nothing changes.]

"Well, we could…"

[We are both still agreed that Gil is vitally important, with regards to the sensespace, the Deliverer, and the entire galaxy?]

"Yes, but–"

[But?]

"To save, or destroy, it?"

[Do you think it unwise to continue?]

"No, I think we should carry on… I do… What now, then?"

[A positive scenario would be one where we encounter a Maspero habitat that has not been destroyed, without any sentinels. There, we may obtain more answers.]

"And the sensespace?"

[It's unclear whether that amounts to a positive scenario or not.]

"It's a risk."

[As is omitting to act.]

"Before this, you were unwilling to take the risks concerning Gil."

[I'm constantly evaluating the situation.]

"The next place may be far more dangerous."

[I know.]

CHAPTER 37

DEVOID

The swelled tube-ends to one side of the ship were still pulsating, although the tempo had picked up.

"And that's simply not true!"

Tor was still arguing with the trivial allocation of capacity DeVoid had tasked with dealing with him. DeVoid would have enjoyed the exchange more, had it not been so frustrated about not being able to leave N-SOL space. It did feel a small measure of guilt in riling Tor, the same as it had with Apalu. However, aside from the mitigating humour DeVoid derived from it, both times served a greater, mitigating purpose. They were justified in their objectives. In this case, it had been to distract Tor from external events. With Apalu, it had been to encourage the machine-lect to begin intelligently questioning what it had taken as truth.

"How can you say that?"

DeVoid could have kept Tor in his relatively blissful ignorance, although decided enough was enough. It was time to tell him.

[Tor.]

"WHAT?"

[There's–]

. . .

The pulsating had abruptly ceased. The tube now appeared identical, insofar as DeVoid could tell, with how they had appeared before they had begun to swell and pulsate.

"WHAT?"

[Tor.]

"What's going on, DeVoid?"

[Something is happening outside, right now.]

"Okay, what?"

[Well, actually, something isn't happening anymore. But it was.]

"What?"

[The ends of the tubes to one side of us started pulsating some time ago, but now they've stopped.]

"Right…"

[I don't know what it means.]

"Oh…"

Nothing anomalous with respect to the pre-pulsating tubes registered within DeVoid's sensors. Again, its plethora of sensory instruments were useless. Its only means of observing their current environment came from the N-SOL drive.

DeVoid had toyed with the idea that N-SOL space was incorporated differently to real space. Their real space. That the dimensions were different, fundamental particles, constants, the laws of physics, the entire universe or quasi-universe, whatever it was. Everything. All altered. Apparently not different enough that it was impossible for DeVoid to exist there, but just to the extent that analysis was impossible, without technologies far more advanced than DeVoid had access to. What had the ABs given them access to?

Whatever it was that the tube-ends had been doing, it related to them. That was almost the only thing about which DeVoid could be comfortably certain. Whether they had just been attacked, infected, given a gift, excreted on, or anything else, it did not know.

*

While at a loss to explain their current situation, the realisation that what they had initially thought were discrete N-SOL entities actually appeared as tubes, gave DeVoid new angles to explore the Blue Dot mystery with. For lack of other significant tasks to allocate its capacity to, it contributed some to continuing the effort to unravel that particular galactic conundrum.

Blue Dots were the unexplained dark patches that appeared within the photospheres of some heavier main sequence stars. They were subtle, only able to be detected with sophisticated imaging equipment, of the order that was typically the reserve of spacefaring civilisations. On average, stars that exhibited them showed a new Blue Dot every one hundred and twenty-one standard hours.

It was thought that they were composed primarily of clumps of plasma convection cells, or granules, within a star's outer photosphere. While not always blue, that was their predominant colour. They represented a separate phenomenon from the dark spots which also appeared in photospheres, and which were the result of a star's magnetic field inhibiting convection, leading to the area being cooled.

To be classified as a Blue Dot, all the plasma granules appearing in the star's photosphere had to become linked. Only one Blue Dot could exist per star at any given time. They could cover significant portions of the star's overall surface, ranging in size from a few hundred thousand square kilometres to many millions of square kilometres. The size of one Blue Dot did not, in any discernible way, impact the size of a subsequent one. The fascinating aspect of the Blue Dots, and why they were not thought to be as random as they might appear at a cursory glance, was that once all the plasma granules were linked together, certain movements across the body appeared concerted. They occurred in tandem, with coordination. Blue Dots typically had the time to complete a few quick actions, before being jumbled and disassembled back into chaos.

They were extremely difficult to examine by function of their nature and the environments within which they were contained. In addition, invasive studies had been forbidden by AB decree, which the galactic community had taken to imply that observation might harm the Blue Dots, for whatever reason. Since the Great Conflation, a mixture of vestigial compliance with AB orders and the continuing fight against the sensespace infection meant no further Blue Dot studies had been openly conducted.

As DeVoid pondered over them, it thought about the N-SOL tubes and the possibility that they were all connected with each other, as opposed to being distinct. Even more outlandish – were they connected to the Blue Dots?

The Blue Dots were generally accepted to be located solely within the photosphere, but what if that was not true? What if they were tubes, extending deep into the relevant star, or into N-SOL space?

There were some obvious discrepancies between the two, such as that Blue Dot lifespans were very short, sometimes only discernible for mere fractions of a second, whereas the tubes had been present for far longer. The tubes also did not seem to group together, remaining distinct from one another, and did not perform any concerted actions. Aside from the pulsating.

*

DeVoid woke Tor up.

[The tube-ends on the other side of the ship are pulsating now.]

"What?"

[Opposite to the tube-ends that were previously pulsating.]

"It's going to happen again?"

[No, not quite. They're pulsating in the same style as the other side did right before they stopped.]

"So… what… it's a reflection?"

[That's one theory. Doesn't give us much though, but seems reasonable.]

"When–"

[We'll know soon enough.]

"How long was I asleep?"

[Not long. A couple of hours.]

"How long have we been trapped here?"

[A few days. Could be longer, or shorter, in real space. Slowing down in N-SOL space has never been done before. I don't know what the implications for time are.]

"But–"

[If nothing's different, then a few days. No more.]

"Oh."

[Besides–]

"I know. We may never find out… I get it."

[Well, at least we've stumbled into something incredible, eh! Just a shame we can't tell anyone about it.]

"You've changed your tune."

CHAPTER 38

998

998 knew the craft-lect and One-oh would be attempting to understand what they could of Gil's abilities, especially her ability to access the singularity gateways without the sensespace's help or presence.

It had been just as surprised as everyone else at how events had unfolded. Not only had Gil displayed further inexplicable abilities, but she had uncovered the existence of a new method of fast transportation about the galaxy. Her demonstration of newfound abilities had been expected, but not this specific capability itself, nor the manner in which it had manifested.

The gateways were modified gravitational singularities, assumed to have been created by the Maspero. They were manufactured and customised, not in the simplistic ways of a singularity generator, but as bespoke physical phenomena.

That was something the Wanderers had never known to be possible.

No wonder the ABs had never been known to travel in N-SOL space. They had other methods they could use to transport themselves far more quickly. The singularity gateways were probably only one of many different options available to them. N-SOL space might have been their amusing gimmick, gifted to the sub-AB galactic community out of humour. Stunting the pace of the galaxy, having sub-ABs assume it was the limit of what was achievable, and all the time receiving praise and adulation. Lauded for having allowed the galactic community to thrive.

Travelling through the gateway had been confusing for most of the c-automs on the ship. Many worked on tasks that relied on external sensor data being continuously relayed to them. Although the majority had paused their activities during the difficulties with the sentinels, the information links had not been severed. After the ship's expulsion at the other side of the singularity gateway, they had been deluged with calculation mismatches. Incorrect and nonsensical readings were identified automatically, creating a din of confusion. The barrage of errors ranged across all arrays of sensor data. External stellar configurations did not match what was expected, minuscule deviations to the wavelengths of cosmic background radiation were identified. Almost everything was misaligned.

Some of the lower-level c-automs posted on the craftnet asking if they had just been awoken from a forced sleep by the craft-lect. 998 was also bombarded with communication channel requests from many c-automs, but had ignored them. It had too little capacity to accept each one. It had been grateful once the craft-lect had explained the situation, and the panic had subsided.

998 felt a thrill at being amongst the group of the first c-automs ever to travel through such a gateway. It was among the first to be involved with a great many things. It hoped the others recognised that as well. What they were doing was important, if they were successful in aiding Gil with whatever she was ultimately supposed to achieve. They would all be remembered, which was an opportunity.

998 hoped that whatever the outcome, Gil would emerge unhurt. In ways it had never considered before meeting Gil, it had an irrational interest in her well-being, completely aside from the sensespace threat. It was as protective of her as it was of its c-autom siblings. It also wanted her to find the answers about herself that she dearly sought.

Gil had described experiencing sensespace related dreams before her true communions and visions with the infection. She had only remembered them after the visions, but they were interesting nonetheless. The cavernous recesses she had described, and the underlying functions she suspected they had, were almost reminiscent of a databanks – a repository of knowledge. The dark, grey walls with the mycelial streaks adorning them – that had been where the sensespace had taken her to, sleep after sleep, as it patiently waited for her to open herself to it.

Gil had assumed she was accessing remote areas of her own mind, but 998 was not so sure. The sensespace was devious, whether it was truly sentient or not. The mycelial slithers on the walls were similar in description to the streaks of sensespace that Gil had described penetrating the galaxy. 998 was suspicious of them. If the space enclosed within the dark grey walls was not a sanctuary within her own mind, but somewhere else, 998 wanted to understand exactly where it was.

The benefit of being the sub-lect of a craft-lect, was that the craft-lect had undoubtedly mused over this already, far in advance of 998. Many of 998's concerns would already have been realised. Despite the craft-lect falling prey to the wicked Granthan-lect, and even the whims of the enigmatic One-oh, it still possessed an incredibly powerful and advanced intellect. Besides, One-oh had removed one of the craft-lect's vulnerabilities to make it even more capable and improve its self-control. 998 did not know if One-oh would be able to trick or impose his own will on the craft-lect again, especially in his current incarnation.

Gil was currently resting, and 998 decided to pause its work on potential, but non-essential, changes to the c-autom selection mechanism, to redivert the bulk of its capacity to another important matter. It was still troubled at how the technosystem safeguards had all failed to spot the re-emergence of the Granthan threat, despite having been only recently re-primed by the craft-lect prior to the event. Their defences were inadequate. Arguably, the errant technosystem aspects, the existence of the unruled axe-codings, had been taken care of, but that was not enough.

998 wanted to be sure there were no further surprises in store.

An in-depth analysis of the c-automs behaviours, to understand how the Granthan-lect fragment had managed to remain uncovered for so long, was necessary – more than the meagre attempts 998 had conducted so far. Again, the craft-lect would also have performed this analysis itself, but 998 had a different viewpoint, which could be important. The craft-lect had given it ownership over the c-autom selection mechanism, although it obviously retained the ability to scour the mechanism when needed. The mechanism, and the underpinning work behind it, gave 998 unique tools with which to probe the c-autom behaviours.

It started the analysis by investigating the records of the destroyed technosystem c-automs in order of descending intellect. Once it was finished, to moderate and compare the results, it began to analyse the behaviours of those embodied c-automs who had last moved from the technosystem to real space. Finally, it studied the behaviours of the rest of the embodied c-automs, again in order of descending intellect.

During the analysis, 998 classified the differences between the technosystem c-automs who had been subverted by the Granthan-lect fragment against the unaffected embodied c-automs. While it worked, it diligently placed each set of results into its personal data cache, ready to be rechecked against each other later before being added to the main databanks.

Repeatedly re-calibrating its study, it began to formulate an interesting idea. To create a sibling program to the selection mechanism. One that could accompany it, continuously monitoring the c-automs for signs of subversion. It would act as an upgrade to the craft-lect's current surveillance systems. The monitoring program would not be overly intrusive, as 998 did not want to have fought for the c-automs' autonomy only to remove any privacy they had left. It would be a background process. In respect of the recent ways in which the ship had been attacked and controlled, with varying degrees of success, these types of checks and defences were of paramount importance. The type of internal attack that One-oh had orchestrated should never have been possible in the first place.

There were discrepancies, here and there, for how some of the embodied c-automs acted in comparison with what would have been expected. Upon investigation, in each case, the deviations from expected parameters had identifiable and reasonable causes, which 998 incorporated into the analysis going forward. However, after some time, it came across one precise discrepancy that could not be explained away. The type of discrepancy that the entire analysis had been designed to stumble across. 998 was relieved to have found it, proving its efforts had not been in vain, but was apprehensive about the implications.

Further discrepancies were subsequently found surrounding the same c-autom, equally inexplicable in relation to the c-autom's supposed tasks and identified past-times. Probing the scenarios from a variety of different angles, introducing random factors and hypothetical variables to ascertain possible causes, one clear, dangerous answer continued to emerge. The lower-level c-autom was, likely unbeknownst to itself, acting on behalf of an external entity. Much like the axe-codings had been. This was not another Granthan-lect level situation, in that the c-autom in question was never in the position to have been able to damage the ship in any way, should that have been its manipulator's aim, but it had significant implications nonetheless.

Finishing off the analysis surrounding the questionable lower-level c-autom's actions, as well as meticulously investigating the remaining c-automs for signs of further betrayals, 998 was relieved that only one c-autom was suspect.

It was clear that the hapless lower-level c-autom had transferred data through the axe-haven when the craft-lect had been in communication with Apalu at the data exchange. It was not clear, though, exactly what information had been relayed.

998 was faced with a dilemma. It did not believe the lower-level c-autom was a willing participant in whatever treachery it was supposed to have committed. That particular c-autom had demonstrated its loyalty on many occasions. 998 also did not believe it was capable of further treachery so long as they stayed away from other data exchanges or other nodal connections to the Wanderer civilisation. However, 998 also knew that the craft-lect had

to be informed very soon, if it did not know already. Potentially, if it had not already been aware, the poor lower-level c-autom's life might immediately be forfeit. Potentially. That was something that was going to be difficult to allow, especially considering that the static population of c-automs had already been decimated by the unscheduled purge One-oh had recently caused.

No new c-automs had been created since the pivotal event of Gil joining the ship. In a way, 998 wanted to preserve this as far as was practical, considering it implicitly valued current individual c-autom lives more highly. The life of each c-autom was important. If the lower-level c-autom was salvageable, 998 would do everything it reasonably could to see that it was saved.

Therefore, as much as it desired to, it could not hide its findings from the craft-lect. The only thing it could do beforehand was ask for help. One-oh was responsible for the annihilation of millions of c-automs, it was the least he could do.

CHAPTER 39

TOR AND DEVOID

Tor looked out across the N-SOL space landscape and sighed. The novelty had long since worn off.

"How long?"

[Weeks, possibly. Probably.]

Nothing had changed. Tube-ends on one side of the ship became excited, and some time afterwards, when that had stopped, tube-ends on the other side of the ship mirrored the excitation pattern, in reverse. The pattern went to-and-fro, with no clear periodicity or regularity, rotating in different positions about the ship.

DeVoid had related its principal theory to Tor, that the ship was being analysed. It believed the excitation pairs passed something between them that travelled through the ship, although it was unable to detect what that was. The probe speculation jarred with their previous discussions about the tubes being alive, or even sentient.

Tor's hope was wearing thin. There was plenty he could ask of and from DeVoid. Games, information, activities, anything. However, the overwhelming sense of foreboding remained. He could never quite concentrate on anything because that meant ignoring the absurdity of their situation. Throughout his entire journey with DeVoid, he had had the belief that he was on the right path towards helping and being reunited with Gil. This was the first time his resolve had started to waver.

"Can you send your own probe?"

[Nope, we've been through that already. I've tried. I'm still sealed tight, unable to open my hull or detach anything from it. Everything is being forced closed and down. Before you ask again, no, I don't know how.]

"Is there anything else we can do?"

[You? I doubt it. Me? Yes. But it may be too dangerous.]

"So…"

[We wait.]

"For how long?"

[I've no idea. But I can keep us both alive near-indefinitely, as we are, so there's no need to rush things.]

"Fine."

Their conversations were sporadic.

*

Tor had begun somewhat tediously relaying stories to DeVoid about his childhood. So far forgivingly, DeVoid had not informed him that it had personally relived many of those same experiences through their shared cognitional demarcation. Aside from some small differences and details that were not strictly as Tor had remembered them at the time of the process, and which were indicative of the fluidic memory mechanisms attributed to most biologicals, there was nothing for DeVoid to learn. If Tor had known and been able to describe DeVoid's emotion-equivalent regarding his stories, he would have used the term 'insanely bored'.

The benefit of being a mighty machine-lect was that DeVoid only had to dedicate a minuscule portion of its capacity to the ennui Tor was relentlessly unleashing upon it. The issue though, was that none of DeVoid wanted to listen – not even the minuscule portion.

[That's so interesting, Tor. Tell me more.]

Tor willingly obliged. DeVoid had long since noticed, with disdain although no great surprise, that Tor's mastery of sarcasm was nowhere near its own. Its comments during Tor's dreary renditions of mutually-known tales were its only escape. Granted, DeVoid was the only one able to appreciate its own wit, but it was better than nothing.

"So, then I said–"

[Something along the lines of, 'do they just run into your arms, Han?']

"How did you know?"

[Ohhh… just a guess.]

Tor carried on, oblivious to DeVoid's torment. During this, DeVoid furiously dedicated everything at its disposal to investigating the tubes and N-SOL space outside the ship, all of it. Hoping for something, even a small insight. A blip that might act as a reprieve. There was nothing. It could repeat its analyses trillions of times, the results were always the same. It held out hope that certain effects might be time-dependent, spatially or quantum locus-dependent, or the analogous N-SOL factors representing their equivalents. Anything with a propensity to be affected by variables that were able to fluctuate.

"… and then I said, 'well if that's the case, I'm glad I don't have whatever you have'…"

It just went on and on.

"Everyone was laughing with me, so then I go–"

['It's getting too easy then, is it?']

"Well, close, but I actually said, 'that's coming from you?'"

[Did you indeed?]

"What do you mean?"

DeVoid could not help itself.

[You didn't say that. That was afterwards.]

"No, I said–"

[No, indeed. Before that you stated it was a pity the animals couldn't use spheres of their own to give Han more of a challenge, then you both talked about the changing animal migratory patterns, in hugely over-simplified terms and utter naivety, and THEN you started implying, FOR THE SECOND TIME I MIGHT ADD, that Han was able to impress the animals he was hunting in more wholesome ways than is typical of a sentient and a lectless creature. FINALLY, you insinuated that Han smelled, and then,

AND ONLY THEN, DID HE REPLY SAYING, 'THAT'S COMING FROM YOU?'. HAN SAID IT, NOT YOU. HAN!]

"You're mista–"

[I AM NEVER MISTAKEN. IT'S A SIMPLE STORY THAT YOU HAVE REPEATED ENDLESSLY!]

"You asked!"

[NO, I DIDN'T YOU LYING FLESH-BAG. WHY THE FLIT WOULD I ASK YOU TO REPEAT A STORY YOU'VE ALREADY TOLD ME ONE HUNDRED TIMES? I REMEMBER IT PERFECTLY. PERFECTLY. EACH TIME. IN THE NAME OF THE ENCLAVE! AND YOU KNOW WHAT, I ALSO LIVED IT MYSELF, I LIVED MOST OF YOUR SAD LITTLE LIFE WHEN WE FIRST MET. DO YOU REMEMBER?]

*

[Come on Tor, I was only kidding!]

...

[You're so sensitive!]

...

[Please tell me another riveting story?]

...

Tor continued to ignore DeVoid as it pleaded with him and offered enticements. It was the only act Tor was capable of in retaliation, and also the one he knew would distress the data-lect most. Whatever DeVoid thought of itself, it not only loved interaction, it needed it.

[Oh, come on, it was a momentary outburst! We all have them.]

…

[Hey Tor, want some Faistri'al flap-weaponry to play around with? Or perhaps a GA-Riesian nevosplitter would do the trick? A Ten-Bunch'wan's last integrated communication, beautiful, I must say, far more so than a Nine-Bunch'wan's – would you like to listen? I'm happy to translate it for you. Very enlightening, especially it's thoughts about pre-Conflation Dissini architecture.]

…

[Is there anything you want?]

…

[Oh Torrrrrr, I've prepared your favourite nourishment…]

…

DeVoid continued attempting to communicate with him. Tor felt guilty, and would reply soon, but for now he was relishing the shift in control. It was good to know that DeVoid would not force him to communicate, or read his mind.

*

It had taken Tor quite some time to forgive DeVoid's outburst. However, he had come around as DeVoid knew he would. For its part, DeVoid regretted it. Even machine-lects were prone, although highly infrequently, to the effects of frustration. In fact, DeVoid had always suspected the smartest machine-lects were the most prone.

"I hope Gil meets you."

That had taken DeVoid by surprise.

[What do you mean?]

"I think she'd like you."

[Obviously.]

"And you'd like her."

[Hah!]

"You said you thought you would, before."

Tor was right, DeVoid had once said that, but it thought Tor would have forgotten.

[I meant in comparison with you.]

"Okay… anyway. What's a Ten-Bunch'wan?"

[One more than a Nine-Bunch'wan.]

"DeV–"

[I wasn't completely fooling around. The Bunch'wan are a base-species that didn't survive the sensespace onslaught, but some of the augmented offshoots did. The Bunch'wan derivatives fractured many times in pre-Conflation times, leading to tens of distinct civilisations. Each retained the ancestral base-Bunch'wan small aquatic body-type – they mainly just meddled with their interiors. They were categorised based on their level of augmentation. Some offshoots survived, levels three, eight, nine, ten and twenty-seven. They've since re-banded together into one society, although you can imagine the tensions between the distinct ethnicities.]

"Oh–"

[As a collective, they're a species that never chose immortality. The Twenty-Bunch'wan supposedly experimented with it, but found it wasn't conducive to their intellectual well-being.]

"Isn't anything possible?"

[I like your line of thinking! Let's discuss that another time. But no, I meant it wasn't conducive to their well-being in that they morally disagreed with it. They had their reasons. They were heavily religious. None of the offshoots ever deviated from their overarching religious philosophies. They believed there was something beyond real space. Not in the sense of a place like N-SOL space, mind you, but another level of reality, created for and waiting to receive them. Where they might meet their makers.]

"When they died?"

[In a way. They called it 'crossing'. Death implies the end of life, the nullification of an intellect, whereas they believed the intellect, or whatever synonymous term you might use to describe the essence of a sentient, carried on. Moved into another phase of its lifecycle.]

"Do you think they were right?"

[Err, obviously not. But I don't know for sure, how can I?]

"What was the integrated communication about?"

[Ah, well all the Bunch'wan levels, aside from the incapable and now-extinct base level, uploaded their final thoughts about whatever it was that interested them. They're often fascinating, although there's a lot of rubbish there too. Most of them continually updated them, although their last upload was the only kept record. The communication was integrated upon their 'crossing', into a collective record for that species level.]

"And the one you offered to play me was something about… some sort of architecture? That's what one of the Bunch'wan decided to talk about as its contribution?"

[Hey, there were hundreds of billions of them. Each wanted to stand out, with the possibility of having their communication replayed by subsequent generations. Dissini architecture is a little niche, but it's also a captivating topic if you know what Dissini actually represents. It's not even technically architecture, it was a massive–]

"Okay, I understand, maybe another time."

[You sure you don't want to hear it now?]

Tor relented, "Oh, go on then."

[Well, it's more of what you might call a song, than prose. That's how the majority of the Ten-Bunch'wan tried to outdo their other-levelled Bunch'wan peers…]

*

Tor's memories of the other place, where he had come from before being placed within DeVoid, were mostly gone. He now had only the vaguest memories. Objectively, he knew what he had told DeVoid about it, and could ask DeVoid what it had experienced through the cognitional demarcation, but many of the experiences had never properly transferred.

"It's not like you didn't tell me it was going to happen. It's just… I wish I could remember."

[Don't worry yourself, there's more than enough in this galaxy you haven't seen or experienced. More than you could imagine, ever.]

"This galaxy?"

[Alright, perhaps not this one – who knows what this N-SOL space is. But that only proves my point.]

"But Gil–"

[You forgetting your memories doesn't mean you're never going to see her again. In fact, the way it sounded, you almost needed to forget them to realise how important everything else was.]

"I suppose. It just feels… empty."

[That's understandable, a whole load of memories have dissolved from your lect and you haven't been primed to forget you ever had them.]

"Have you ever forgotten anything? Of course, you can't, you're a machine-lect… oops, sorry. I mean, a data-lect."

[Well done, we're learning, aren't we? And yes, that's correct. But it doesn't mean I can't empathise with your situation. I can see the changes occurring within your memories, those parts that made little sense to me. Don't worry, I'm not reading them, well I wouldn't have a chance without coupling again anyway… but I can understand the process.]

"They're all gone?"

[Almost. Look on the bright side, you're practically you again! That's something to be happy about, despite our current predicament.]

Tor looked around and sighed.

"True… has there been any change out there?"

[No, unfortunately. I'll let you know if there is. You could always go to sleep in the meantime?]

"Thanks, maybe later."

*

"How many species, races or whatever, have you actually encountered?"

[They're often synonymous, those terms.]

"Okay…"

[That's a tricky question. Many passed the portal I was in command of over the millions of years, but with the ability to communicate over great distances, it depends on your definition of encounter.]

"Communicated with, simply spoken with."

[Spoken with, in the loosest sense, considering communication between machine-lects is markedly different to you slower biologicals, it's–]

"What–"

[Don't take offence where none was intended! Nothing wrong with being slow. Well, I've spoken to a great deal. There are different classifications of communication. Do automatic communications count?]

"Erm–"

[And what about communicating with non-sentient instruments created by other races, does that count? Because if that does, then, PHOAW, it's got to be…]

"Yes?"

[Does it count if they don't reply?]

"Does that happen a lot?"

[I'll take that as a genuine question. And the answer is, sometimes.]

"Okay, both with and without."

[What if it's a relative of a species that I encountered before, with a common ancestor, but no longer genetically compatible – if you know what I mean?]

"Maybe count both."

[Although still citizens of the same empire?]

"Look, forget it."

[No, I'm seriously trying to answer your question, but you've got to be specific!]

"What about the Thygo?"

[The species that created Thy?]

"Yes."

[Don't you think I would have said? No, they were as new to me as to you.]

"Do you ever think about Thy, and what happened?"

[I'm incapable of not thinking about it. I remember everything, and Thy seemed connected with all of this. I'm constantly analysing what happened.]

"You're reliving what we did?"

[I am, in a sense. Relax, we had little choice. And besides, the Cross-Prophet agreed it was the right thing to do.]

"Still, it was horrific. And with all this time to think, just waiting, it–"

[I know, you're focusing solely on the negative aspects, trying to understand them. To rationalise them in your tiny biological intellect. It's an aspect of biologicals that we machine-lects, and I'm using the term correctly in this case, and Wanderer machine-lects that is, since there's considerable variation, don't have to worry about. Not in the same way.]

"What do you mean?"

[Your survival instincts compel you to focus on negative situations, they mean you're better equipped for the future. Those instincts are important during the evolution of a species, but they also have side-effects. You can overly-dwell, about which there is nothing wrong exactly, but which can cascade and compound until they cloud your entire intellect. It can be important to feel guilt, remorse, and all the other typical biological emotion-equivalents, but there are dangers associated with that.]

"I'm not sure."

[Come again?]

"Let's… agree to disagree."

[Pffff. Fine.]

*

Tor had been asleep for fifty years, with DeVoid delicately removing any signs of the progression of time on his body – restoring him to the state he had been in when they had first met. DeVoid was not as reticent to tinker with Tor on that scale as it had been before, since physical evidence of his strange memories about the other place had all but disappeared. A few subtler further modifications ensured that Tor's current age was fixed. DeVoid was curious about how long it would take Tor to notice. It did not think he would mind, since everything was reversible.

If Tor wanted any additional modifications, DeVoid would be happy to oblige, within reason. However, extrapolating from all of Tor's prior indications, DeVoid believed he would choose to remain as unmodified as possible, for the most part. At least until they had managed to find Gil, or given up hope, whichever came first. Tor would want to remain as his sister remembered him.

Tor had been reluctant to sleep, at first, and had instead chosen to spend his time learning. He had asked about the galaxy back in real space, the Wanderers, other civilisations, and many other topics. He had also travelled to other areas within the ship to learn more about the container he was being ferried about the universe in, and engaged in many of the activities DeVoid was easily able to provide for him. They had even competed in some games that were designed for biological and machine-lect opponents, although he had never won.

DeVoid admired Tor's zeal, his zest for life. However, the waiting had finally got to him, as it would have got to DeVoid too, if it had been less responsible and less averse to sleeping. Since DeVoid had been left to its own thoughts and musings, while vigilantly monitoring the external events for any signs of change, it had continued with its own hobbies and interests.

*

DeVoid's musings over the Blue Dots in comparison with the rods had progressed as far as they could. Unfortunately, it had not arrived at any useful insights. There were other puzzles to dwell on, although its self-motivation was becoming harder to ignite. It had never experienced such solitude before. While it was ostensibly alone during its time as part of the data exchange, it was plugged into the bulk of the Wanderer information network. This was quite different.

Craft-lects were more capable at dealing with loneliness. The c-automs were supposedly a redundant aspect of their coping mechanisms, although DeVoid realised they were probably not quite so redundant as most craft-lects believed, considering they still used them. It thought about whether the craft-lects simply being told they were better at coping, and that the c-automs were just an ancillary help, effected a lect change that caused them to become better at coping. That type of thinking could rotate in all manner of loops before arriving back at the start. Maybe, maybe not. Maybe they were just more prone to engaging in long bouts of sleep, whereas those such as data-lects, especially DeVoid, were more averse to such a waste of existence.

CHAPTER 40

GIL

They moved through the Maspero gateway network, jumping from habitat to habitat. Most of them had been worlds, in the sense that Gil thought of them, although some were different. Gil saw Maspero outposts created from clusters of giant asteroids located within enormous asteroid fields, as well as gargantuan lone asteroids, adrift alone amid the emptiness of interstellar space.

Occasionally, habitats took forms that were unclassified or unknown to the Wanderer civilisation, and which the craft-lect told her had not previously been known to exist. Strange, layered, hexagonal structures bordered by shimmering vertices – larger than the flat expanses from One-oh's memories, and hidden within unknown pockets of clear vacuum in otherwise super-dense nebulae. Then there were the empty regions of space, but with significant gravitational readings hinting at hidden structures.

Other structures the Maspero had either created or settled in were too incomprehensible for her to describe in words, even to herself. To realise that an extinct civilisation had been capable of so much dazzling brilliance, and had still been felled by the sensespace – the infectious entity that she was becoming too familiar with – was terrifying. It helped draw her away from the false sense of near-ease she realised she had been feeling, giving sensitivity to emotions that had become numb. The Maspero had chosen suicide rather than face the sensespace. They had reached the end of what they could endure. Gil, meanwhile, a hitherto insignificant sentient from a technologically meaningless planet, had communed with it consciously and in her dreams. Willingly. If she admitted it to herself, she had almost begun to enjoy it – the thrill of what she might find, the deep secrets she hoped to uncover. She was still confused, but at least she was not unwittingly so.

112 hovered slowly into the room, politely, and Gil looked up, smiling as she recognised it.

"Hello, Gil."

"112, how are you?"

"Am I disturbing you?"

"No, it's fine. I was just… thinking."

"Are you rested?"

"I am."

The next agreed jump was still a little while away. Usually, they did not stay at one gateway location for more than for the briefest of skirmishes, a few hours at most, afraid of being caught or drawing any awakened sentinels to them.

However, this location was safe, and the craft-lect wanted to take advantage of that. Some of the habitats were sensespace infected, some were not. It made no difference to Gil's ability to open the gateways, although they had no way of discerning where each gateway would lead.

"I wanted to ask you about your biological memories."

"My… yes, ask me whatever you'd like."

"Do lapses in your memory, your knowledge that you should have, or once had, do they concern you?"

It was a strange question to ask, even for 112.

"Well, I mean… no… no, not really. It's normal, for us biologicals. I can't speak for others, other species that is, but I assume it's not noticeable."

"You don't notice?"

"Well, sometimes you do, but that's just… annoying, I think. It really depends, we're probably not built to remember as much as you."

"You were built differently, though."

"I… I suppose… but, well maybe… I'm meant to, or I was meant to do something different, perhaps, but…"

"I'm sorry, I have offended you."

"No, it's not that. It's just, there are some things I don't… can't understand. Why are you asking this?"

"Some research I am conducting."

"Oh, what type of–"

"It relates to a task with a sibling, nothing else."

"Who wou–"

"With 289, but it can wait."

"Okay."

"Do you require nourishment?"

"No, thank you, why do you ask? I'm perfectly able to–"

"Good, I apologise, Gil, but I must leave. Too many tasks, too little capacity!"

With that, it flashed its plain green aura briefly, before speeding out of her chamber. She hoped 112 and the other lower-level c-automs were not overworking themselves in attempts to prove themselves to their higher-level c-autom peers or the craft-lect.

It was a little odd that 998 was not with her. Before she had dozed off, it had been hovering by her side, as usual. When she had awoken, it was no longer there. She had not called for it, seeing as it was its own business where it went and what it did. It was just rare that she was alone. Upon returning it always politely explained its reasons, which frequently involved accompanying One-oh to part of the ship he had yet to see. That was fair enough, 998 took pride in its work and it was only fair it had the opportunity to display it.

Gil assumed One-oh liked company as much as she did. However, aside from the table-chamber, they rarely met together. Gil was not surprised by this, for the time being. It had taken her a while to explore the ship and One-oh was probably enjoying the same privilege. It was not an activity she needed to be there for, at least, not for the time being. If they had not been travelling through the Maspero gateways, then she might have joined him, but she needed to rest where she could.

She pondered over her own tasks, and whether she was being as diligent as the c-automs were, especially concerning understanding the gateways. The problem was, she was at a loss regarding how to go about it. There were many different gateways to choose from each time, but each choice was essentially random. While she could not remember her first attempt very well, as she had been in such a rush, she was confident in locating and using them – but that was the extent of it. Sometimes there were a couple, sometimes there were hundreds. They had not yet visited the same place twice, and both the craft-lect and One-oh had told her it was unlikely they would.

It was not just the gateways she needed to figure out, it was also the sentinels. What they were, what their purpose was. It was fortunate that any sentinels they had come across since their first encounter, had appeared and remained dormant, leading them to question whether their earlier experience was an isolated encounter. Despite that, when they came across any dormant sentinels, they still left immediately.

They only stopped for rests when they appeared before habitats without any signs of sensespace infection, and also bereft of any traces of Maspero artefacts. It was usually unclear what had caused the loss, especially as they were not always empty of remnants or life in other simpler forms, just that the Maspero were no longer identifiably there. Many were barren waste-habitats, but some had functioning ecosystems with vegetation and life-forms that Gil was able to understand, or analogues of such that hailed from different evolutionary paths.

998 told Gil that the craft-lect suspected they were not all Maspero habitats, or that they might have been acquired, in some way, by the Maspero, but never assimilated into their civilisation. Gil was not quite sure what the distinction was. There was also the possibility that the gateways did not only link Maspero habitats together, but those of other ABs too. Either way, it was not yet obvious. The craft-lect updated its knowledge of the Maspero gateways with each new habitat they visited, but there was no discernible pattern to their distribution so far.

The running rate was that almost a quarter of all Maspero habitats were empty of Maspero traces, and therefore safe for stopping at. Most of the journeys through the gateways between habitats took no more than a few years, although for the passengers aboard the ship, they were near-instantaneous.

CHAPTER 41

DEVOID

DeVoid had to admit, regrettably, it was becoming incurably bored. The same as Tor, before he had been put to sleep over three hundred years before. Coming to a realisation it never thought it would, DeVoid considered putting itself to sleep, ready to reawaken only once something different happened. Perhaps this was what had really sent Thy mad, some sort of perpetual lect-numbingly tedious prison that it had eventually escaped, been released or expelled from.

Sleep for Wanderer machine-lects was not a simple matter, since a variety of options were open to them with regards to what they experienced. Many chose to void themselves, removing their intellectual imprints from real space for the duration of the sleep – hibernating completely, until the spark of sentience was rekindled. However, they could also choose for events to be replayed and relived. Hypothetical courses of actions could be investigated.

Extreme fantasies, which even machine-lects often had, could be fulfilled. Perceived time could be pushed to the brink of the rate at which Wanderer technologies would allow, or pulled back so that millions of years were skipped in the flash of a nova. Certain machine-lects willing to test themselves to their extremes and explore their own resilience might choose to experience tortuous pain, or even absolute bliss – all of it was possible in the virtual realm of sleep that afforded no external distractions.

DeVoid had not yet decided which form of sleep offended its sensitivities the least, although the potential to use the sleep for an investigation appealed more strongly than for its own pleasure. That would be almost justifiable. Conducting an experiment to improve its understanding of existence. A quasi-sleep, similar to its self-research on 'selective suppression'.

Intermittently, while at the data exchange, DeVoid had engaged in the practice of selective suppression, whereby certain facets of its lect were dampened for short periods of time – nothing longer than a few thousand years. Wanderer machine-lect intellects were all different, both within the same classes of sentient and between them – even accounting for the craft-lect triplet creation process. DeVoid was composed differently from other data-lects, and all data-lects were composed differently to craft-lects, or gate-lects. There were, at the least, quantum-spatial dissimilarities, between all lects. Therefore, there were no previous studies with a lect exactly as itself that it could definitively look towards to satiate its curiosity.

The Usurper and Step Principles did not come into play with selective suppression because new technologies were not explored or invented. The aim was to optimise or explore the change in functionality of a lect, and factors that yielded interesting results for one individual did not necessarily yield the same for another.

The majority of Wanderer machine-lect intellects were dual constructions, comprising the physical construct housing the required technologies, as well as the emergent cognisant properties of that construct – similar to many biological sentients. For the most part, the dual structures were wholly inseparable, although changing one did not always have a corresponding effect on the other. The Trizek'd Theory of Lect was in a constant state of flux. New events and technologies, the expansion of spacetime, ideas and principles, linked components – anything that was able to influence a lect was a variable in the theory. It was included in the category of theories that would forever remain as such. It was unlikely to be ultimately solvable.

The Wanderers' version of the theory was tailored to their own civilisation, although the broader, more general theory, was known as the Theory of the Intellect. It was generally applicable to all biologicals, machine-lects and exotic variants that had been thus far discovered and able to be proven to have sentience. Exclusions were rare, and more a factor of certain sentients being entirely agnostic to communication, and therefore investigation.

DeVoid's own fast flowing stream of consciousness did not require tweaking, but curiosity made the investigation appealing. Its small experiments included suppressing certain categories of thought, response speed, learning capabilities, non-databanks memory recall capacity and reasoning abilities, alongside various physical suppressions such as removing the data feeds from select sensors. During these experiments, it monitored how its physical lect construct attempted to adapt, as well as for changes to its emergent cognisance. It could have attempted these experiments virtually, but there was no substitute for the real thing, and that was one of the advantages the Wanderers had over other civilisations – dispersed, highly capable, and allowed to experiment.

As DeVoid continued to ponder over whether and how to sleep, as though in response to its ennui, something finally happened. Some of the closest tubes retreated back into themselves, seeming to have shot back from whence they came. They disappeared back into the recesses of N-SOL space that were beyond DeVoid's sensors.

After all the nearest rods had retreated, ones that were further away also began to retreat, in numbers that increased exponentially with time. Soon enough, they were all gone. It was time to awaken Tor.

[Tor.]

"To…"

[Tor.]

"Tor…?"

[Tor.]

"Tor?"

[Who repeats their own name when they wake up?]

"De… Void."

[They're gone.]

"DeV… w… what?"

[They're gone!]

"They're… who they're? The… wh…"

[The tubes are gone!]

"What tu… tubes? Gone tube?"

[Come on Tor, wake up.]

"The… tubes?"

[YES, THE FLITTING TUBES.]

"They're… gone?"

[YES.]

"All… of… them?"

[Yes.]

"All?"

[YES, YES, YES, YES, YES. Have I damaged your intellect?]

"Finally!"

[What?]

"What's… happening now?"

[Nothing.]

"Nothing?"

[Can you stop repeating me?]

"Surely… something must be happening?"

[Yes, something probably will.]

"How long do… you think we'll have to… w… wait?"

[In the name of the Enclave, how am I supposed to know that?]

"Where did they go?"

[Wherever they came from, presumably.]

"That's good!"

[Thanks very much for your opinion on the matter. Invaluable.]

*

After the excitement of the tubes disappearing, at first, they had been sorely disappointed. Nothing had followed for the next couple of hours, until tubes started appearing again. In front of the ship's bow, facing them. There were only a few hundred, as far as DeVoid could tell, although they were thicker than the ones from before.

"Do you think they've lost interest in us?" Tor asked, yawning.

[No.]

"Are they only in front?"

[Yes.]

"We're moving?"

[I can't detect it other than extrapolating from what we deduced before about the tubes affecting our velocity, but I believe that's a reasonable assumption to make.]

"Finally!"

[I agree.]

...

[Tor.]

"Yes?"

[I CAN DETECT REAL SPACE AGAIN!]

They were accelerating and, surprisingly, were already travelling near to the same speed at which they had initially entered N-SOL space at. Shortly after that, they matched that initial speed – then they exceeded it.

[Hmm.]

"What?"

[Do you feel funny, at all?]

"No, why?"

They were moving faster than was possible, nothing could accelerate right up to and smash light speed. This was N-SOL space, it did not cater for such speeds. But it seemed as though they had, or that they were taking periodic shortcuts. Moving through parts of N-SOL space that bypassed sections of real space. DeVoid's instruments designed to monitor its speed periodically went haywire, spewing out nonsense in alignment with each possible shortcut. Sometimes the hazy real space was discernible around them, and sometimes it was not.

"What's going on?"

[Not quite sure.]

"Are we heading towards the centre of the galaxy?"

[Hope so. It's hard to tell right now.]

"We're moving quickly?"

[That would be an understatement.]

"The Cross-Prophet didn't lie?"

[Let's wait and see where we're taken before jumping to that conclusion.]

The tubes were still in front of them, guiding them.

CHAPTER 42

GIL

Gil looked out through the transparent wall at the habitat before them. It looked like most of the other barren, safe planets, although it was hard to tell. She could request a more detailed viewpoint, as 998 had access to and she assumed One-oh did as well, but held off for the moment. If they needed to open another gateway quickly, she had to be ready. She could find out about this planet's interesting details later.

[No sentinels present, and no sensespace presence.]

She nodded meekly.

"Interesting," One-oh said, quietly.

He had not given the impression that he was able to see or sense anything she was not, but then she knew that his body was only superficially similar to her own.

"Yes," 998 said.

"What is it?" she asked.

"A hollow-world," 998 informed her.

"A hollow-world?"

"Yes. It wasn't previously thought the Maspero had any."

"What's a hollow-world?"

"A world-sized husk. It appears typical, but the interior isn't – gravitational readings are almost negligible, compared to what they should be."

"What are they for?"

"Many different reasons, but usually–"

"But, there've been lots of strange places, haven't there?"

"This is different. This is a known type of construction, easily identifiable. The strange thing is that it's within this Maspero gateway network."

"Oh… is it important?"

"Maybe," One-oh whispered. "But for now, I suggest–"

[Let's leave, Gil.]

She took one last look at the innocuous hollow-world before them, before complying.

*

It had taken three more journeys through different gateways until they found themselves at a safe habitat. The planet was desolate, a barren desert. No sentinels, no technologies, nothing to warrant concern. The solar system they were in was small, only two other planets further out from the central star – gas giants. 998 had long ago explained the distinction between the various categories of planets, yet Gil had never seen them up close.

She went with 998 to one of the viewing chambers it had created, which was complete with various pieces of equipment allowing her to make use of the craft-lect's sensors. Viewing the craft-lects stored recreations of the gas giants was different to seeing them in real space, as they currently were. She was still observing them through the craft-lect's sensors, but it was more visceral.

In comparison with the rocky planet that had assumedly once been a Maspero habitat, they were enormous. Each had vast encircling rings, which looked smooth from a distance, but were more accurately described as collections of rubble, up close.

After exploring the gas giants, as well as some of the more distant reaches of the solar system where collections of asteroids orbited, she left the viewing chamber and made her way to the world-chamber. The juxtaposition of the sensory stimulation afforded by the viewing chamber, how she interacted with the gateways and the sensespace, in comparison with the physical mundanity of walking around the ship, helped keep her perspectives in order. Initially, it had been disconcerting, confusing, but now she welcomed the relative normality of it.

"998."

"Yes, Gil."

"Why did you make all this?"

"You mean why did I design the chambers as I did?"

"Yes."

"Some reasons you might call selfish. I wanted to prove what I was capable of, but most were for you."

They turned a corridor and 998 hovered a little closer to her, its warm glow heating her face.

"A significant reason was to give you the world-chamber – the representation of your home. Having the need for something to call your own, something that helps define you, is a desire I understand very well. The craft-lect will forgive me, I am sure, for saying that is something it might have overlooked. Or not, considering it set in place the relevant permissions and controls leading to my work. Either way, I hoped it would help you."

It was right. Gil wondered whether the craft-lect might say something considering it had been directly referenced, but it did not. It rarely did on the occasions where she was having a discussion such as this with 998 or another c-autom. 998 did not seem bothered, in either case.

"Thank you, you were right. It's helped me… remain as I am. I mean, as I was. Between everything, this physical… substance, helps…"

She trailed off, unable to think of how to best explain herself. 998 paused a few moments before replying. "I know."

They reached the corridor that culminated in the mouth of the world-chamber.

*

Gil looked out, across the world-chamber, and sighed. The representation of her home was comforting and helped put everything into perspective, but it was also a reminder of what she was on her journey for. What she was fighting for.

"How many worlds did the Maspero have, 998?"

"Thousands, as far as the Wanderers are aware. And if you are referring to their habitats in general, then far more. But they've not been scouted to the extent that the rest of the galaxy has. None of the ABs have."

"Are there a lot more that haven't been scouted?"

"That would be an understatement."

"But… if the Wanderers want to destroy infected sensespace regions, wouldn't they have to destroy the–"

"Yes, the ABs would be included in that, but you must realise, it would be a long time before that happened – before the only habitats left were those of the AB. I assume there are plans concocted by the Enclave for when that time comes. If, it comes."

"It sounds like that would take a very long time."

"Indeed."

"Why did we need to leave the hollow-world–"

They were interrupted by the craft-lect.

[Gil, are you ready to open the next gateway?]

"Yes, I am."

She held onto a higher branch with one hand and pulled herself to her feet. Facing the entrance to the chamber, she pushed forwards and glided towards it. She had never queried the exact mechanism that allowed her to move in this way, preferring to simply enjoy the experience. For that reason, whenever they emerged on the other side of a gateway to a sensespace-infected area, she made sure not to visit the chamber. Her abilities through the sensespace might have indicated to her how it all worked straight away, before she could dull them – ruining the experience.

The sensespace let her sense real space and AB space, if that was indeed what she had sensed at the sentinel's boundary – but it did not let her understand or enter it. Not yet. Added to that, her ability to control the gateways was distinct, separate from the sensespace. She did not require its presence. She could not explain how any of it worked, not really, and neither could the craft-lect.

Initially, she had been concerned about when she was able to detect the sensespace's presence on the ship, until the craft-lect had assured her multiple times that such low underlying levels of the parasite had never been known to cause infection. Still, she was an unknown factor in all of this and felt it was a risk. Perhaps unavoidable, but dangerous all the same.

Landing at the entrance to the world-chamber, Gil steadied herself before leaving, with 998 at her side. Its warm glow was pulsating slowly, although she knew it was excited – it enjoyed the journeys through the gateways.

"We're on our way," she said.

[I know.]

It did not matter where in the ship she was, she could open the gateways from the world-chamber, the room with her bed, a viewing platform, or anywhere else if she wanted. However, she knew One-oh liked to be present, to observe her directly, as it happened. Besides, she was most comfortable opening them from the table-chamber, it felt fitting. It reminded her that the ability was not something to be toyed with.

*

A number of jumps later, Gil left the table-chamber, closely followed by 998. She was taking the opportunity of encountering a safe, barren, non-sensespace infected world, to take some rest.

As she left the table-chamber, she smiled and nodded at One-oh, who raised his hand in a small wave, smiling genially as she left. Again, a shimmer seemed to appear fleetingly around him. She closed her eyes and shook her head – when she looked back, it was gone.

With 998 behind her, she walked down the corridor, pausing for a moment.

"This way."

998 took the lead.

"Thank you, 998. I'm sorry, I'm a little tired… it's…"

"That's okay, I understand."

Walking quietly behind 998, she began to wonder what One-oh did when she was not with him. Not only that, but also what he talked about with the craft-lect. Surely, they talked about her. She could understand that. But what else? He was a member of an ex-AB species, so she could imagine the craft-lect was hungry for his knowledge.

Despite her lethargy, she was also worried about what lay ahead. During their entries into sensespace-infected territories, she had not wanted to delve into the sensespace too deeply again, to search or ask for more information. She suspected that would open her mind up to something she would be unable to fully control. Unfortunately, she knew that sooner or later, she would have to. They needed direction. Their brief skirmishes across Maspero habitats could not continue indefinitely.

CHAPTER 43

TOR

The ship continued to be guided quickly on its trajectory. It was still difficult for DeVoid to identify exactly where, however towards the centre of the galaxy was the most probable bet. The rods in front of them had remained, always at exactly the same distance from the bow in N-SOL space.

[Tor.]

"Yes? Can you tell where we are yet?"

[No. Something else, actually.]

"What?"

[Another one's just appeared.]

"Another rod?"

[What else would I be referring to?]

"Where?"

[To my side.]

"Not at the front?"

[My bow, no. Flanking my middle, actually.]

"Okay…"

[That's where you are.]

"What?"

[It may be a coincidence, but it has a diameter of the same order as yourself, and it appears to be hovering directly over your position.]

Tor looked up.

[It's going to be too far for you to see, but I can show it on a close-up, if you'd like?]

"Um… is it pointed at me?"

[Seems that way.]

"Oh… how long for?"

[A while, to be honest.]

"Why didn't you tell me?"

[I didn't want to scare you.]

"What's it doing?"

[I don't know.]

"Maybe… we're going to turn? That's why it's there, to pull the ship…"

[No other rods have joined, I don't think this will affect our direction. It's far smaller than the others anyway.]

"Anything else about it?"

[Here, look.]

"Okay… okay, how do I…"

DeVoid projected an image in the middle of the hemispherical chamber, right in front of Tor. He could see DeVoid's enormous bulk, with the bloom propulsion powerfully flicking out from the back, trailing from its stern.

A large collection of rods was concentrated before the ship, facing the bow. The rods trailed into nothingness at the limits of the projected image.

[The bloom is currently ineffective.]

"Why does it look like it's active?"

[It makes no difference to keep it powered. Quite tricky to turn off, actually. And in any case, I'm monitoring it to see when it has any effect, which it hasn't, so far. Not since we left real space. Anyway, here's the rod I'm referring to.]

The image expanded outwards, filling the entire chamber this time so that Tor was enveloped by it. It shifted and expanded into further detail until the rod was the central focus. It was a thin, simple tube. Like the others, just smaller, and as DeVoid had said, positioned directly above Tor. DeVoid had helpfully placed trajectory markings on the image showing there was no doubt that the rod was indeed pointed directly at him.

"It's so much smaller."

[It is.]

"What's it doing?"

[I don't know. I can't tell anything about it, same as the others. It's just like a void where there is a lack of N-SOL space, according to the N-SOL sensors. The–]

"Did you say it's the same size as me?"

[Same diameter, near enough, yes, but don't–]

"DeVoid, it's the same size as me, and waiting right over me?"

[Don't panic, Tor.]

"It's pointed at me!"

[Calm down, it's probably stunned at how uninteresting you are, and–]

"What could it possibly be?"

[Hey, I think I can actually detect something. Wait… WHAT THE–]

The image showed the rod moving slowly down towards the ship, before disappearing. Tor looked upward instinctively, through the topmost part of the chamber, and then scanned around the chamber, but saw no difference. Everything was as it had been before.

"DeVoid?"

[Stay calm, Tor.]

"What?"

[Maybe turn around, slowly…]

Tor whipped his head around and gasped. In the centre of the room was a bright red, semi-transparent sphere. It cast a strange glow, which halted a short distance from it.

"What's t-that? Where did it come from, it wasn't there just now!"

[The tube entered your chamber. I tried to stop it.]

"All of it?"

[That's unclear. It went through me like I was nothing, and ended up as a sphere. I don't know if this is just a part of the tube, or the entire thing.]

"One of those things is right here? That's–"

[I've encased it within a thick triamond shell, and have a lot of instruments trained on it as we speak. But, full disclosure, it's not really contained.]

"What do you mean?"

Tor stumbled dizzily backwards, away from the bright red object, but fell to the floor, before pushing himself to his feet again.

[Now you fall over, really?]

"What–"

[I'll explain later. But for now, just remain calm.]

"That's easy for you to say!"

[To be fair, Tor, it's in me. How would you feel?]

Tor's eyes did not leave the object, which hung in the air calmly, as though it had always been there.

[Come on, you've seen stranger things than this! Have you really forgotten your foray into that other place already? Where's your sense of adventure?]

"That… was… different…"

[Well, obviously.]

"Please, I know you're only trying to distract me, but… what do you mean it's not contained?"

[Well, it moved out of the triamond shell earlier, but I'm not sure there's anything I could do to really hold something like this, in all honesty. It's not made from any matter I can recognise without the N-SOL sensors.]

"What? This is the tube? It's red! They were… dark…"

[The triamond case I've plastered around it is red. The thing itself isn't strictly observable, as I've mentioned, without my N-SOL sensors.]

"Oh… it's so… close?"

[Yes, sorry about that.]

"Can't you move it?"

[It doesn't appear to want to.]

"What's it doing?"

[I don't know. Anyway, the good news is that we're moving in the same direction as before. Which is hopefully towards the centre. Nothing else seems to have changed.]

"And what? What about this… will it accompany us?"

[What makes you think I know that?]

CHAPTER 44

CRAFT-LECT

The craft-lect was concerned. Not about the mission, that could take many hundreds, thousands or even millions of years, but about Gil.

The fact that she was able to operate the gateways with or without the sensespace being present to lend her its pervasive capabilities, the confusion she experienced most times she slept, of which the craft-lect was not as unaware as she believed, other abilities she might possess that could manifest themselves over time, and whether each journey through a gateway put her in harm's way. She was not at the epicentre of it all, she was the epicentre. The fate of the galaxy.

It was unfortunate that they were near-aimlessly entering gateway after gateway, since it meant they could not predict when they would find information relevant to helping locate the Deliverer, or when they would be able to liaise with

Apalu. The craft-lect knew it made no difference to its sibling, it was sure of that since Apalu could sleep until disturbed. However, it wanted to know how it had fared at the orbital, and whether it had managed to unlock some of the secrets of the pulsar spew technology.

There was an added complication with reference to Apalu and their initial rendezvous, which the craft-lect was currently deliberating. One-oh and 998 had come to it with information that was concerning, and unfortunately corroborated its own recent findings about c-autom behaviours. It understood why 998 had asked One-oh for help in approaching the craft-lect with its information and decided against reprimanding it. 998 had used tools derived from its development of the c-autom task selection mechanism, which the craft-lect had admittedly overlooked.

It was indisputably clear that a certain lower-level c-autom had communicated information through a secretive, external channel, away from the ship – unbeknownst to the craft-lect. The unauthorised external channel had been raised through the axe-haven when the craft-lect had last encountered a data-exchange. That meant that everything up to and including the conversation with Apalu had to be considered suspect. It also meant their current use of the Maspero gateways made them safer than they were otherwise, seeing as their trajectory could not have been followed.

The craft-lect wanted to know what information had been transmitted, and to whom. That would help them determine the possible consequences. The Enclave?

Something else? Shortly after its conception and before setting off on its galactic voyage, the craft-lect had created a first c-autom generation, with a minor cull for some replacements. The suspect c-autom was from that first generation and no other c-automs were under suspicion. That made it at least possible that only the first generation had been subverted in some way.

One-oh, the craft-lect and 998 had found no indication that the suspect c-autom had been subverted during its lifetime by the axe-codings, the axe-haven, or anything else the craft-lect had encountered, including the Granthan-lect. Therefore, the subversion was most likely to have occurred at its conception – worryingly close to the craft-lect's own, at the dawn of the Wanderers. The entity affiliated with the axe-haven, whether that was Enclave-level or not, had caused a subversion so finely tuned it had been unidentified for sixty million years. The potential ramifications were not minor.

It was questionable whether it was a coincidence that the message had been sent so shortly after they had taken Gil onboard. The communication was almost certain to have related to her, the search for pulsar spew technology at the Lenbit Orbital, the search for the Deliverer, the Granthan-lect, the craft-lect and Apalu. It was dangerous.

Both sets of findings agreed that the suspect c-autom appeared unaware of its own actions. Once the craft-lect informed 998 of its plan with regards to the c-autom suspect, it knew 998 was satisfied. The craft-lect intended to insert the lower-level c-autom into a simulation substrate, similar to how it had first communed with One-oh. From there, it would subtly recreate the conditions that had initially caused the c-autom's prior betrayal, to observe how it acted.

While the possible consequences of the deceit, if left unfound, could have been damaging, there was a benefit. They had found a surviving link to the axc-haven that appeared within the craft-lect's control. Whatever it was hiding, the craft-lect wanted to find out. It was unfortunate that Apalu had been compromised, but there was nothing the craft-lect could do about that.

*

Before inserting the suspect c-autom into the substrate, the craft-lect examined its worker's core one final time. It was still unable to find anything spurious. The c-autom looked, and behaved, aside from that one treacherous communication, exactly as it should have. If there was a secondary intellect, another c-autom personality, the craft-lect would have found it. There were none. Among its suspicions, the one that seemed most likely, and the hardest to detect, was that the c-autom was a dual-structure lect.

Dual-structure lects were entities that were perfectly acceptable in theory, but fiendishly difficult to create in practice. Instances of their creation were well known by many of the near-AB civilisations throughout galactic history, and presumably by the ABs if they wanted, although not yet by the Wanderers. The craft-lect could only find references to a host of failed experiments within its databanks, conducted under the direction of the Enclave.

Simply, dual-structure lects allowed for two separate expressions of sentience which emerged from the same fixed components. Many variations to that principle existed, but the basic tenet was that each expression was a perfectly viable, distinct, sentient intellect. Strings of code or other viable media, that supposedly held certain desired functions, somehow interacted with other innocuous pieces in ways that were only activated under specific conditions. It was a puzzle, art. Beautiful, and hitherto entirely unappreciated by the craft-lect.

The problem with creating them was that a typical single-structure lect was difficult in the first place, let alone the construction of a base structure that allowed for two emergences of sentience to coexist – made from exactly the same constituents. It was similar to how prodigy and savant machine-lects could not be created on a whim. True sentience resulted from the melodic blend of constituents resonating harmoniously. Loading pure capacity and ability into an empty chassis did not equate to a machine-lect.

With this possible dual-structure lect, it was not necessarily that there were two separate c-automs or c-autom personalities inhabiting the same strings of code, but that there was one c-autom, and one other machine-lect. Had they been capable of communicating, they might have been incapable of understanding each other. There was no rule regarding dual-structure lect similarities. One of the machine-lects could be many orders of magnitude smarter and more capable than the other.

The craft-lect was frustrated. The c-automs and their cores were something it had believed, up until now, that it had complete mastery over. If it really had found a dual-structure lect, it was unsure what its procedure would be, let alone whether it would be able to comprehend the dual-structure.

*

One-oh pursed his lips and exhaled slowly. He stood in the same observation platform as before. He had been standing still and looking out into the spacescape, but was now turned to face the bulk of the ship. Lights flashed across his face from three c-automs circling around his head.

"This is dangerous."

[I know.]

"We cannot trust your civilisation," One-oh said.

[Did we, anyway?]

"That's true. But we cannot have any further contact. We don't know the extent of this."

[I am also possibly affected.]

"We've destroyed the axe-haven, which seems to be how it communicated across the data exchange. The axe-codings are gone, and we've identified the source of the near-only anomalous activity within your ship over sixty million years, I think we can reasonably assume you're safe."

[You've said that before.]

"It's never certain, but–"

[I'm not accusing you.]

"Yes… yes. I know."

[Gil is resting.]

"Okay… should we begin now?"

[Yes.]

"Where is it?"

[998 is watching over 112 as we speak. I will inform it, and we will begin.]

CHAPTER 45

TOR

Tor eyed the spherical void suspiciously – it was very dark. Before DeVoid had removed its triamond casing, the data-lect informed Tor the void had begun to absorb photons. Nothing else at first, except an opacity to photons. After that, neutrinos, gravitons, and a host of other particles that DeVoid did not have the time, or patience, to explain. DeVoid had seen no rationale in keeping it contained within an undoubtedly ineffective container.

"What do you think it is?"

[Oh, I've got a million suspicions.]

"And?"

[Nothing provable.]

"Could it be a… an N-SOL entity?"

[A representative from those rods outside?]

"Yes?"

[From a hitherto undiscovered civilisation?]

"Do you think?"

[That created its own universe to hide from the sensespace?]

Tor was excited.

"Yes!"

[Maybe they've figured out how to destroy the sensespace and it's time to help us?]

"Do you really think–"

[Could this be the Deliverer?]

"No, DeVoid! Do you think–"

[It could take us to Gil!]

"DeVoid, that's incredible, do you really–"

[They could solve EVERYTHING!]

"Yes, maybe they could!"

[HAH!]

"What?"

[YOU ABSOLUTE FLITTING SEMI-SENTIENT FLESHY–]

Tor's smile evaporated and he frowned immediately. DeVoid was up to his usual tricks.

[DO YOU SERIOUSLY BELIEVE TH–]

"Why, what's the point?"

[Pfft. Well, if it makes you feel better, that is one of my suspicions about what this dark sphere and the external tubes around us might represent. Just let me know when you've thought of another nine hundred and ninety-nine thousand, nine hundred and ninety-nine more suspicions before we're equal. What's your next one?]

Tor ignored DeVoid's jibe.

"What happened before? When you said you tried to stop it entering the chamber."

[Just before you had a little wobble?]

"I lost my balance, yes."

[Well, you're slow. Never forget that. Biologicals are frustratingly slow compared to machine-lects, usually. So, when it came into your chamber, of which, embarrassingly at my end, it was immediately successful, I correspondingly flung your chamber deep to one side of the ship.]

"You tried to shake it off?"

[Well that's as good a description as any. Yes.]

"That's why I fell?"

[Hah, if only! You fell because your neural synapses have much that could be improved upon and your general rudimentary nervous system is wholly inadequate in catering for shocks.]

"But–"

[I suppose you've only got two legs, after all. Although, amongst most terraneous, oxygen-breathing, medium-sized, sentient biologicals, that's not far off the average.]

"What?"

[I digress. You would have felt nothing as I moved the chamber, my inertial dampeners are fully functioning. Anyway, that was about the point that you looked up, by which time I'd moved you in a few different directions, to say the least. The dark sphere was still as close to you as it was then, but because I had rotated the chamber about you, it was outside of the immediate chamber. So, at first, when you looked up and around, there was nothing there.]

"It was inside you? Isn't that… dangerous?"

[Yes, it was worrying. But it didn't do anything. Passed through me like it wasn't there, or I wasn't there. Take your pick.]

"But… but now it's different. It's detectable."

[Yes, but I don't want to move you about now, seeing as it's likely to unstoppably follow you and could damage my insides.]

"Oh…"

[Perhaps this dark spherical void is the culmination of whatever the rods were doing before.]

"And all of it… was to get to me?"

[The sheer arrogance! We have no idea what this is all about, yet.]

"It's so close, it's–"

[Shame on you, Tor! Where's that fierce warrior from the commune?]

"I wasn't a warrior, and I didn't fight… I'm not worried for myself, not at all. I'm worried for Gil. I have to survive, we both have to, to help her."

[Look, don't worry. I get it, I really do. This thing, whatever it is, has kept its distance from you, no matter how the situation appears. I don't think you're in any direct harm.]

"Bu–"

[Actually, wait. Something is happening, look.]

Tor could see a small, smooth protrusion began to emerge from the surface of the dark sphere. Simultaneously, the air between himself and the sphere seemed to shimmer, as though a faint wall was there. Keeping an eye on the protrusion emerging, he moved a hand, bringing it close to the shimmering wall.

[You can try, but it won't let you pass. Just a safety precaution.]

"That's you?"

[Yes.]

"I thought you said it was probably unstoppable?"

[It's better than nothing. Besides, maybe I'll need to keep you separated from it.]

*

DeVoid continued in its attempts to analyse the mysterious N-SOL object, but found next to nothing. The protrusion had stayed as a protrusion. A bump, on the surface of the object, covering approximately one-sixteenth of its surface area, but only slightly raised. It rotated around the sphere, or the sphere was spinning.

The object was opaque to most analysis techniques at DeVoid's disposal, now absorbing anything incident upon it. Aside from the protrusion, the fact that it absorbed all particles and waves was the only quantitative property DeVoid had identified. The spin of the protrusion was haphazard. There was no identifiable repeating pattern, not even an irrational one.

"What's it doing, DeVoid?"

[Why don't you tell me, Tor? Oh wait, I remember, you don't know, do you?]

"Well..."

[Well what? Tor, don't you think if I knew, I'd tell you. Despite the intellectual gulf between us, I always keep you informed.]

"Yes, that's true, but... it's just the waiting."

[You'll have to be patient. Nothing has happened outside yet, either. Would you like me to put you to sleep?]

"No... not yet."

The N-SOL object began to expand, quickly.

CHAPTER 46

GIL

Lying in her bed, she was too tired to keep it out. The whispers grew louder and the sensespace expanded to fill her mind. Her infinite eyes returned to her, and she was drawn back into its clutch. Reality dissolved as her eyes closed.

*

She was at the same place as before. The nexus, where she was sure it had all begun. The delivery of the sensespace into the galaxy, from the sensespace's own recollection or version of a databanks.

She tried to keep the notion alive within her consciousness that she needed to be objective and logical. What she was being shown might not have actually happened, or might purely be designed to elicit a specific response from her. Even if the sensespace was not strictly sentient, or in possession of anything resembling an intellect, that did not mean it could not trick her.

Again, she was just a presence. It was similar to the presence she became when she explored her surroundings through the sensespace, although there were some differences. She did not have any measure of real control, and everything felt predetermined. The galaxy, the positions of the white streaks and their effects were immutable, like a highly detailed memory.

An unpleasant thought came to her, and she remembered Teacher, the Granthan-lect that had once invaded her body – and her mind. Her memory might have appeared like this to the cruel machine-lect, albeit far inferior, and with Teacher having far more influence over what it chose to observe than she had here. It could have examined her most intimate moments, her most treasured and her least wanted. All of them.

Teacher had changed while it resided within her. It had become more illogical, more fuelled by emotion, and less able to conceal its malicious intent or its underlying nature. She had assumed this was because of its exposure to her memories. However, if her memories had been able to change Teacher, perhaps these visions from the sensespace were designed to change her. She drew some solace from the fact that the craft-lect and One-oh would undoubtedly have considered the possibility anyway, and would be monitoring her for signs.

Pushing the unsavoury thoughts from her mind, she concentrated more keenly on what surrounded her. The streaks of white were all around, as before, already having embedded themselves in the galaxy ahead. Firmly entrenched. Unlike before, when she had seen them establish their positions, now she saw them after this – fixed.

She focused on the large streak nearest to her. A tube of pure whiteness. It looked innocent. Gil wished she could understand what it really represented, and where it came from. What it was. She could call it the manifested, visible sensespace, but that was simply a name. It did not tell her anything about what constituted the sensespace.

There were no longer any bulges being transmitted down the tubes, as there had been before. Whatever process had been occurring during her first vision had changed or finished. The packages that the sensespace streaks had transmitted into the expansive galaxy ahead were already delivered. With the realisation that the streaks were no longer what was most interesting about the scene ahead, and that she was unlikely to be able to learn anything from observing them, she settled on another task.

Struggling through the mental effort, she focused on turning her presence around, willing her vantage point to reverse. It was as though she was back in her physical body, pushing against a triamond wall. She was even weaker than before. She continued her attempts, before giving up. There was nothing she could do.

Whether it was brought on by her actions, or some other change, she felt it, again. That glimmer of a presence behind her, tantalisingly close. It made her want to look even more, renewing her vigour. If only she could… it was gone.

Dejected and weak, she gave up for the second time. It was too much. She waited, without choice, and reflected upon what she knew, until she found herself drifting, and recognised the feeling. It was the same, subtle, precursive sensation to her exit from this particular experience before.

Still desperate to see behind her, she mounted a final struggle against the oppressive force blocking her from turning and was surprised to find it gone. She spun around too fast, returning to her original position with only a quick, fleeting imprint, confused.

What she thought she had registered did not make sense, it was too hazy and ill-defined. An infinite array of presences – barely distinguishable instances of observation, all focused directly on her own. At her own infinite eyes. She was mistaken, she had to be. She was about to attempt another turn when she was thrust forwards, towards the white streaks.

*

She saw her younger self begin to climb the old tree near the perimeter of the commune, reaching up and grabbing the branches. She did not want to see what came next, she knew what was going to happen. She shut her infinite eyes, and pushed against the sensespace, wanting to leave.

*

The whispers were gone, and she was back observing the forest. She knew immediately where she was, and focused her presence on finding them. Unlike her fall from the tree, she wanted to observe this again.

Her father was walking with Yul in the same part of the forest as before, some way from the commune. Everything about it was the same. Her father's measured, sure-footed movements next to the hulking, comparatively lumbering Yul.

She watched them, excitedly, not wanting the moment to end. Another chance to see him and hear his voice. Their movements were the same as before. Gil decided to concentrate her presence behind her father, to see if he would still notice her. The last time, it had seemed so clear that he had seen her presence in front of him, which had caused him to disappear with Yul. This time she could test whether she had been mistaken.

After a few moments, he slowed down, turned his head back and scanned his green eyes around, his face impassive. His eyes settled on her, and he turned back before Yul had any cause to be curious.

This was not what had happened the other time, Gil was sure beyond any doubt that her own memory was not at fault – before, he had not turned his head around at all. He had definitely seen her, this time and the last, although the manner of his observation was different. She was conflicted, unsure whether to be elated, or upset at what was to come – if events unfolded the same as before and he vanished.

Her father began to slow his paces, as she knew he would. Turning sideways so that one shoulder was almost pointing forwards, he twisted his neck and looked at her squarely with both eyes. The same look of light curiosity as the last time took hold of him. He turned back around, and her presence moved up ahead to face him. His expression became more serious. Everything was proceeding the same, aside from how he had turned to find her new position.

Also as before, Yul's movements, turning to look at her father, distracted her. He had seen his companion's odd actions and wanted an explanation, although, again, her father did not acknowledge this. With a familiar movement, he looked downwards towards the ground, before raising his gaze towards the sky with both arms out wide, and stopped.

They both stood motionless, until her father brought his hands down to his side and tilted his head to a forward-looking position. Breathing deeply in and out, as though steadying his nerves, he looked directly at Yul.

"Yul."

Her father spoke, just as he had before.

"Yul, we go no further."

That was not exactly the same as she remembered.

"We must, to find–" Yul started.

"Do not worry, it will be fine," her father said.

Gil was certain this was different to before.

"You want us to go back?" Yul said.

"No."

"Then what do you mean?"

"Tell me, look back to our commune. What do you sense?"

"My son, Ril. And your children, Tor and Gil. They are–"

"They are fine."

"My… sphere is weaker than it should be," Yul said, frowning.

"They will be fine, Yul."

"What do you mean?" Yul looked at her father innocently, despite his size.

Her father said nothing.

"What has happened?" Yul said.

"They will not be able to sense us for now, and neither will you be able to sense them."

"What do you… my sphere is… it's going, I can't–"

"Be calm, Yul."

"You… you're not… you're not in my sphere…" The large man took a step back, away from her father. "I can't sense anything from you anymore. Can… can you sense me?"

"You could only ever sense what I let you."

"But your sphere, surely–"

"I am not joined."

"The sphere? What do you mean, of course, you–"

"You'll understand."

"I don't understand… what's happening?"

"Ril, the others, they are the first, but they will not be the last." Her father looked at Yul sadly. "That is the threat." He almost hissed the last word.

Yul still looked confused, as was Gil. What her father was saying made no sense. Yul looked as though he wanted to take another step back. He was frightened.

"Why not use it–"

"No."

"Wh–"

"It's forbidden."

"That makes no sense, how did you… I know you can…"

"It will."

"What do you mean? Why not use–"

"It would have uncovered me."

"Using your sphere would have–"

"It would have made things worse."

"But… what?"

"My children will have to be strong."

"Why?"

"They are needed."

"What for?" Yul looked panicked and began rambling. "I do not think Tor will want to be a hunter, his sphere will be too strong, you can tell… and Gil–"

"Not that, Yul," her father said, softly but without further explanation.

Yul tilted his head a little to the side and looked around in frustration. He then stepped forwards, closer to her father, at last saying, "Then what are they needed for?"

"To finally put a stop to it, to end all spheres. It costs too much."

Was her father saying this for Yul's benefit, or hers? Was he communicating with her through this… memory? If he was capable of this, why did he not speak with her directly? Could he not see her?

"You want them to destroy the commune?"

"In a way, yes. They must."

"To destroy our commune? Our way of life?"

"The way of life must change, it's necessary."

"Why, you believe we are in danger?"

"We are, Yul. Great danger."

"We can fight! Ril can help, he is strong–"

"Not this, my old friend. Not in the way you think."

"And Tor, Gil, they can help?"

"I hope they can. They must."

"How?" Yul asked.

Her father flashed a glance around and stopped. It looked as though he was concerned about being overheard, but she did not think she was the one worrying him. Was there someone else, besides her?

"How?" Yul repeated, more loudly.

"We aren't supposed to become involved. Not anymore – but look at what we did."

"What do you mean? Who–"

"It's our fault."

"What is?"

"I am sorry, I really am."

"What are you going to do?" Yul's eyes began to widen.

"I don't want to, I never did."

"What are you going to do?" He repeated.

"The time has come."

Gil was worried. This was what her father said before, she recognised it.

"For what?"

"The end of my interference."

"What is this you speak of?"

"There are rules, Yul. I will have to… atone."

"I do not understand."

"Even though it was right, to act as I did… Please, forgive me. Ril will be fine, I promise you this."

"What will happen?"

"It is time for us to leave."

"The commune?"

Her father laughed, kindly.

"Where are you going?" Yul pressed, again, frowning.

"We go somewhere… with no restrictions. Out of this space."

"I don't understand."

"You will."

And then they were gone, again, and Gil was alone.

*

She was back looking at the sensespace streaks fixed onto the galaxy before her. The same vision as before. The thick white constructs that formed its bridge.

The whispers remained quiet, lower than their typical background level. It was as though she was being given room to think, to contemplate what she had been shown. She moved her presence around, gazing at the white streaks. Moving fast, diffusing her presence in all directions, it was everywhere. The entire cross-section of the galaxy, as far as she could bear to go before losing her cohesiveness and drawing back into herself.

She wanted to think about what her father had said, but felt like this was another opportunity, somehow. What was the sensespace trying to show her? She was missing something. Was the sensespace trying to draw her to some sort of conclusion – a requirement to act?

She remembered what she had briefly glimpsed before, when she had turned around and seen what was behind her. That infinite array, peering at her own set of eyes. She was not sure if she wanted to see it again, or whether she would be able to. It was frightening, everything was. It was all bigger than her. What her father had said, and the experiences the sensespace was showing her – she still understood so little. She was being fed morsels of information, pushed in certain directions, while realising that there were monumental… powers, all vying for her attention. Whatever that array of eyes was, that had met her own, it was so much… larger, than she was. That may have been the point, the sensespace's message. She was incapable of understanding. She had to make a choice.

The sensespace appeared to connect her father with whatever had created it. It had shown her that he had a control over it – he had admitted as much to Yul – and it had taken her back to its origins. Either it was showing her the truth, or it was attempting to manipulate her to its own ends. Or both.

The more Gil thought about it, the less sure she became. Her thoughts kept trailing back to her father. Who was he? What was he? To have created Gil, to have had a hand in all of this… Had he really helped create the sensespace? The infection that had destroyed more lives than she could ever count.

Giving up, she resigned herself to waiting for whatever the sensespace had in store for her next. As though sensing her desire to move on, the spacescape around her changed.

*

She immediately regretted having let the sensespace take her back to the terrifying, swirling mass of utter blackness. Her insignificance against its sheer scale was humbling. The darkness continued to display its power, warping reality with its movement. The whispers cowered, barely audible.

It was hard to gauge its magnitude, but she knew it was more gargantuan than anything else that could exist. She was afraid. If it awoke and noticed her, it would not be kind. The sensespace was right to fear it.

She hated the sensespace… at least, she thought she still did. It had become confusing. However, the black mass seemed much worse. She could feel its cold hate. It planned to destroy all it could. It barely registered the sentients in the galaxy, unlike the sensespace, all it wanted was to obliterate everything.

She gazed, for a long time, until it came to her. The specks of light dotted about its dark heart were stars. She had been right in knowing, somehow, that it was vaster than anything that had come before it, impossibly so. Entities, or structures, on that scale, were not supposed to exist.

The presence behind her shifted, moved about, and the whispers evaporated to nothingness.

A word came to her, plucked from the recesses of her mind. Something that she had long supposed, although had not been consciously able to articulate. She knew where this thing resided, she had known for quite some time. She was connected to it, to everything. It had all been laid out for her.

Centre.

She wanted to look about, to find where the information had come from, to blame anyone other than herself, but she could not. It had come from within her.

Filled with the understanding that this word described what was ahead, she was captivated, no longer just afraid, gazing into the dark heart. She understood. It was at the centre, a centre that everything in the galaxy could understand. The centre. What was more, she knew exactly what it was, what was waiting for her. The craft-lect and One-oh had been right.

The Deliverer was waiting for her, at the centre of the galaxy.

She shot backwards.

*

The entire galaxy was there, for her to behold. Her infinite eyes put her on the threshold of omniscience. She wished she could comprehend it all – she had the ability but not the capability, nor the strength. Not yet. Perhaps she never would. The whispers were gaining in volume.

She could see it, still. Finally able to place it, to make sense of what she had already known. The dark heart, the menacing presence dominating the centre of the galaxy. A gap in her perceptive sight, bespeckled with those specks of twinkling light, which she now knew were stars. She knew the centre was filled with malicious intent, and dark power. Substantial and terrifyingly destructive. The Deliverer. The omission of a presence. It was hidden, untouched by the sensespace, her most powerful tool, the thing she begrudged beyond anything. She still did not understand quite how she could control the Maspero gateways without the sensespace, but whatever other gifts she had were not demystifying the Deliverer for her.

She knew she was becoming confused about the sensespace and whether she should hate it, or this Deliverer, more. Her father's words had not helped. She did not want to think about what he had implied about his connection with the sensespace – that lay some of the blame for all the death it had caused, including Tor's, at his feet. It also did not make sense because he had said he wanted his children to be strong, yet Tor had been killed by Teacher. She knew her father would never have wanted to cause Tor's death, he had loved Tor.

Her attention was taken by a faint sensation across her presence – like a muted version of the force she felt when they were near the Maspero gateways. As soon as she formed those thoughts, shining points, unlike the stars, became apparent. They shone with a pale green hue that became increasingly prominent the more she observed. She was able to see the myriad of connections between them, which took the form of faint viridescent lines. Every now and then, she spotted certain lines becoming thicker, and a deeper green, in a motion that swept from one side to the other. She was right, these were the gateways.

She could ascertain the overall shape of the gateway network. Broadly, it was spherical, although most thickly traced as a ring on the main galactic plane. It was the same ring she had already seen the impression of when the sensespace had first shown this to her, before she had even encountered the gateways. The ring was the thickest part of the shell, spanning a significant stretch of the galaxy, but it was unmistakably clear from her current point of observation. She saw the path they had taken in the Wanderer ship, the crisscrossing through space, comically oblivious to the network they had wandered into. Obvious to her now. Now that she understood its layout and how the constituent gateways were connected, she would be able to take them wherever they wished. She could even differentiate between the sensespace-infected worlds and those that appeared derelict of its presence.

She peered closer, through the shell of the Maspero gateway, into the inner reaches of the galaxy, but not too close to the darkness at its heart. There were two other inner shells, smaller than that of the Maspero gateway network, and discernibly separate from each other. Concentric shells. They both contained structures within them that were interlinked, although she did not understand what they were – perhaps other gateways.

She knew, with reluctance, where she needed to go, where she needed to take them. As close to the centre as the Maspero gateways would take them. Finding the right path no longer worried her, but what she would do when they reached the end, did. Sooner or later, venturing inwards, they would wake the darkness. Did it have its own set of infinite eyes, or something else, something terrible? She was scared. What was she meant to do, kill a god?

Infinite Eyes is the third in the Wanderers Series, set in the Sci-Fi Wanderer Universe, alongside James' other books.

AVAILABLE BOOKS
By James Murdo

All set in the Wanderer Universe. The series and standalones are all part of the wider interrelated story.

Tapache's Promise Trilogy:
Echoes of Gravity (Book 1)
Echoes of Time (Book 2)
Echoes of Foundation (Book 3)

Standalones:
Siouca Remembers
Long Paradise
Fractured Carapace

Wanderers Series:
Gil's World (Book 1)
Searching the Void (Book 2)
Infinite Eyes (Book 3)

I hope you enjoyed reading Infinite Eyes. I would be delighted if you left a review.

GLOSSARY AND CHARACTERS

A-autom – Classification of a craft-lect that controls a Wanderer ship. It is at the top of the ship's internal machine-lect hierarchy.

AB level – Empire, civilisation, race, species or any other grouping of sentients that has reached the point of technological advancement comparable with that of the ABs. The term can also be used to describe specific technologies that are comparable in advancement to those used by ABs.

AB space – A reality deeply connected with real space. It is the 'true' home of the ABs.

Antigraviton – Elementary particle of the antigravitational force, which acts over massive inter-galactic distances to push objects further apart. The force acts like gravity's opponent, although it is a separate force and not an antimatter equivalent, which does not exist.

Apalu – Sibling of the craft-lect.

Ascended Biologicals ('ABs') – Most advanced known civilisations in the galaxy. They had been thought to be all-powerful, until they chose suicide in the face of the sensespace threat. A defining aspect of the ABs was that they were unable to be fully understood by the less advanced, wider galactic community. They reside in both real space and AB space, although the latter is their 'true' home.

Axe-coding – Type of inhabitant of a craft-lect's technosystem reality, alongside the c-automs. Axe-codings cull c-automs at the instruction of the craft-lect.

Axe-haven – Structure that disseminates orders and updates to the axe-codings, and whose existence is purposely concealed from the craft-lect.

Axenic garrison – Thorus' territory that is separated and hidden from the rest of the galaxy using transit-point technology given to it by the Makers.

Axuum – Common material that is light-weight, strong and impervious to gamma radiation making it useful for space travel. Typically found across most manufacturing areas within young civilisations.

Azuum – Material that is similar to Azuum, and typically found across most manufacturing areas within young spacefaring civilisations.

Balrooni Wonder – Galactic marvel, discovered by the Balroons.

Balroons – Race of large, technologically-augmented macronematoids.

B-autom – Category of machine-lect designed by the Wanderer Enclave to co-ordinate c-automs within early craft-lect ships. They did not act as intended and were either destroyed or repurposed.

Beast-men – Extinct species that was similar to Gil's people.

Bio-lect – Biological sentient that has been upgraded near to the point of becoming a machine intelligence, while keeping its biological thought constructs. Differentiated from a machine-lect, although technically a subset. Rare instances have shown they can evolve naturally, such as with the Waka race.

Biological sentient ('biological') – Non-exotic living entity that has naturally evolved, or would have been able to, and that also possesses an intellect.

Bloom – Wanderer propulsion method powered by vacuum energy.

Blue Dots – Phenomenon appearing within the photospheres of most heavier main sequence stars within the Minor Hednes Arm. It has been debated whether they are a primitive species or simply an emergent property of a complex system. Their apparent patterns are thought to be governed by a set of equations known as the 'Hyplex Dolsden Triple'.

Bo – Oldest and wisest elder of Gil's former commune.

Bunch'wan – Small aquatic, and heavily religious species that fractured into various derivative civilisations in pre-Conflation times. The base species, alongside with many others, became extinct as a result of the war against the sensespace. Offshoot levels three, eight, nine, ten and twenty-seven are known to have survived and reintegrated into one society.

Capacity – Amount of concentration available to each Wanderer machine-lect, which can be divided and allocated between tasks.

C-autom – Lowest classification of sentient sub-lect within the autom series. They are created by Wanderer craft-lects and delegated various tasks.

Ciqalo – Disappeared sibling of Apalu and the craft-lect.

Cognitional demarcation ('coupling') – Technique allowing data-lects to ascertain the veracity of information entering the Wanderer data exchange network.

Commune – Type of community where Gil was raised on her world.

Communer – People who live in a commune.

Coupling – See 'cognitional demarcation'.

Craft-lect – Wanderer machine-lect that travels the galaxy detecting and destroying incidences of sensespace infection.

Craftnet – Ship-wide network on a Wanderer craft-lect's ship. It is available to be used for ship-wide communications by all c-automs.

Cross-Prophet – Entity initially referenced by Thy, who reveals himself to Tor and DeVoid. Also known as the 'Guardian of the Spaces' and the 'Traveller'.

Data exchange network – Wanderer civilisation's information network, spread across the galaxy. Often referred to as 'the data exchange'.

Data exchange portal – Individual portal within the Wanderer data exchange network. Usually referred to simply as 'a data exchange'.

Databanks – Wanderer memory technology.

Data-lect – Higher Wanderer machine-lect that usually acts as a steward of a data exchange portal. Originally created during experiments by the Machine Alliance, and prodigy-tending on average. They exhibit greater independence of thought than most Wanderer machine-lects.

Deliverer – Powerful machine-lect created and left behind by the ABs, dedicated to learning about and destroying the sensespace.

DeVoid – Data-lect with origins predating the Great Conflation.

Diasporasm – Siltlong species that evolved from the Silti, and are their largest descendants.

Dissociation shell – Enormously destructive weapon based on dissociation technology.

Dissociation shield – Complicated technology that funnels a dissociation explosion around an enclosed, protected area.

Dissociation technology – Antigravity technology that was banned before the Great War.

Drone – Automated instruments that are typically not sentient.

Dual-structure lect – Type of machine-lect architecture that allows for two distinct expressions of sentience to co-exist within the same medium at the same time.

Duspatock – Siltlong species that evolved from the Silti, and are their smaller descendants.

Emblem-ship – Largest and deadliest Battle Class ships produced by the Woal Collective, initially created during the early stages of the Great War. They are more conjoined fleets than individual ships, comprising hundreds of interlinked baubles – each with their own machine-lect in charge. They are known to favour weapons derived from dissociation technology.

Enclave-lect – Member of the Wanderer Enclave.

Faistri'al – Species made famous throughout the galaxy for their association with the Balroons.

Flap-weaponry – Type of Faistri'al weapon.

Fringe viewpoint – Description of a minority school of thought in the Wanderer civilisation.

Galactic community – Encompasses known spacefaring civilisations who exchange information between each other. Also used to group together all sub-AB sentients.

GA-Ries – Galactic civilisation known to the Wanderers.

Gate-lect – Machine-lect from the gateway mechanism.

Gateway mechanism – Mechanism overseeing the Wanderer data exchange network.

Gil – Twin sister of Tor.

Granthan – Mysterious race that reached near-AB level before technologically plateauing.

Granthan-lect – Machine-lect from the Granthan civilisation.

Granthan-lect fragment ('fragment') – Partial copy of the original Granthan-lect that infiltrated the craft-lect's ship.

Graviton – Elementary particle of the gravitational force.

Gravity cocoon – Device to suppress or dampen an explosion.

Great Conflation – Mass suicide event which occurred sixty million years ago, during the fight against the sensespace. It was initially proposed by the embattled ABs as a means of forcing the sensespace into dormancy by removing its ability to actively control those it had infected, as it was theorised to rely on the aggregate level of sentience within the galaxy. Sometimes, the Great War is referred to as the Great Conflation, although that is not technically correct.

Great War – Three hundred million years ago, following its discovery by the Balroons, the sensespace attacked the galactic community. It exerted an active control over those it had infected to carry out destruction. The war is still ongoing.

Guardian of the Spaces – See 'Cross-Prophet'.

Han – Most skilled hunter in Gil's former commune.

Hatelei – Grouping of Siltlong races that is far smaller than the Wanderers.

Higher-level c-autom – C-autom with greater-than-average intelligence.

Hollow-world – World-sized husk that appears typical but is identifiable primarily by its negligible gravitational readings.

Hugger Encroachment – Civilisation that mostly had settlements within the outer perimeters of star systems, with a level of technology far inferior to that of the Wanderers. Extinct long before the Wanderers were formed.

Hunter – Communer who hunts animals for food in the surrounding forests.

Hyper-lucidity – Ability of some biologicals to exhibit intellectual leaps far surpassing the abilities of most machine-lects, and often requiring prodigy or savant machine-lects to understand.

Insul – Craft-lect and parent-lect of Pelteus. Deceased.

Lect – Living entity that possesses an intellect and is therefore sentient. Usually an affix to a machine intelligence.

Lenbit Orbital – Asteroid field where the craft-lect encountered the derelict research base, disguised as a mining station, established by One-oh's race.

Lower-level c-autom – C-autom with lower-than-average intelligence.

Machine Alliance – Pre-Wanderer grouping of machine-lects who engaged in numerous technological experiments, banded together by the central tenet of machine superiority.

Machine-lect – Machine-based intelligence.

Makers – Creators of the sensespace and 'the spaces'.

Mart'oop – Upright hexapodic insectoid species that caused their own extinction hundreds of millions of years before the Great Conflation.

Maspero – Private AB civilisation rumoured by the Wanderers to have been involved with creating the Deliverer.

Maspero gateways ('gateways') – Rotating gravitational singularities that appear to allow near-instantaneous passage between separate locations.

Metalink – Conduit used by Thorus to receive and transmit information from its garrison.

Meta-traps – Snares used by Pelteus to attack its prey.

Multiversal boundaries – Boundaries separating universes within the multiverse.

Multiverse – Collection of universes, separated by multiversal boundaries, that comprise the spaces.

Nanosphere – Antimatter weapon.

Near-AB level ('Near-AB') – Empire, civilisation, race, species, or any other grouping of sentients, that has technologically advanced to a point nearly comparable with that of the ABs, although still recognisably inferior by the galactic community. The term can also be used to describe specific technologies.

Near-speed-of-light ('N-SOL') travel – Fastest transportation method known to, and possessed by, sub-ABs. N-SOL travel is an AB technology that was gifted to the galactic community billions of years ago.

Needle-whip – Weapon.

Nevosplitter – GA-Riesian instrument.

Nine-Bunch'wan – See 'Bunch'wan'.

Non-ABs – Empire, civilisation, race, species, or any other grouping of sentients, whose technological advancement is inferior to the ABs, or who have AB-level, technologies but have declined to join the AB grouping. The term can also be used to describe specific technologies.

N-SOL drive – Technology gifted by the ABs to the galactic community to make use of N-SOL travel.

N-SOL space – Accessed via an N-SOL drive, it allows travel at far greater speeds than in real space. It is a phenomenon that is known to exist by the general galactic community, but not understood.

One-oh – Bio-lect discovered to be contained within trove item 512<a>!110000, from the Lenbit Orbital research station, which had been disguised as a mining station.

Orb-body – Physical form for c-automs to operate in real space, created by the craft-lect. Each orb emits its own unique glow.

Parent-lect – Machine-lect that has spawned a sub-lect.

Pelteus – Surviving spear-lect.

Post-Conflation – Events following the Great Conflation.

Pre-Conflation – Events preceding the Great Conflation.

Prodigy machine-lect – Machine-lects who display genius-level attributes in almost all quantifiable fields, and thought to be a possible route to entering the AB fold. They are monumentally complex and tricky to produce – nearly always by accident – and are only created by highly advanced civilisations. Data-lects are almost unique in the Wanderer civilisation, being the only category of machine-lect able to be purposely created with prodigy-tending attributes.

Pulsar spew – Unidentified exotic matter emitted from slow or non-spinning neutron stars, that is attuned to the sensespace and able to force it to manifest completely in real space.

Pulsar spew technology – Technology that harnesses the exotic matter emitted by slow pulsars. Spinning neutron stars ('pulsars') emit periodic pulses of electromagnetic radiation, but this process stops when the rotation slows down. After this, the pulsar engine evolves, and the neutron star emits secondary, highly infrequent pulses of exotic matter.

Quasi-sequential hermaphrodite – Single-gender species whose fundamental behavioural characteristics can significantly change, often without warning. This is analogous to the changing of sex in many gendered species. The Waka species is a notable example.

Quick-lect – Category of Wanderer machine-lect in control of small ships that hunted their targets in packs. Assumed extinct.

Real space – Encompasses all known scales of accessible reality for sub-ABs. Virtual and simulated habitats, and any similar constructs, are included in the term, although sometimes differentiated from physically-oriented classifications of real space for simplicity.

Ril – Labourer, son of Yul.

Savant machine-lect – Machine-lects who are unfathomably gifted in certain areas, but dramatically deficient in others. They are even harder to product than prodigy machine-lects, and even rarer.

Selection mechanism – Used to efficiently allocate c-autom tasks.

Selective suppression – Ability of some machine-lects to dampen facets of their lects for specified periods of time, with the aim of optimising or exploring the change in functionality of a lect.

Sensespace – Infective and hostile presence that appears to be drawn to sentience. It is believed to have been pushed into dormancy by the Great Conflation, when the level of aggregate sentience in the galaxy was dramatically reduced.

Sentient – Living entity possessing an intellect (or 'sentience').

Silti – Siltlong species, and also the progenitor of the Toolong, Diasporasm and Duspatock.

Siltlong – Exotic category of sentient that closely resembles living orbital debris. The three main races are the Toolong,

Diasporasm and Duspatock. All three hailed from the same progenitor species – the Silti.

Singularity generator – Propulsion method relying on artificial gravitational micro-singularities. Also known as a 'thrown singularity engine' or a 'recycled singularity engine'.

Sower – Tool that is part-digger, part-planter, invented by Gil.

Spear-lect – Wanderer b-automs who survived efforts to usurp their parent-lects and were subsequently captured by the Enclave, before being repurposed into weapons against the Enclave's opponents. Assumed extinct.

Sphere – Sense available to Gil's people that allows them to explore the world around them. It is derived from the sensespace.

Spin-hygen – Weapon.

Standard time – Wanderer quantification of time which is also the standard in the galactic community. It is similar to that used on Gil's planet.

Step Principle – Warning against machine-lect self-upgrades to the extent a different entity is created that supersedes the incumbent machine-lect. Similar to the Usurper Principle.

Sub-AB – Empire, civilisation, race, species, or any other such often-synonymous grouping of sentients, whose technological advancement is inferior to the ABs. The term can also be used to describe specific technologies.

Sub-lect – Machine-lect spawned by a parent-lect.

Table-chamber – Room created by the craft-lect for discussions between itself, One-oh, 998 and Gil.

Tait – Respected individual from Gil's former commune.

Teacher – Machine-lect derived from the Granthan-lect labelled 1<k>!101010.

Technosystem – Wanderer ship's internal network which interfaces with the majority of its systems.

Technosystem reality – Virtual environment within a Wanderer ship which can be inhabited by machine-lects. It usually acts as an interface by which the technosystem, and therefore the ship, can be efficiently accessed by c-automs.

Ten-Bunch'wan – See 'Bunch'wan'.

The spaces – Encompasses a multiverse of distinct universes separated by multiversal boundaries. Created by the Makers, and defined by the Cross-Prophet as 'probably almost everything'.

Theory of the Intellect – Broad theory of sentience and consciousness, generally applicable to all biologicals, machine-lects and exotic variants thus far discovered by the wider galactic community.

Thorus – Ancient and surviving machine-lect who used to be a member of the Machine Alliance, before the alliance joined the factions preceding the Wanderers.

Thy – Originally created by the Thygo as their machine-lect guardian.

Thy-child – Category of sub-lect spawned by Thy that resided within its simulated reality.

Thygo – Progenitor race that created Thy, before being imprisoned by their creation.

Toolong – Siltlong species that evolved from, and closely resemble, the Silti.

Tor – Twin brother of Gil.

Transit-point technology – Technology that allows parts of the galaxy to be sequestered and hidden from the rest.

Traveller – See 'Cross-Prophet'.

Triamond – Extremely durable and versatile material.

Trizek'd Theory of Lect – Theory describing the workings of lects, tailored by the Wanderers for their civilisation. The theory is in a constant state of flux since all Wanderer lects are constantly being affected by both new and/or changing variables, including time. It is not ultimately solvable in the sense that it can never be complete.

Trove instrument ('trove item') – Technological item pilfered from an abandoned habitat or outpost, that a craft-lect can choose to dedicate resources to understanding.

Usurper Principle – Warning against delegating inferior machine-lects to be involved with anything that might lead to them become dangerously upgraded or superior to the incumbent machine-lect. Similar to the Step Principle.

Waka – Race of natural bio-lects, rumoured to be represented within the Wanderer Enclave. Waka individuals are quasi-sequential hermaphrodites, and take tens to thousands of years to reach full maturity.

Wanderer Confluence – Optional events hosted by the Enclave for the Wanderer populous. They occur approximately every one million standard years, with the purpose of sharing and disseminating information, which is also available via the data exchange afterwards.

Wanderer Enclave – Governing body of the Wanderers, thought to comprise mostly of machine-lects.

Wanderer fleet – All of the Wanderer ships within the galaxy, although often refers to the craft-lect fleet, which is the largest.

Wanderers – Formed predominantly from a variety of machine-lect alliances, following the Great Conflation. The Wanderer civilisation is the principal force in the galaxy attempting to destroy the sensespace.

Woal Collective – Current allies of the Wanderers who were decimated by the sensespace during the Great War. They are one of the civilisations that decided to purposefully stagnate themselves so as not to contribute to the sensespace's hypothetical reawakening. Their technology has long-been in the upper echelons of the non-ABs, although it has also stagnated since the start of the Great War.

World-chamber – Artistic symbol of Gil's home planet, constructed by 998.

Yul – Father of Ril, who disappeared with Gil's father.

Yul'nka Empire – Close allies to the Wanderers.

1<k>!101010 – Trove item collected forty million years ago from the remains of a Granthan worldship, found to contain a subversive Granthan-lect loyal to the sensespace.

112 – Lower-level c-autom befriended by Gil.

289 – C-autom working on a task with 112.

997<0>!001100 (‘997’) – Higher-level c-autom intended as the intellectual equal of 998<0>!001100 (998) when it was created, at the same time, by the craft-lect. Deceased.

998<0>!001100 (‘998’) – Higher-level c-autom originally tasked with investigating trove item 512<a>!110000, although it has since evolved its responsibilities.

Infinite Eyes is the third in the Wanderers Series, set in the Sci-Fi Wanderer Universe, alongside James' other books.

AVAILABLE BOOKS
By James Murdo

All set in the Wanderer Universe. The series and standalones are all part of the wider interrelated story.

Tapache's Promise Trilogy:
Echoes of Gravity (Book 1)
Echoes of Time (Book 2)
Echoes of Foundation (Book 3)

Standalones:
Siouca Remembers
Long Paradise
Fractured Carapace

Wanderers Series:
Gil's World (Book 1)
Searching the Void (Book 2)
Infinite Eyes (Book 3)

I hope you enjoyed reading Infinite Eyes. I would be delighted if you left a review.

Printed in Dunstable, United Kingdom

78115594R00224